Praise for Lorenda Christensen

"Lorenda Christensen has created
a really fabulous world where humans and dragons
live side-by-side in semi-peace."
—*Smexy Books*

"I was drawn in by the first line,
then the first chapter of this book."
—*Dear Author*

"*Never Deal with Dragons* is a fast read
with a wonderfully likable heroine."
—*Fiction Vixen*

dancing
with
dragons

LORENDA CHRISTENSEN

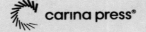

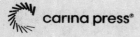

carina press®

ISBN-13: 978-0-373-00252-8

Dancing With Dragons

Copyright © 2014 by Lorenda Christensen

Recycling programs
for this product may
not exist in your area.

www.CarinaPress.com

Printed in U.S.A.

Dear Reader,

One of my favorite downtime activities—other than reading, of course!—is going to the movie theater with my husband. And while my husband has been known to considerately sit through "chick flicks" because he loves me, they aren't his first choice.

Lucky for him, I love action thrillers almost as much as the latest Nicholas Sparks adaptation. It doesn't take long before I'm sucked into the world shown on the screen. And with the amount of popcorn I'm shoveling down my throat, you'd think I was the one chasing bad guys, skidding my motorcycle under a conveniently placed eighteen-wheeler or sweating profusely while holding my gun steady on a questionable associate.

For *Dancing with Dragons*, I wanted to re-create the same heart-pounding sensation of an action thriller in print, and focus on what it might actually feel like to be chased by dragons who wish you bodily harm. And what you'd be thinking when a handsome stranger offers you help in return for information. Especially if you're someone like Carol Jenski, who—unlike Myrna Banks from *Never Deal with Dragons*—can count on one hand the number of times she's had to deal with a roomful of angry dragons and a complicated political situation, as well.

I hope you enjoy your time with Carol and Daniel... and I hope that should we ever meet in a movie theater, you can hear the film over my popcorn crunching!

Happy reading,

Lorenda

Dedication

For Nathan Patteson,
because you're the coolest ER dude I know.

dancing
with
dragons

Acknowledgments

There are some books that are easy to write,
and there are some that you wish you could bury
in the backyard and never see again.
And then there is my editor, Kerri Buckley, who
is willing and able to take those backyard books
and turn them into something that people might
want to read. Trust me when I say that even if
Carina Press pays her ten million a year,
she's still not making enough. Thank you.

To my Firebird sisters, thank you for the laughs,
the support and the brainstorming sessions.
I couldn't do this without you.

To my sister-in-law, Jaria, thank you for loaning me
the use of your house and keeping my kids alive
while I sat in your guest bedroom and typed out
the last half of this book. I owe you a kid-free trip
to the spa. It's in writing now. Take advantage.

And finally, to my husband, who reads every book,
even though he'd rather be watching football.

ONE

THE POUNDING IN my head kept perfect time with my footsteps as Richard pulled me by the hand through the wide hallways of Budapest's most elegant hotel. Only minutes ago, I'd been in the middle of a more-than-minor disagreement with an enraged dragon who'd wanted to eat my best friend Myrna. The fact that I'd also just accused her of sleeping with my boyfriend seemed like a minor point, especially since said boyfriend and I were currently running from another dragon. Except this one was smarter, older, and held the title of Dragon Lord of North America.

Unfortunately, I was in no condition to sprint; the spots dancing in my vision refused to get out of my way long enough for me to actually see where Richard was going.

"Richard. I need to stop." I was afraid I might throw up if we went much further.

"Shhh. We're almost outside."

A part of my brain, the part that hadn't been slammed against a wall by a giant, scaly-clawed fist, was worried that the lights, floor and walls were bleeding together into one large blob. I put a hand on my stomach and gagged. Before I knew it, I'd shifted my body until my face was pressed against the most heavenly patch of carpet I'd ever had the privilege to lay upon.

"Carol." Richard gently shook my shoulder. I tried to turn my head toward his voice, but the carpet suddenly became much less heavenly as it scraped along the surface of my scalp.

Richard grabbed for my wrist. "Oh God, Carol! You're bleeding. A lot." He sounded a little scared.

Exhausted from the effort it had taken to raise my head, I forgot about the rubbing and simply blinked as Richard yanked a blindingly white handkerchief from inside his suit jacket and gave it a hard shake to unfold it.

I tried to push him away when he pressed the cloth to my temple, because it made the single bongo playing against my skull turn into a full-fledged university drum line, complete with cymbals and gong. But I was dimly surprised to realize my hand wouldn't obey me.

"I'm okay." A lie. But a necessary one. "We don't have time to play doctor." *Play doctor.* I chuckled at my own stupid joke, fully aware that the quip was guided by hysteria rather than humor. But I didn't laugh for long. The motion made the drumming in my skull even worse, and I bit my lip against the pain.

I managed to focus long enough to grip the door's safety bar and haul myself up. I squinted at the green sign hanging from the ceiling, hoping it said EXIT, because the buzzing in my ear had upgraded to a ring. I fought another bout of nausea. "Just get me outside. We'll worry about the blood in a sec."

Richard muttered something under his breath, but did as I asked. The cold wind slapped me in the face, and helped me refocus my muddied thoughts. Richard half carried, half dragged me toward a small maroon sedan and batted my clumsy hands away from the latch.

"Here, let me do it." His voice was quiet, but I heard the tremor underlying his words. I must be bleeding badly for it to scare Richard this much. He was used to working with dragons.

Crumpling gratefully into the passenger seat, I put my head between my knees and tried to will away my dizziness. I felt something warm on my neck and I swiped at it, only to have my fingers come back covered in blood.

"Richard, I'm not feeling so well..." I concentrated on holding the cloth to my head, my fear mounting as I realized the material was nearly soaked through.

"Carol, baby, I need to you to stay awake for me. I'll get you to a hospital, but I need to find one a bit further away from the hotel."

The car came to life with a shudder. When Richard pushed hard on the gas, we shot forward, jerking my body forward and causing me to groan.

He glanced into the rearview mirror and winced at whatever he'd seen. "Sorry. I'm afraid I'll be breaking some speed limits in the next few minutes."

Normally, I would have protested, but the roar of an angry dragon and the unmistakable thump as something slammed into the side of our car led me to admit that Richard might be right.

I cried out as he made a hard turn into a narrow alleyway, and my left arm was bashed against the car's electronic window control. That was the point where my body decided I'd had enough, and the contents of my stomach landed in a wet heap right between my mismatched socks.

"Oh, Richard! I'm so sorry!" The words, which had made perfect sense while still inside my head, tumbled from my mouth in a mix of unintelligible syllables.

Richard's fist hit my knee as he shoved the engine into a higher gear. "Hang on!"

I'd barely had a chance to get my hands on the dashboard when the car's tires squealed as we turned in another wild circle, and razor-sharp fangs appeared in the windshield right in front of me. My mind couldn't make sense of what I was seeing, until I realized: the dragon's face was upside down.

Oh crap. He must be perched on the top of the car.

That fact was confirmed when a giant orange claw slid through the gap in my window.

Orange?

"Who's chasing us?" The dragon who'd attacked

me and Myrna had been green, and had been pretty up front about the fact that he'd been sent by Hian-puo, the dragon lord of China. Hian-puo hadn't exactly been fond of Myrna, since she's the one who'd uncovered his plot to murder the rest of the world's dragon lords with a bioweapon designed for just that purpose.

I didn't get a chance to think about it much longer, because the roof of our car made a metallic screech as the orange dragon tried to rip it off. Panicked, I finally located the window control and pushed. The dragon roared again, and our car fishtailed sideways as the claw disappeared and the dragon shifted its weight. I had a second to hope we'd managed to dislodge him, but my hopes were dashed when that same claw punched through the roof as if it were tin foil.

Richard yelled as he punched the gas, and I heard a sickening thud of flesh on stone as we shot into a tunnel. I turned my head as quickly as I dared, just in time to see a dragon lying motionless on the road behind us.

The movement made my stomach roll, and I closed my eyes in an attempt to hold the nausea at bay. "Richard, I think I'm going to…"

I heard the faint sound of Richard screaming as I felt consciousness slip away.

TWO

THE BEEPING OF the heart monitor was driving me insane. I'd been forced to listen to the sound for what felt like forever, and I couldn't figure out why I was the only one who was bothered by its incessant squawking.

I'd panicked a bit when I'd tried to tell someone to turn it off, because no matter how much I concentrated, I couldn't seem to get air to push past my vocal cords. I wondered if this is what death felt like. Trapped in a body that no longer functioned.

Except for my hearing, which I prayed would malfunction.

Then again, at least it kept me awake. I'd started to dread sleep, because every time I succumbed to the urge, my memories of how I got here would come rushing back to swallow me whole. Well, at least they were partial memories.

I think. Everything was really confusing lately.

I remember being slightly buzzed, and I'd been climbing onto the enormous bed in Myrna's room when a dragon had burst into the room.

And I mean that literally. Even though the door

had been several feet away, I'd instinctively ducked as large chunks of the hall-facing entry spewed toward my face. Myrna—who just forgiven me for accusing her of sleeping with Richard—did the same, and I must not have been moving as fast as I thought, because she was at my side and pulling me to the floor before I was able to do it myself.

The bedframe dug into my hip, and my right elbow was bent rather uncomfortably against my stomach, but I didn't complain. The dragon was bigger than any I'd ever seen before.

Even with the hole he'd blown in the wall, the green beast still filled the doorway, his thick scales scraping against the damaged construction and his clawed feet sinking into the plush carpet as he stepped fully into the room.

The dragon paused and, as if he hadn't just caused thousands of dollars of damage to the hotel room, took his time looking over the furnishings, like he was a prospective buyer looking for a new home. Or maybe he was just hoping to find something else to crush into bits. If his scars were anything to go by, the bruiser enjoyed that type of thing.

Myrna and I had spent a week working around angry, human-hating dragons, and while the job was old hat to her, I still wasn't used to the sight of their long pointed teeth and flaring nostrils.

I tried to scoot further under the bed. No luck.

My friend worked with dragons at Dragon Relations, Arbitration, and Cooperative Interspecies Mediation—DRACIM for short. She'd been working for the North American dragon lord, Nir Relobu, to try and negotiate the release of a team of scientists who had been detained by Lord Hian-puo of China, because they'd come too close to discovering the Chinese dragon lord's plan to engage in biological warfare with his fellow dragon rulers.

We'd gone in without knowing this important fact, and Myrna's team, me included, had barely escaped with our lives. We were in Budapest to witness the Chinese dragon lord's trial, and—based on how the proceedings went—likely his execution as well. Dragons really have no problem with the death penalty.

And now it appeared that Chinese dragon lord had—perhaps rightfully—decided we were to blame for his current plight. The green dragon had made it very clear he wasn't in Myrna's hotel room by accident, and that Hian-puo of China had sent him there. We'd done our best to fend the creature off, but even with two of us, the odds were firmly in his favor. I made the mistake of trying to stop him from killing my friend, and he'd slung me against the wall in response.

This was the point where my memories started to get hazy. Unfortunately the fear of the experience was still all too clear. I remember Richard arriving, and me stabbing at a dragon with a fireplace poker, but not much else.

I BLINKED TWICE and waited until my vision was something other than a mass of wet, shimmering bubbles of light. The wait was much longer than I expected, but at least my eyes were working.

And they were staring at a ceiling. A large water stain marred the white surface above my head. The panel looked a little soggy, and I wondered idly whether anyone was aware of the leak. *They should send someone to fix that.*

"Carol?" I heard Richard's voice just before his face appeared above me. His hair was a mess and his face unshaven. "You're awake. You had me so scared." I felt his hand grip mine, and I gave his fingers a reassuring squeeze.

The movement caused pain to shoot up my arm.

"Ow. What happened?" I raised my hand to find it nearly twice the size it should be and covered in scabbed skin and bruises. It looked like I'd gone toe to toe with a brick wall and lost. Badly.

Richard's forehead creased. "You don't remember?"

I searched my memories. "I remember leaving Hian-puo's trial, and coming to look for you…" I glared at him. "You were ignoring me and hanging out with Myrna's good-for-nothing boss."

Richard worked for the North American dragon lord, doing everything from hiring Lord Relobu's house staff to negotiating business deals with foreign nations on the dragon's behalf. Though Trian—

Myrna's boyfriend and the head of Relobu's security team—had recommended Myrna as DRACIM's best mediator to work through the prisoner exchange with China's Hian-puo, Richard had been the one to actually hire her for the job.

She'd introduced me to Richard soon after, and we'd started dating. I'd thought things were going well between us, until Richard had pulled out the silent treatment at the Budapest hotel. At first I'd assumed he was busy with the week's cleanup—a bomb, a homicidal dragon, and a dragon lord's criminal trial wasn't exactly normal, even in his line of work. But when all of that had been taken care of and he still hadn't talked to me, I'd started to worry. Then I'd started to get paranoid.

And when I say paranoid? I don't mean the normal, run-of-the-mill version where I thought Richard was just staying with me for the sex. No, I tipped completely into crazy-land. After the last day of the Chinese dragon lord's trial, I got drunk, got dressed in the world's most ragged set of pajamas, and turned my impressive skills of ass-hattery toward blaming Myrna for pretty much everything. I blushed as the memory of accusing Myrna of sleeping with Richard popped front and center in my mind. The shame of it almost felt worse than my injuries.

I had to give her credit—she didn't laugh in my face, even though any fool could see that she was head over heels in love with her newly reclaimed boyfriend, Trian.

Nope, Myrna was a stand-up gal who also had the benefit of knowing me for years. She was well-aware that I didn't have the best track record with guys.

It was my fatal flaw: I was attracted to good-looking men.

My preference for the card-carrying members of the eye-candy club doesn't sound like a flaw. In fact, most people would likely consider my tastes normal. Probably nine times out of ten, if I asked a woman whether she was more attracted to the hot dude shooting hoops on a basketball court or the hefty, middle-aged man running the concession stand, she's gonna go with the attractive ball player.

But if you told that same woman that the ball player lived out of his car, beat his dog, and stole money from every girlfriend he'd ever had, the concessions manager would start looking pretty darn good by comparison. But me? I was always the idiot who offered to share an apartment, watch the dog, and sign up for a joint checking account just because the hot guy looked even hotter when he was about to kiss me.

Like I said, my fatal flaw.

Usually Myrna was there to knock some sense into me before I did something irreversible like marry one of these jerks. But she'd seemed to almost approve of Richard.

But here I was, barely conscious and already throwing blame around like it was rice at a wedding.

I looked down at my hand once more. Despite my angry outburst, Richard had put his palm over mine.

Maybe I was overreacting. Again.

I sighed. "I'm sorry, Richard. I'm sure you had perfectly good reasons."

Richard's cheek twitched and he looked to the window. "Of course. Emory and I were simply discussing DRACIM's role in Lord Relobu's future mediation projects now that Myrna's assignment is complete. That's all."

I started to snort, but the effort made my head hurt. Emory was Myrna's boss at DRACIM, and quite possibly the biggest idiot on the face of the planet. "You'd have been better off asking Myrna. If Emory had his way, DRACIM wouldn't be involved at all. You should have seen the stack of liability releases she had to sign in order to come on this assignment."

To be fair, Lord Relobu's offices had insisted on almost as many for me. When DRACIM had flatly refused to provide one of their own agents to serve as the engagement's dragonscript expert, I'd volunteered my services. The trip had been Myrna's chance to get out from under her manager's thumb, and I'd been happy to help. Especially when taking the position meant I'd get to spend more time with Richard and see China at the same time.

Myrna had warned me the trip might be dangerous, and I thought I'd understood what she meant.
My friend worked around dragons every day, and had
to be constantly on her toes to avoid being crushed
or eaten by the much larger creatures. But she'd been
at DRACIM for years and had always managed to
come home in one piece, and I figured I'd do the
same, especially since Relobu was sending us with
a security team. And I hadn't expected our hosts to
actually make plans to cause us harm.

Oh how wrong I'd been.

"Myrna's job sucks. Did you *see* how the Chinese
dragon walked right up and threatened her? At his
own trial, for God's sake."

The lines on Richard's forehead became a bit more
pronounced. "So you remember Hian-puo's trial. Can
you remember what happened after that?"

I frowned. I could picture the dragon lawyers
making their last remarks to the ruling council, and
the trial concluding just before dinner. I'd milled
around the groups of formally dressed "party" at-
tendees looking for Richard, but I'd quickly given
up when I realized there was no way to see over the
enormous dragons crammed into the room.

When I'd finally caught sight of him in the hall
talking with Emory, I'd called his name, but they
were already halfway inside the elevator. That's the
point where I, angry, headed to Myrna's—

"Oh crap! A dragon busted into Myrna's room!

Oh my God, is she okay?" I only realized I'd been trying to climb from the bed when Richard pushed me back toward the pillows.

"She's fine, Carol. She's fine. Calm down."

I let him help me settle back into the pillows, wincing when he got too close to my knee. While he fussed with my bedding, flashes of the attack ran through my head, right up until the moment the dragon had slammed me backwards into the wall. But interspersed in these memories were pictures of Richard and Myrna's faces above me, tense and angry.

"What were you and Myrna fighting about?" The question seemed silly, considering I'd just woken up in a hospital with no memory of being brought here, but for some reason my subconscious was screaming that the answer was important.

But Richard didn't answer. Instead he reached down to my bed railing and hit the nurse call button.

"Yes?" The disembodied voice was young and buried under a heavy foreign accent. So I was still in Budapest. Good to know. At least I wasn't suffering from amnesia. This trip had been my first—and last—trip to dragon lord Lady Adelaida's Pearl of the Danube. I'd found international travel wasn't to my liking.

"She's awake. Carol is awake." Taking his hand from the button, he smiled at me and ran a finger along my cheek. "Don't worry about any of that right now. Let's make sure you're going to be okay."

Richard didn't meet my gaze as he spoke. He was hiding something, but my head was throbbing and I admitted that I didn't want to deal with anything heavy at the moment. So I changed the subject, which was harder to do than I thought it would be with my muzzy brain refusing to cooperate.

I flicked my eyes to the soggy ceiling. "What kind of dump did you bring me to?" The hospital equipment looked new enough, but the stained ceiling, combined with the general smell of damp made me think this wasn't exactly a state-of-the-art facility.

As I was speaking, a nurse stepped into the room and closed the door behind her. Dressed in standard blue scrubs and tennis shoes with her hair tied into a high ponytail, she looked fifteen years old.

It must be the middle of the night. They always stick the newbies on the night shift.

Regardless of her age, her manner was totally professional as she wrapped my arm in a blood pressure cuff and checked the levels of the IV bags hanging from a hook beside my bed. Everything must have been fine, because she turned back to me with a forced smile.

"You are awake. We were beginning to worry." Her tone suggested otherwise.

I probably should have found something other than the soggy ceiling to talk about, because she'd clearly taken offense.

Only then did I process her words, and it suddenly occurred to me that I may have been out for a long while. "Could you tell me where I am? And what's the date?"

Richard, who'd stepped away from the bed at the nurse's arrival, stepped back into my line of vision. "You're at the Péterfy Sándor in Budapest. It's a hospital."

I shot Richard an exasperated look. The monitor pretty much gave that one away.

"We are a very good hospital." The nurse's expression was almost militant, as if she dared me to disagree with her. Yep. She'd definitely heard my "dump" comment.

I was an idiot. It was like the restaurant rule, only more important. Instead of simply spitting into your food for bad customer behavior, hospital workers could unplug some pretty important machinery. Like the IV currently feeding me much-needed pain medications. I had a feeling that the dull headache I had was only the tip of the iceberg.

The nurse was right. The Péterfy Sándor was one of the oldest hospitals in Budapest, and also one of the most well regarded. When I wasn't being chased by dragons or puking my guts up in rental cars, I worked for an international advertising and publicity empire, CreaTV. I'd actually art-directed a spread for the facility, highlighting the fact that it had managed to survive all three World Wars as an active medical operation throughout. It had become one of Budapest's national treasures and a source of national pride.

And I'd just insulted it.

"Of course. You're right. I apologize for the insult. Can you tell me what day it is?" I gave her my best smile. Based on her sniff, I was far from being in her good graces, but the comment must have done something to appease her because she answered my question.

"It is Thursday."

Thursday? The "party" we'd attended, the trial of Chinese dragon lord Hian-puo, had been on a Saturday. I turned my head to find Richard. "I've been out for five days?"

His lips tightened into a thin line. "Carol, today is the 23rd. You've been unconscious for a week and a half."

The shock of his statement seemed to worsen the thumping in my skull. I raised a hand to inspect the wound on my head. But instead of the frizzy hair I expected to encounter, my fingers touched a not-so-small amount of gauze.

Good Lord, that was a lot of gauze.

The nurse frowned and captured my wrist before I managed to run my fingers around the entire expanse.

"Do not touch. It needs to heal." She eyed me closely, her hand holding firm, and waited until I nodded.

"I want to see it." I blinked and returned her stare, relaxing my arm to demonstrate my intent to follow her directions.

Only then did she release my wrist and enter the attached bathroom.

Returning with a small hand mirror, the nurse turned the glass toward my face.

For a moment I didn't recognize myself. And when I did, I fought a strange urge to cry. Bruises spread under both my eyes, so big and dark that I almost reached up to try and wipe them away. They looked drawn on, as if I were just another girl with ruined mascara, albeit mixed with a faint tinge of navy blue and purple eye shadow. The spot along my cheek where Richard had run his finger was similarly decorated, except that it had already started to heal, giving me that weird yellow-green tint under pale white skin.

But the thing that had caused a catch in my heart was the huge surgical pad balanced high on the left side of my skull. It was bigger than my hand, and taped firmly to my head with copious amounts of tape. But it wasn't the amount of adhesive that had me feeling dizzy with rage. When I looked back to Richard, I knew I was shooting daggers.

"You let them shave my head!?"

My shriek startled the nurse, and I was more than a little startled myself to see the mirror I'd been hold-

ing shatter against the far wall. Both she and Richard turned to stare at me as if I were a wild animal.

Richard treated me accordingly, both of his hands
palm out in a conciliatory gesture. "There was so
much blood, they couldn't be sure you didn't have
other wounds."

"I don't care if my brains were leaking from
my ears, Richard! You let them shave my head." I
knew it was stupid, and childish, to scream at Richard about something that likely saved my life, but I
wasn't exactly reasonable at the moment. I couldn't
help the tears welling in my eyes. I looked around to
see if there was a tissue within reach, with no luck.

In fact, my nurse had made a point to roll the
room's dinner cart a few feet away from my bed.
She continued to watch me suspiciously, and I found
myself suddenly annoyed at her presence.

I took a deep breath and turned my head to look
at her. "Did you need anything else?" I struggled to
keep my voice even, but failed miserably.

Her lips thinned as she shook her head and turned.
Walking a large circle around the broken glass, she
stalked out the door, every inch of her body tele-
graphing her affront at my attitude. With my luck,
she was probably off to find a member of hospital
security. Or a doctor from the psychiatric wing to
come and evaluate the crazy American. I couldn't
dredge up enough energy to care.

They'd cut my hair. My long, curly, red hair that

I spent a fortune every six weeks to maintain. It had taken me years to get the length I wanted without the split ends. And now it was gone. Shaved close to my head just over my right ear, and hacked into uneven hanks of curls everywhere else.

Richard murmured something about me being beautiful no matter what, but I didn't believe him. I looked like a dress-up doll who'd fallen into the nefarious hands of a mean older brother. Combined with the bruises and bandages, I could barely even recognize my own face.

I sniffled. "Where's Myrna?" With Richard's twitching and empty words, I wanted—I needed—someone here who would understand how I felt. Or at least someone who wouldn't lie to me and pretend everything was okay when it wasn't. Somewhere in the back of my mind I understood that it wasn't just my hair that had me bothered, but that I'd lost control of just about everything in my life.

Richard was quiet for a moment, as if he were weighing his words carefully. "I talked to Trian last week. A bomb went off in the Tulsa DRACIM offices, killing eleven dragons. Myrna's back in Tulsa trying to get things cleaned up."

"Oh my goodness. That's terrible. What about the humans?"

"No humans were injured."

My eyes widened. Eleven dead dragons and no human casualties? Impossible. Unless… "The bomb.

It was a biomatter bomb, wasn't it? Just like the one Hian-puo tried to use on Lady Adelaida."

He nodded. "Specifically formulated to affect only dragons. It didn't cause a single human injury. But DRACIM is involved nonetheless." Richard sounded frustrated

I'd assumed Myrna was still here in Budapest, and was a little hurt when she hadn't been by to see me since I woke. But now I realized she had much bigger problems.

"Do they know who's responsible for the attack?"

Richard walked to the window and jammed his hands into his pockets. "How much longer do you need to stay here? I'd like to leave as soon as you're able."

His frequent changes of subject were giving me whiplash. "I don't know. I just woke up." My tone was more than a little petulant; it's not like it was my fault a dragon had tossed me against a wall like a broken puppet. I'd expected a bit more coddling on his part before he started rushing me out the door. But here he was, only minutes after I'd woken from a freaking coma, acting like a husband waiting for his wife to put on her lipstick before heading out to church.

Relobu probably needed him back in Tulsa and helping Myrna, so I understood his impatience. But I was bothered by the fact that he seemed to be blaming me for the delay.

"It's fine, Richard. If you need to get back to Tulsa, I understand." I didn't. Not really. But all his brooding and snapping made me feel guilty for keeping him here. "I'll just call a taxi to take me back to the hotel for my things before I catch a flight back stateside."

At least I hoped I could do that. Commercial flights, especially to and from international locations, were rare. Flying was just too dangerous. In addition to the cost of fuel, salaries, and maintenance, airlines had to hire dragon guards to fly with them for protection from rogue or distracted dragons who might collide with them midair. Combining the cost of service with a severely low demand—there weren't many people willing to take the risk of death-by-dragon—and the airlines were simply no longer cost effective.

We'd originally flown to Europe by private charter and with a Relobu-supplied dragon escort. I would just hope that one of the dragon lord's staff would be available to help me make similar arrangements.

He sighed. "I'm sorry, Carol. I just have a lot on my mind. Let me go see if I can find your doctor." He didn't quite make it out of the room before I caught him checking his watch.

My head—my patchy, half-shaven head—was hurting again, so I said a mental good riddance to my irritating boyfriend, and drifted into a medically assisted nap.

THREE

IT SEEMS I'D made an enemy. My nurse walked into the room and sniffed with disapproval when she saw I was awake. Her expression told me that after my mini-breakdown over the haircut, she'd done her best to be assigned elsewhere, and failed miserably.

The nap had done enough good that I was embarrassed about my earlier rudeness, so I made a point to greet her properly this time around. "I'm sorry, but I didn't catch your name, what with the freakout over my hair and all. I'm Carol." I held out my palm to shake her hand, doing my best to showcase my sanity. I didn't need the entire hospital thinking I was a crazy American with a hair fetish.

"Rosa." She took my hand, but eyed me warily as she shook it, as if I might rip hers off and throw the twitching digits against the wall.

Though my entire face seemed to ache with the effort, I tried to look pleasant, but it only made Rosa quickly back up a step. I realized that at this point, there was no way Rosa was going to become my new best friend, and a simple handshake wasn't going to make her want to stay longer. Instead of wasting any more of her time, I pointed my chin in the direction of the heart monitor and asked the question all hospital patients want to know. "So. How am I doing? Any news on when they might let me out of here?"

Rosa, still giving me the wide berth you'd give a caged tiger, walked cautiously to the foot of the bed and grabbed my chart. I was impressed with how she managed to keep one eye on me as she read. "Your head is better. You are having no issues with pain." Her accent was thick, and it was a moment before I realized the last sentence wasn't in the chart. She'd asked me a question.

"Other than the injury to my vanity, and the occasional mirror tossing, I'm fine." I chuckled a little at my attempt at a joke, but stopped when the movement jostled my sore knee.

She stared at me in silence for an uncomfortable amount of time, and I had the strangest urge to tell her about the candy bar I stole from a convenience store when I was six.

"You are American?"

"Uh…" the question itself wasn't odd, as my unusual accent telegraphed the fact that I was not from around here. But Rosa's interest didn't seem to stem from friendly curiosity. Instead, she looked as if she'd just solved a puzzle that had been worrying her for a while.

Nevertheless, I answered her question. "Yes. I'm from the state of Oklahoma. Southern United States."

Her eyes widened slightly, and she looked once more at her chart. "I will speak with the doctor." She dropped my file back into the plastic holder and hustled from the room, the set of her shoulders and the brisk squeak of her shoes broadcasting her haste.

I wasn't doing a very good job of making friends.

Which would have been fine, except Richard had disappeared. I figured he was either still out looking for my doctor, or had left to go get some coffee. So when my door opened, I assumed it was him. Instead, a different sandy-haired man, around my age, entered the room and gave me a polite nod before settling himself comfortably in the chair beside my bed.

Out for coffee it was. Apparently my surgeon was right here.

"Nice to see you're awake. Carol Jenski, correct?" Unlike Rosa, he was very easy to understand. In fact, his accent was almost non-existent. I found myself worrying once again about my appearance. Why is it that I could only meet a doctor this good-looking when I actually looked like I needed a doctor, and not in some cozy coffee shop where I could flirt with abandon?

"That's me."

His lips crinkled at my response, and I felt my heart flutter. This man was gorgeous. And more importantly, he was impeccably dressed. The shirt he wore was a crisp, pale green, and it complemented his skin tone perfectly. Not to mention it was the

exact same color as his eyes. He'd combined it with a
pair of dark khaki slacks and a brown leather jacket.
The combination was a one-two punch to my libido.
Nothing was sexier than a good looking man who
knew how to dress himself.

He stretched to shake my hand. I took the opportunity to peek at his third finger, and my heart did
more than flutter. He wasn't wearing a wedding ring.

His grip was firm, and warm, and I gave myself
a moment to be glad my boyfriend was occupied
elsewhere. Just because I was off the dating market
didn't mean I couldn't take a look at the local wares.

"My name's Daniel Wallent. Are you feeling up
to answering a few questions?"

I gave him an overly enthusiastic smile, mostly
because the condition of my teeth was the only thing
I was positive about. My upper lip was busted and
still a little swollen, but at least the dragon hadn't
knocked loose any of my dentist-enhanced pearly
whites. Smiling was all I had left. So long as he
didn't get close enough to smell my breath. Based on
some quick mental math, I hadn't brushed my teeth
in over a week. "Sure."

Dr. Wallent settled back into his chair and pulled
a notepad from the briefcase at his feet. "Tell me a
little bit about yourself, Carol. What brings you to
Budapest?"

Odd question. But then again, I'd never had a serious head injury before. Maybe he just liked to make

sure patients weren't suffering from amnesia. Or loss of motor function. Heck, maybe my smile looked better than I thought, and Dr. Daniel was flirting with me.

"I came with a friend. She had some business in China, and we stopped by Budapest on our way back to the U.S." I wasn't sure how much of DRACIM's involvement in the China situation had been shared with the general public, so I did my best to keep my explanations generic until I could consult with Myrna about the DRACIM projects that were public domain—like the translation services at the trial— and the parts that weren't—like DRACIM's help with the relocation and employment of Hian-puo's abused human servants.

At the trial, Lord Relobu had publicly taken credit for most of the trip's activities, so DRACIM might well prefer to remain safely in the role of facilitator instead of show runner.

"And what were you doing in China?"

My frown pulled at the wound on my scalp, and I had to make a conscious effort to smooth my expression. His question was a valid one, especially if he was checking to see whether I was mentally competent or not. International tourism hadn't fared so well since the Third World War, partly because a lot of the touristy scenery had been severely damaged by the bombs lobbed back and forth across the oceans. When the dragons were discovered, many

nations turned their military efforts toward the an-
nihilation of the species worldwide. The dragons
didn't like this, obviously, and several more of our
tourist hotspots had been destroyed by the reptiles'
fits of rage.

China wasn't exactly business or vacation friendly
anymore. Hian-puo had been the dragon lord since
the beginning of dragon rule, and he'd made it very
clear that he wasn't fond of visitors. It was rare to
see a human deliberately book travel to that area of
the world. In fact, most people spent a lot of time
trying to *leave* China, not enter it. Unlike Relobu,
Hian-puo had offered no protection from possible
dragon attacks. More often than not, Hian-puo had
been the one ordering the strikes.

Still, I couldn't give him specifics until I was certain DRACIM would approve. "I'm sorry, but if it's
okay with you, I'd rather skip that question until I
can talk with my friend. She sometimes deals with…
sensitive issues. I'm not sure how much I'm allowed
to talk about."

Dr. Wallent studied me intently, and I stifled the
urge to burrow further under the thin blanket. Maybe
he wasn't my surgeon. Maybe Rosa really had noti-
fied the psych ward, and he was a shrink. Or he was
my surgeon, and he now assumed I actually did have
amnesia and would never sign the discharge order.
I made a conscious effort to stop my wildly spinning thoughts.

"I can assure you, I remember the entire trip. And I'm not making it up, the trip was real."

I regretted the words as soon as they were out of my mouth. There's nothing that makes a person sound crazier than insisting they aren't crazy. He was silent for another few seconds. "Very well, Ms. Jenski. What do you do for a living?"

I breathed a sigh of relief. This was a question I could answer. "I'm a manager at the Tulsa branch of CreaTV Marketing. The company as a whole is involved in public relations and media pursuits across several industries. I head up the fashion department. We're in charge of ads and magazine spreads, and recently, we've market-tested a few television commercials as well."

"Ms. Jenski, are you a dragonspeaker?"

The tension had barely left my aching shoulders before my muscles were once again bunched in response to my renewed urge to flee. Outside of DRACIM, dragonspeakers are extremely rare. There were very few people who knew I understood the dragon language. I'd dabbled in it while I was at college, but learned pretty fast that I wouldn't cut it as a full-time expert. The job required far too much time spent in stuffy old libraries hunched over barely legible scraps of paper. I was a people person; that much time alone would have killed me. So I contented myself with the occasional bit of home study. Later, when Myrna started bringing home paperwork full of the familiar language, I got curious. Within a few months, I was helping her decode some of the dragonscript in her contracts and such. Until recently, my interest hadn't gone much further than that.

It wasn't exactly something to brag about. The general public did their best to ignore dragons entirely, so admitting you were one of the few who understood their language automatically labeled you a dragon lover, and society's doors closed pretty quickly after that. If I knew anything, it was fashion, and it was *not* in fashion to be a friend of the dragons.

In Tulsa, politicians paid lip service to the North American dragon lord, but they made sure it happened behind closed doors. With Hollywood coming back to life after the war, mostly due to dragon financial assistance, I expected that attitude to change somewhat—movie stars historically pandered to the moneymen, and the general public followed suit. But until then, interacting with dragons outside an official DRACIM capacity pretty much made you persona non grata in most human circles. Even with the protection of Myrna's chosen career, some people still treated her as a traitor to her own race. As a public "dragon lover," Myrna'd been very careful to keep her address under wraps after she moved in with me. It was safer that way.

"Ms. Jenski? Did you hear my question? Do you

understand the dragon language?" Dr. Wallent was waiting for my answer, his green eyes seemingly burning a hole in my head.

"I—I don't. I don't understand. Why would you need to know that?"

"Ms. Jenski, I'd appreciate it if you'd just answer the question." The easygoing gentleman was gone and his attitude had become tense, driven. Almost angry as he leaned forward in his chair.

I was getting that way myself. "I don't see why that's any of your business. If you're asking whether I regularly hang out with dragons, the answer is no. And I'd appreciate it if you could tell me why you're so interested in what I do in my free time. How exactly is this supposed to help me heal, Dr. Wallent?"

His left eye twitched, and if I didn't know any better, I would have said he was startled by my response. He settled back into his chair, steepling his hands under his chin.

"I'm sorry, Ms. Jenski. I'm just trying to figure out what happened. Can you tell me what were you doing at the Hotel Gellért a week ago?"

I'll admit it. My feathers were a little ruffled by his questions. My expectations for this conversation—a few easy medical questions interspersed with a lot of flirting—were obviously off target. That, coupled with my bald head, bruises, and severely deflated ego had made me a little cranky. I took a deep breath. The poor guy was just trying to do his job. And I'd always heard that the better the doctor was medically, the worse he was at achieving a pleasant bedside manner. If I had to choose, I'd take the medical expertise.

"Like I said, I was there with a friend."

"Were there dragons present?"

That fact was no secret. Lord Relobu had long attempted to foster goodwill between the two races, and had sponsored or hosted many parties in an attempt to calm the tensions among both species. But Hian-puo's trial, oddly enough, had done more to bring humans and dragons together peacefully than all of Lord Relobu's attempts put together. As soon as the trial had been announced, news of the accompanying gala had spread like wildfire through every major newspaper in the world.

I wondered how the bomb at DRACIM had affected those budding attempts at a real peace.

"Yes. My friend works for DRACIM. She was at the hotel on a translating assignment." A lot more had been involved in the assignment than translation, including Myrna's testimony against a power-hungry, insane dragon lord, but it was as far as I could go without speaking with Myrna first. The public was used to DRACIM translating for dragons. What they weren't used to was DRACIM tracking down bioweapons and taking point on international dragon political disasters.

DRACIM, especially the Tulsa office, did their

best to work closely with an area's reigning dragon, and I didn't want to damage the company's relationship with Relobu by sharing details he hadn't vetted for public consumption until I had a chance to find out what the two organizations were running with as an official story. Richard hadn't exactly given me a detailed play-by-play on the current media environment, and I was nearly two weeks behind the rest of the world newswise.

If I'd learned one thing in my years at CreaTV, it was that people talked, and turned tiny bits of information into full-blown panic-worthy explosions. I'd rather err on the side of caution than make a dragon lord angry. A DRACIM official working for Lord Relobu at a function, even an international one, was nothing out of the ordinary. So until Myrna told me different, that was the limit of DRACIM's involvement.

Dr. Wallent nodded. "Your friend. Is she available for a few questions?"

"I'm afraid not."

"Who was the man with you earlier? Is he also a DRACIM employee?" He must have seen Richard in my room while I'd been in a coma.

I briefly wondered whether he thought I was making the whole DRACIM thing up, and wanted someone to corroborate my story. Someone without a head injury.

DRACIM North America, operating under the

purview of Earth's most human-friendly dragon lord, was by far the largest branch of the company. Maybe the one here in Adelaida's territory wasn't as well-known as the one back home. Or maybe this doctor just needed to get out more.

Either way, I wasn't in the mood to be helpful.

"That was my boyfriend. And no, he doesn't work for DRACIM." Which was the truth. Richard worked for Relobu. And as one of Relobu's top human employees, anything Richard said would be taken as if it came directly from the dragon lord's tongue. I didn't want to accidentally set loose a rumor if I could help it.

Where in the heck did Richard run off to?

This conversation was making my head ache. Something just didn't feel right. I wasn't familiar with foreign medical routines, but even allowing for cultural differences, this conversation seemed a bit extreme. I felt more like a suspect accused of a crime than a medical patient. "Shouldn't you be taking my blood pressure or something?"

He ignored my question and circled back to my earlier explanation. "Would your boyfriend be Richard Green? CEO of Relobu Holdings?" The intent look in his eyes was back, and I felt the hair rise on the back of my neck.

"I don't understand how that's—"

Before he could answer, my door swung open and

a woman dressed in a business suit and white jacket walked in, with Richard trailing a few steps behind.

I smiled, grateful that Richard was back to speak for himself in my conversation with Dr. Wallent. My gaze went back to the woman who'd entered before him, wondering how she fit into this increasingly confusing situation.

"Carol, it is delightful to find you awake! I am your surgeon, Doctor Garay." The woman walked to the bed and held out a hand.

Mystified, I gave it a perfunctory squeeze. "Um, hi. Nice to meet you." I looked to Richard, who was oblivious to my confusion. He was too busy frowning at Dr. Wallent, who currently watched our exchange with ill-concealed impatience.

Dr. Garay was likewise ignoring my look of bewilderment. "Rosa tells me you are anxious to be discharged. I have been looking over your chart. I see no serious problems, but do you mind if I perform a quick examination?"

The doctor finally met my eyes, and her chirpy demeanor dimmed slightly. "Is everything okay? Are you in pain?" She reached out as if to pull back the bandage on my head, but I waved her away, instead leaning forward so I could see "Dr. Wallent."

Daniel Wallent—the man who'd walked into my room like he owned the place, who was now lounging arrogantly in my chair, and who had spent the past several minutes grilling me like a cop—gave me a small shrug as if to say "so what if I've been found out? You're the idiot who fell for it."

I wanted to send my scabby fist straight into his nose.

"Who the *hell* are you?"

He laughed. "Don't worry, I'm not here to kill you or anything." He glanced at Richard, who stood frozen just inside my room with an expression of terror on his face. "The same can't be said for your boyfriend. Word is, he has no issues with doing whatever it takes in the name of revenge. I wonder how Lord Relobu feels about his employee's recent activities?"

Richard went white, and I could practically hear his teeth grinding. Daniel's comment had struck a nerve, but for the life of me I couldn't catch the undercurrents. I looked at the doctor and was relieved to see that she seemed just as confused as I was.

Daniel stood and slid past the IV stand. "Tell me, Mr. Green, would you be interested in giving me something I can quote for my article tomorrow?"

Article?

I felt the bandage move on my head as my eyebrows shot up. "You're a reporter!" My heart clenched as I mentally ran through our conversation.

I'd been focused on keeping the inner workings of DRACIM safe from the curious public, not from a man with knowledge and experience taking tiny bits of information like this and digging up the full story behind them.

If word got out about all that had happened, we'd have another World War on our hands. Hian-puo's trial had been a step in the right direction for human-dragon interactions. DRACIM's media arm had done a great job presenting the trial as proof that the dragon council cared about the Chinese dragon lord's treatment of his human subjects, and had taken action to stop it.

Despite their efforts, our human governments were still highly hostile to the dragon nations. They didn't play by human rules, and we didn't have a good way to make them. DRACIM was doing its best to change that fact with the few human-friendly dragon lords willing to attend talks about human rights.

But according to Myrna, the idea of worldwide dragon laws against human mistreatment was still little more than a pipe dream. Despite what DRACIM was trying to make the public believe, most of the dragon council, Relobu excluded, had taken an interest in Hian-puo's actions because he'd been building a bomb that harmed dragons, not because he was routinely rude and dangerous to the humans in his territory.

At the trial, I'd agreed with the approach. It was better for dragons in general to appear in a positive light while DRACIM worked behind the scenes. Nicer dragons meant the human world would more likely take a "wait and see" stance for Hian-puo's successor, instead of panicking about the remaining dragon lords tearing a hole through the world in a battle to determine who got the remaining territory. We had too many world leaders with itchy trigger fingers, and if we had another war, I was almost positive the humans wouldn't come out the winners.

And I'd just blabbed information directly to the press. Sure, I'd been somewhat circumspect, but Daniel had obviously done his homework. Trips to China were rarer than black dragons. The only course left open was to find out how much the reporter knew, and get the information to Myrna in time for her to play a little damage control. Taking a moment to mutter a silent apology for adding to Myrna's workload, I straightened my shoulders and met Daniel Wallent's eyes. "I'm afraid now isn't the best time for an interview. But I'd be glad to discuss your story after I've been discharged. Perhaps sometime next week, when I'm feeling a bit better?"

"I am afraid I must agree. She is in no shape for interviews." The doctor jumped into action, crossing the room to retrieve a small set of scissors from a drawer.

Daniel Wallent angled his body toward my bed and leaned in close, exposing a dimple in his left cheek. "Next week, hmm?"

I nodded, embarrassed and annoyed when the heart monitor registered the increase in my heart rate at his proximity.

"Well, Ms. Jenski, I'm afraid next week will be too late. A dragon-killing bomb went off at DRACIM's Tulsa offices, and I have reliable sources who say your boyfriend was the one who shipped it there. So if it's all the same to you, I think I'll be speaking with Mr. Green."

Richard shipped a bomb to DRACIM? Mr. Wallent's information was completely wrong. Richard worked for Lord Relobu. No way would Richard purposely kill dragons. I was reevaluating my assumption that Mr. Wallent had been thorough in his research.

Glaring at the amused reporter, I wondered how I'd ever thought this man was cute. "Mr. Wallent. I'm afraid speaking to Mr. Green just won't be possible."

He gave me an indulgent smile. "And what makes you say that?"

"It appears he had another appointment."

FOUR

THE AMUSED EXPRESSION dropped from Daniel's face when he turned toward the spot where Richard had been standing only a moment before. While Daniel had been gloating about his impersonation skills, Richard had sneaked from the room.

All trace of his superior attitude gone, Daniel shot me one last glare before he bolted out the door in pursuit.

I laughed, then groaned as the movement jostled my head. Richard wasn't stupid. There was no way Daniel would be able to track him down today.

Then it occurred to me—Richard was my ride out of here. My injury had left me with little memory of the route we took to reach the hospital, so I had no idea how to get back to the hotel.

Any cab driver worth his salt could get me there, of course, assuming I had money to pay for a taxi. Which I didn't. Also, I wasn't sure I wanted to return to Hotel Gellért, especially if Hian-puo's dragons hadn't cleared out.

What I really wanted to do was find the next plane headed for North America. But I couldn't go straight to the airport; my passport was still in my suitcase. Earlier, Richard had seemed more than eager to leave Budapest as well, so it was possible I'd get to the hotel only to realize he'd grabbed my stuff for me while I'd been unconscious.

I chewed my lower lip, trying to decide whether I'd be better off waiting until Richard returned to the hospital, or whether I should take my chances on a quick flight to Tulsa.

I much preferred the second option; homesickness was a sick weight in the pit of my stomach, and I really, really wanted out of this hospital bed. But I certainly wasn't up for another round of avoiding Hian-puo's thugs. And how would I leave word for Richard on where I'd disappeared to?

Dr. Garay cleared her throat. Still holding my chart, she peered at me over the rims of her reading glasses. "Mr. Green still works for the North American dragon lord?"

"Well, um…" Richard *had* worked for Lord Relobu the last time I checked, but I was beginning to realize I'd missed a lot more than I thought. The idea of Richard as a bomb-maker was laughable. He'd worked for the dragon lord for years now without even a hint of a problem. In fact, he was surprisingly well-adjusted to navigating in a dragon-rich environment considering his father's history.

His dad—paralyzed from the waist down in an attack by angry dragons—had been Richard's responsibility since he turned fifteen. But Richard hadn't seemed to mind, much less blame Relobu for it.

But since I'd woken up, Richard was acting strange. What if Daniel Wallent wasn't as crazy as I thought he was? Maybe Richard really had been involved with the bomb that went off at DRACIM—

And then it hit me.

The rest of the dragon experts were back in Tulsa dealing with the bomb cleanup, both Lord Relobu's teams and the agents of DRACIM. As Relobu's top ranking human official, Richard would have been expected to personally direct the dragon lord's resources in dealing with the aftermath. But Richard had stayed behind with me in Budapest, something even Myrna hadn't been able to do.

Relobu had almost certainly ordered Richard back to Tulsa with the others, and Richard had decided to stay here with me instead.

I flushed with guilt that I was considering Richard was involved. He wasn't acting strange because he'd set off a bomb. He was acting strange because he'd refused a command from a dragon lord. Nobody did that.

Relobu was probably furious. No wonder Richard was ready to get me out of the hospital as soon as possible. He probably expected the dragon lord to send someone to "convince" Richard he'd made a bad decision with some claws or teeth. Dragons weren't exactly the subtle type, and they definitely did not handle rejection well.

Dr. Garay was still frowning, so I rushed to put her at ease.

"Please don't worry. I'm sure Richard will work everything out. Lord Relobu isn't aware we're even here. No harm will come to your hospital."

I certainly hoped I wasn't lying through my still-attractive teeth.

Dr. Garay looked startled for a moment, then laughed. "This hospital has been here for over one hundred years, and through three World Wars. I'm confident it can survive much worse than a few angry dragons. We're no strangers to dragons here. In fact, Hungary's dragon lord, Lady Adelaida, provides generous financial support for the Péterfy Sándor."

I blinked, surprised. "That's—" I wasn't sure what to say. Ridiculous? Unheard of? Outside the realm of possibility?

The doctor smiled at my expression. "Your dragon lord isn't the only one with a positive interest in humans. We make up the largest facility for dragon-related trauma in all of Europe. Lady Adelaida feels it is her responsibility to ensure we are able to provide top-notch service to those who have been victims of her more aggressive subjects."

That was the nicest way to refer to creatures prone to murderous rage that I'd heard in a while and I fought the urge to roll my eyes. Myrna had regaled me with stories of "unreasonable" dragons. In a human, similar bursts of anger would be seen as out of the ordinary, but mostly just annoying. But a temper tantrum from a dragon often meant damage to property, and sometimes loss of human life.

I hadn't fully understood the constant stress Myrna was under as a DRACIM agent until I'd experienced a dragon temper tantrum firsthand. I fought the urge to shiver at the memory of the green dragon bursting through Myrna's hotel door as if it had been made of tissue.

No wonder Richard took off when he realized I'd been talking to the press. Nothing would bring Relobu to our front door faster than our pictures being pasted above the fold in a major newspaper. Even now, after I'd accused him of cheating on me *and* likely cost him his job, he was still trying to protect me. Unfortunately, that protection had left me momentarily alone in a foreign country.

Dr. Garay had her gaze directed once again at my chart. She made a few notations to the papers before glancing up with a smile. "I have good news, Carol. I believe your injuries have healed enough that I can process the discharge papers today, so long as you promise to avoid situations that would cause strain for at least ten days. Also, you must call me should you have any issues."

"Absolutely. That's wonderful news." And it was. Except for the part where I wasn't sure of my next move.

While I wasn't comfortable leaving Richard alone

to deal with his issues—especially since I'd indirectly caused most of them—I was doing more harm than good sticking around here. It was time for me to find my way back to Tulsa.

I hoped there would be something I could do stateside to help him. I had no desire to do anything but get back to my regular life. I'd come along on the trip as a favor to Myrna, but I wasn't cut out for this kind of work. Give me a quiet cubicle over formal dragon ceremonies any day. I might be bored with the first, but at least there was a greater chance I'd manage to keep the pieces of my skull intact.

To be perfectly honest, I had no wish to be around should Relobu decide to show his irritation. I just didn't have the stomach for it. Going back home would be the easiest way to allow Richard to do what he needed to do to get back into Relobu's good graces without having to worry about me. At this point, the only thing I could do to help was to remove myself from the role of the simpering princess who needed protection. I had no doubt Relobu would welcome Richard back with open arms as soon as the dragon lord realized Richard wasn't deliberately ignoring his orders.

Besides, with Myrna's boss Emory being the idiot that he was, my friend was probably hoping Richard would come back and help her pick up the slack in what had to be the public relations nightmare of the century.

A dragon-killing bomb at DRACIM. I shivered at the amount of public panic she was likely dealing with right now. DRACIM was as close to neutral territory the humans had in their dealings with dragons, and I couldn't imagine how people would react to the news that it was no longer safe.

Speaking of Myrna… "I don't suppose you have a telephone here at the hospital I could use?" I needed to give her a heads up that I'd be home soon, and that an incompetent reporter was chasing our China story under the mistaken impression that Richard had more sinister intentions.

"Of course. Just speak to the charge nurse." Dr. Garay made a final notation on my chart before looking up. "I would greatly prefer to keep you here for another two or three days for observation, but if you feel strongly about leaving today…"

"I do." I was getting itchy sitting in a bed that was literally being paid for by one of the very dragons my boyfriend had supposedly tried to kill. I snorted. Even if Richard's involvement was a mistake, it was super-bad karma.

The doctor pursed her lips, but she didn't push. "Well, looks like we have everything in order here; I've given you a script for the pain, and you'll need to have your stitches removed in a few days. You're likely to experience mild dizziness and slight nausea, but make sure and give us a call if you feel confused, or you experience loss of motor function, no matter how small."

"Will do." I paused, hoping she'd be able to fill me in on the most important detail of being discharged, but when Dr. Garay remained silent and started gathering her things to leave, I cleared my throat and took the plunge. "What about my clothes?"

The doctor raised an eyebrow in question.

I moved the blanket off my legs to display the hospital-issue white gown, ragged at the hem and, even freshly laundered, dotted with stains of things I knew hadn't come from me. "Where are my clothes being kept?"

They hadn't been in the restroom when my ponytailed nurse had helped me hobble in there earlier this morning. Not that I was too excited to put them back on; I'd been in a set of mismatched pajamas when Myrna and I were attacked, and I wasn't looking forward to hitting the streets in them. But at least they would cover my butt until I could get something decent.

Unlike the hospital gown.

Dr. Garay smiled and reached out to pat my hand. "I'm afraid we had to cut your clothes off when you arrived. There was a lot of blood, and we couldn't be sure it wasn't yours without taking a look. But don't worry, dear. We have arrangements with a local business to provide clothing in these situations." She reached over and pushed the call button on my bed, and seconds later Rosa's head popped through the doorway. Dr. Garay filled her in on my predicament, and Rosa assured me that all my unmentionables would be covered in no time. The nurse closed the door behind her.

The doctor made one last effort to convince me to stay, then handed me what looked like a ream of paper filled with directions for continuing my care at home and dire warnings should I not follow said directions explicitly. Thank goodness I had a head for foreign languages, because the sheer volume of Hungarian paperwork I'd been given made me blanch.

I was feeling pretty cheery, considering. Sure, my boyfriend was currently MIA, my most comfortable pair of pajamas were in shreds and stuffed in a bio-waste container somewhere, and my hairstyle was far from ideal. But the doctor had given me a good amount of painkillers, and I was on my way back to America and away from this dragon business forever.

Not to mention I was about to get clothes—for free. Well, probably not for free, but covered by insurance. How often does that happen? I wondered whether I'd get lucky and they'd bring me something European-branded that's super expensive in the United States. I hoped Rosa was a good guess on sizes; I didn't think my bruises would appreciate a marathon try-on session.

The doctor had been gone around five minutes when Rosa opened the door. The monitor once again registered my excitement, this time at the sight of the red shopping bag dangling from the crook of her arm.

I love clothes. Even though I spend every day at work choosing outfits for our models to wear, I never get tired of shopping for myself. In fact, that's how Myrna got me to volunteer for this trip. She needed someone who could read as well as speak the dragon language, and I needed to experience firsthand shopping in Europe—the only continent still creating quality new fashion after the war. Hian-puo's hissy fit had kept my dreams of flying to Paris from becoming a reality, but maybe this hospital trip would have an unforeseen bright side.

I might not have been able to pick them out myself, but I was still going home with a new outfit from a foreign country.

The nurse reached into the bag and I felt my sore body protest as I sucked in a deep breath. Rosa pulled something from the top.

The material was…some sort of cotton, and colorful. The cotton I didn't mind. But the color? It wasn't my favorite. I preferred to even out the flame red of my hair with more neutral tones. But, I reminded myself with an inner eye roll, since I was missing most of my hair, I could handle more color than usual.

She shook out the folded fabric and my mind went completely blank. It was the most hideous thing I'd ever seen.

"Oh, my God. Is that—" Despite the pain, I shook

my head, hoping the vision before me was a side effect of my recent injury.

It didn't do any good. The colorful fabric wasn't just colorful, it was Hawaiian print. And it wasn't a cute little dress. Or even a pair of trendy, cropped pants.

And then Rosa smiled for the first time since I'd met her. "Miss Jenski, you are American, yes?"

I nodded, unable to speak. My brain couldn't make sense of what it was seeing.

"I hear Americans prefer to dress according to their own style. Things that reflect their personality. This," she said with a challenging lift to her brow, "is what I see of your personality. Noisy, rude, and not at all pretty."

Rude? What had I ever done to her? I was beginning to think she had me confused with someone—

My thoughts were interrupted by the big clothing reveal. A heavy jolt of shock slammed into my belly.

It was a muumuu. A long, painfully colored sack that—even in the loose-fitting housedress style— was still at least three sizes too large for me. "Is this a joke?" I just couldn't comprehend what was happening. I'd been more than hesitant to wear my ratty pajamas, but compared to this outfit, my pajamas were Chanel's latest dragon-proof design.

"No, this is not a joke." Rosa said with a triumphant smile, her tone very clearly mocking.

I looked again at the red package she'd carried through the door. What I'd thought was a fancy, designer shopping bag was actually emblazoned with a familiar white logo. Rosa noticed I was straining to get a better look and turned the package toward me.

"The Salvation Army? There's a Salvation Army in Hungary? And they carry Hawaiian print muu-muus?"

Rosa's smile grew wider. "No. The Salvation Army doesn't carry anything this ugly. The hospital has an arrangement. We are given the clothes that aren't good enough for their stores." She pushed the muumuu toward me. "Of course, we do offer you the option of a hospital gown."

"Of course you do." The hospital gown fit like all hospital gowns—not at all. So this was spitting in a customer's food…hospital style.

FIVE

ABOUT AN HOUR later, I walked slowly toward the information desk at the entrance of the hospital, Dr. Garay's sheaf of discharge papers clutched in my hand. Despite the very drafty back, I'd chosen the hospital gown. The muumuu had been truly hideous, and once Rosa brought it closer, had emanated a distinct mothball fragrance.

I'd told myself that at least I'd be able to blend in with the rest of the hospital patients until I could pick up something else. I'd cinched the thin material as tightly as I could around my waist and prayed the well-worn fabric held together long enough for me to find some decent underwear.

The elation of outsmarting Daniel Wallent had worn off. Now the reality of being alone in a foreign country at a hospital at which I barely remember arriving hit me hard. Richard hadn't returned yet, and it was becoming harder and harder to feel good about my decision to wait for him here. But every time I decided to take my future into my own hands and get a flight out of Budapest on my own, I'd remember that Richard had braved a dragon's fury in order to remain in the city with me. The least I could do was stick around until he came back.

If he came back. I realized my hand had an unconscious stranglehold on the small bottle of pain medication prescribed by the good doctor.

Luckily, the woman seated at the reception desk looked much friendlier than Rosa, so I swallowed the panic and asked to use the phone.

"Of course. Anything we can do for our patients." She lifted both headset and base onto the narrow vinyl lip of the nurse's station. I dialed the number to the apartment Myrna and I shared in Tulsa, and was surprised when a male voice answered. It took me a minute to place it.

"Trian? Hi, um, is Myrna around?" I felt awkward talking to Myrna's ex-boyfriend. We hadn't spoken since Myrna told me he regularly morphed into a two-thousand-pound dragon and started tearing things apart. It would be weird to greet him with "Hey, I hear you turn into a reptile, that's cool." But not mentioning it at all felt like I was somehow hiding the fact that I knew, or basically admitting to him that dragons were still somewhat terrifying to me. I'd actually hoped to ease into the discussion during a series of casual double dates or something.

So much for that. It looked like Trian had moved out of ex-boyfriend status, and I now had a dragon morph living in my apartment.

"Carol? Is that you?" Trian's voice crackled

through the old telephone system as he sighed. "Oh Carol, you shouldn't have called here." He sounded disappointed, and more than a little resigned.

"I've run into a little problem…" I trailed off, unable to explain my current situation without sounding mentally unhinged. "I'm actually at a hospital right now, but I'm being discharged. Richard was supposed to come and pick me up, but I'm not sure where he is. I'll tell her about it as soon as I'm back, but I wanted to give her a heads up about a reporter I accidentally talked to."

"Before you say anything else, you really need to give Myrna a call." There was an uncomfortable pause.

"Ookaaay…" I waited for him to tell me what he meant by that, but he either didn't want to tell me, or didn't notice my discomfort. I heard him rustling papers on the other end of the line before he rattled off a string of digits and told me they were Myrna's new number at DRACIM.

"Trian, what's going—"

"If anyone asks, you didn't speak with me. Call Myrna." The call disconnected.

Frowning at Trian's abrupt sign off, I gave the receptionist an absent smile as I punched the phone's worn keypad.

"Myrna Banks." My friend sounded flustered.

"Myrna, it's Carol. I just got off the phone with—"

"Carol. Thank God you're okay. I'm so glad you

would he want with me?" Did the dragon lord think I'd have some insight into why Hian-puo had sent the dragon after Myrna? If so, he was going to be sorely disappointed.

"Relobu made an announcement on all the public radio stations that if he finds you, he's planning on charging you with the DRACIM bombing."

"What?" I'd been experiencing a lot of "I can't believe this" moments lately, but this one took the cake. "Why in the world does he think I had something to do with it? I wasn't even around. In case no one has noticed, I've been laid up in a hospital bed for a while now. Unless I developed an ability to spirit-walk and possess people while being in a coma, it wasn't me."

Myrna sighed. "I know. It's ridiculous. But someone mentioned to the dragon lord that you flew dragonback to Budapest ahead of the rest of the China team. Alone."

"I did, but it was to buy clothes, not to orchestrate the theft of a weapon of mass destruction!" I made a conscious effort to lower my voice. My hysterical tone had managed to draw the eyes of several hospital occupants, and the last thing I needed was to make myself more visible. "Myrna, you and Richard used Relobu's jet to go after the bomb Hian-puo shipped from China into Adelaida's territory. Relobu ordered another to carry the human members of the team Hian-puo had been holding captive, but it was going to take at least twenty-four hours to get the plane to China, and then the plan was for it to fly straight back to the U.S. When one of Relobu's dragon's offered me a ride to Budapest, I took him up on it. That's all."

"I have a hunch I'm tracking down, but it's going to take a while. I don't have time to explain exactly why, but you need to leave. Preferably without Richard."

I was stunned. "Without Richard? Myrna, I'm a foreign country! My clothes and passport are still at the hotel, and I don't even have money for a cab. Maybe it's better that when Relobu's people show up, I simply explain how there was no possible way I was involved."

I knew the words were stupid as soon as they were out of my mouth. There was no way any of Relobu's subjects would dare disobey him, even if they did believe me. Richard was as close to the dragon as any human could be, and even he had been a nervous wreck in my hospital room. And if Relobu sent actual dragons to pick me up? I seriously doubt they'd even give me time to try and explain. Dragons weren't exactly known for their patience. And the fact that I was accused of killing some of their coworkers— likely a friend or family member at that—did not help the odds that they'd be inclined to friendliness.

"Myrna. I didn't do it. You have to believe me." My voice broke as a sob threatened to break free.

"I do. And I'm doing the best I can to make him see reason, but I need some time. Which means I need you to get out of there. Quickly. I've done what I could to keep your location under wraps, but I'm hearing chatter that one of Lady Adelaida's teams has received a tip that you're at the hospital, and she's sending someone to check it out. With all the recent disturbances, she's being careful to demonstrate that her allegiance with Relobu is still very strong, so if she finds you, it's a given that you'll end up in a Relobu holding cell as soon as they can strap you to the back of a dragon. Someone must have ratted you out. Frankly I'm surprised she hasn't found you already."

Just then, Rosa entered the hall and gave me another glare. Suddenly her attitude made much more sense. She was the rat. And she'd turned me in, not because I'd insulted her hospital, but because she thought I was a murderer.

Oh crap.

"You need to get out of the hospital."

I couldn't agree with her more. But that was easier said than done. I could barely walk without becoming dizzy. I'd have no chance with a group of trained predators.

I needed to get to the hotel, find my passport, and find a plane heading west...

It was as if Myrna read my mind. "You can't come back to the United States. Relobu is in charge, and I can't guarantee your safety here. Right now, Adelaida's dragons are the ones you need to avoid. But when Relobu's team gets there...the only reason there isn't a swarm of North American dragons dragging you out of there right now is because Trian told Relobu he needed more time to recover before going back out on assignment. The instant Trian is back in command, he'll have no choice but to come and get you himself."

And I'd basically told Trian where I was. No wonder he hadn't been in the mood to talk to me. He'd been doing his best to play dumb, and I had to go and ring him up on the telephone, leaving him no choice but to fly straight to Budapest as soon as he was cleared for duty. I'd jumped out of a frying pan, directly into a freaking volcano.

"But I don't understand." Things were moving faster than I could process them. "Why is he after me? I need to talk to Richard. As soon as he gets back, I'll—"

"Carol, don't wait on Richard. You need to leave, now." The thumping from Myrna's office had started up again, only this time it was accompanied by a human voice shouting profanity in very loud dragon-speak. "Honey, I have to go. There's a dragon tearing my waiting room into bits. Stay safe. Call me when you can." The line went dead.

I was still staring at the phone when I heard a familiar voice. "Trouble in paradise, little girl?"

Daniel Wallent was propped against one of the

hospital's stone columns only feet away, giving me a smug smile of his own.

"What are you still doing here?" Daniel Wallent was the last person I wanted to see while I was still trying to absorb what Myrna had told me. Lord Relobu made an announcement, and now I was a fugitive? It just didn't make sense.

I was Myrna's best friend, for goodness' sake. Until moments ago, I was still technically employed by the dragon lord as a dragonscript expert in an ongoing investigation. It was the reason I was in Budapest to start with. Well, that and the fact that I'd self-appointed as Myrna's fashion adviser. Shopping was the only part of the trip I'd actually enjoyed. And now, because I'd hopped on a dragon's back to fit in an extra couple of hours of my favorite activity, I was a wanted fugitive? Even the idea was insane. I didn't think my confusion was unfounded.

"Is Richard still here in the hospital? I'd still like to get a quote for that story." Daniel's expression was open and expectant, and despite the fact that most of my current predicament wasn't his fault, his obvious good cheer was more than annoying. It was downright infuriating.

"Even if he was, I wouldn't tell you."

He shrugged as if he'd heard that same response a million times before. "Fair enough. However, I couldn't help but overhear your conversation. Sounds like you're in a pickle. Are there holes popping up in Wonderland?"

I leaned my forehead against the cool surface of the reception desk. My head was throbbing, I was dizzy, and apparently there was one dragon army after me and another on the way. Not bothering to lift my head from the desk, I rolled my face around to look at the reporter.

"Can we please not do this right now?"

Daniel studied me silently for a moment. "Tell you what. I'll get you out of here. Tomorrow I'll help you figure out how to get your stuff from the hotel, or get you in contact with your boyfriend."

I raised my head. "You'd do that? Why?" Visions of Daniel hauling me to the nearest police station and turning me in to Adelaida's dragons jumped to mind. We'd make a quick stop to pick up his photographer, of course, so the story he wrote about my capture would be properly illustrated. There was no way he'd be doing this out of the goodness of his heart. The guy had no qualms about interrogating a girl fresh out of a coma. He was an unrepentant shark.

My feelings must have shown on my face because he nodded. "Oh, I'm not doing it out of the kindness of my heart. I find you someplace to sleep tonight, and in exchange—"

"I knew it." I took a step closer and stabbed a finger into his chest, so angry I could hardly speak.

What had I done to deserve all this? The dragon

attack, the coma, and now being forced to trade who knows what for some temporary safety—it was infuriating.

So I took it out on Daniel Wallent.

"I knew it was too good to be true, that you could be a decent human being. I didn't just fall off the turnip truck, you know. I've heard this one before. You'd let me stay at your place, in your bed, and in exchange, I show you the night of your life?"

Why my mind went straight to sex, I have no idea. Maybe it was the stress of the last week that had been building in my system with no physical activity to release it, or maybe it was the arrogant way he simply stood there and watched me, his relaxed position displaying a wide set of shoulders, flat stomach, and a set of delicious khaki-encased legs. The leather jacket he'd been wearing earlier was hanging from a single finger on his left hand, while a pair of dark aviator glasses were in the other. He was just a guy standing against a wall. But for some reason, my hormones had decided this guy was the thing to have.

Evidently my accusation made him angry, because his lips tightened as he raised his hand to run a finger lightly across the bandage strapped to my head. "Babe, trust me, at the moment your sexual favors are the last thing on my mind. I'm not sure whether you noticed, but you're too skinny, half bald, and in possession of a whopper of a busted lip." His finger continued past the gauze and along the outer shell of my ear before tracing a lazy path down the side of my neck to my shoulder.

I was so surprised by the gentle touch that it took me a minute before I heard him, and when I did, I sputtered, partly shocked and partly humiliated by his dispassionate cataloging of my flaws.

"I...I am a very attractive woman! Where I'm from, guys are practically lining up for sexual favors from me. I work for an advertising agency with strong ties to Hollywood, and they always ask why I waste these looks on a desk job instead of becoming a model."

His angry expression morphed into amusement when he gave me an all-out belly laugh. "I'm sure they do. Now, were you coming with me, or did you plan on sticking around to talk to them?"

Daniel's eyes flicked to something behind me in the hall. I turned to see two dark-haired men enter the hospital through the extra-large doors installed at the main entrance. They stopped at the information desk and said something to the man on duty. The taller of the two humans pointed to the insignia on his jacket. The employee nodded once before pushing away from the desk, probably to find a supervisor.

"The badge he just pointed to? That's Lady Adelaida's crest. They work for her. She's the dragon lord of this territory."

"I know who she is," I snapped. "What I don't understand is why you and Myrna are both convinced everyone is after me. Maybe you are right, and they are looking for me. But what if they're just trying to piece together other stuff that happened? What if I'm the witness, and not the suspect? Did you ever think of that?"

Just then, the wide doors opened, and a mottled-yellow dragon lumbered in to stand beside the two humans. From the movement of their bodies, it appeared that the two thugs exchanged pleasantries with the new member of their group before settling in to wait for the hospital employee.

I started frantically looking around for convenient places to hide. Dragons were never sent on assignments where combat wasn't expected. Peace-time talks, at least outside of reparations discussions, were rare.

Daniel gave me a look. *I told you so.*

The group continued to stand at the entrance, bored, as the employee scrambled to find some help. I fought the urge to duck as the dragon took in his surroundings with a slow swivel of his long neck. He was much smaller than the green dragon that had attacked Myrna and me at the hotel, but he looked no less dangerous for his size. Even without a badge, it was clear from his color that he was one of Adelaida's. The European dragon lord was known for her canary yellow scales, and made certain whatever outfit she'd chosen for the occasion displayed their gleaming perfection. With his odd mixture of yellow and brown, there was no doubt he was a direct descendant.

Before I'd spent much time with dragons, I'd thought Lady Adelaida was the most interesting of all the lords, because we shared an interest in fashion. I'd half hoped to meet her during Hian-puo's trial, but she'd been too busy with arranging the accommodations for the other lords and their traveling companions for me to feel comfortable approaching her.

Now, with her dragons hunting me on Lord Relobu's behalf, I found I had no regrets on the matter.

"Carol?"

Daniel raised an eyebrow in question. "Are you coming with me, or taking your chances with them?"

I weighed my options. Which is to say, I studied every possible solution to my problem, took one more look at the dragon, and finally admitted that I had no options.

"I'm coming with you."

SIX

DANIEL TOOK MY hand and pulled me a few feet down the hall before pushing open the door to the stairs. My knee wasn't fond of all this walking, but at least it was holding my weight. Mostly, I was amazed at my body's general weakness. After a week in a hospital bed I'd already lost a good portion of the muscle I'd put on during the mandatory combat training required by Lord Relobu in order to join the team in China.

At the time, the exercise had been a lot of fun. I'd learned some moves that weren't taught in my weekly kickboxing class, and I'd been pleasantly surprised to see how good my newly toned arms had looked in a halter dress. But now that I think about it, the training had been a complete waste of time. I knew five or six ways to severely injure a dragon, but not one of those methods had kept me from being thrown against the first handy wall my attacker had found.

And now I'd lost the toned arms. Go figure.

I stumbled as I was trying to reteach my legs how to work, and my paper bag of medicines crumpled against the concrete wall.

"Here, let me hold them." Daniel took the sack from my hands and set it on the floor before he tossed me his jacket. "Put this on. Your hospital gown is so thin it's transparent."

I scowled at him, but took the jacket and stuck my arms through the sleeves. He'd already picked up the medicine and was halfway down the stairwell before he turned to check on my progress.

"Are you coming, or not?"

I muttered something uncomplimentary under my breath as I followed him down to the ground floor and out the door to the employee parking lot.

It must have been around noon, because I had to squint at the blinding sun reflecting off rows of shiny expensive cars. Where did people find the money to buy new these days? With the price of gasoline, and electricity, and…well, everything after the war, I felt lucky to have a car at all. It looked like medicine was still a lucrative profession.

Which shouldn't surprise me, based on my own personal experience. I hadn't even needed to go outside to have a dragon whack my head against the wall. I wouldn't be surprised if serious injuries had probably multiplied ten times over since dragons had entered the world. And I'd bet the Péterfy Sándor was even more successful than most, if the majority of dragon-related injuries were sent here.

As I did my best to keep up with Daniel's long-legged stride, I mused about the probability of my heart exploding from the exertions of simply walking in a parking lot. Extended comas apparently aren't great for staying in shape, and I was walking proof. I'd broken out in a clammy sweat, and my stomach was protesting at all the movement.

Daniel fished in his pocket for a set of keys, and pointed.

"This is me." He stopped in front of a sleek black motorcycle, kitted out with chrome bars, chrome exhaust, and a gleaming black helmet hanging from one side of the handlebars.

I stood and stared, trying to determine whether I could be lucky enough have hit my head so hard that I'd just hallucinated the entire thing—hospital, dragons, motorcycles and all. This could not be happening. I was still trying to formulate a question that didn't start with "what the hell" when he made an impatient sound in his throat. He swung a leg over to straddle the machine before sliding a pair of sunglasses onto his head and reaching out a hand to help me on.

"What's the problem?" he asked when I made no move to join him.

"Are you crazy? I'm not riding on that."

I could see my bruised and battered face reflected in the lenses of his sunglasses as he considered me. Daniel pushed the bag of drugs he'd been carrying against my chest, turned the key in the ignition, and started the bike with a kick. "Suit yourself. Tell

Lady Adelaida—and Lord Relobu—I said hello."
He tipped his head toward the door we'd just exited.
The dragon lord's men had slipped outside and were
scanning the parking lot. The dragon must have been
forced to take another route as the door was standard human size.

Daniel knew what he was doing when he took
the garage exit.

One of the men caught sight of me and tapped the
other on the arm. They yelled, and started to run in
our direction.

"Okay, okay. I'm coming." I crawled onto the bike
awkwardly, trying to figure out how to keep the edge
of my hospital gown firmly underneath my rear instead of free to fly up over my head once we were
moving. As soon as I was settled, Daniel revved the
motor. I grabbed him firmly around the waist, my
white paper sack of medication dangling over his
stomach.

The world went dark for a moment and I felt Daniel's abs ripple as he twisted to awkwardly shove my
head into his bike helmet. I winced as the pressure
pulled on the stitches in my scalp, but I didn't plan
on complaining. If we wrecked, my already broken
skull needed all the help it could get.

With the helmet properly in place and just a little
too big, I could see again, provided I didn't make any
sudden movements. I looked behind us to check on
the progress of Adelaida's men. They were only a

few feet away, and one of them reached out to grab me when the motorcycle jumped forward in an awesome burst of speed. I involuntarily tightened my already snug hold on Daniel.

"I can't drive if I can't breathe," he yelled.

I reluctantly loosened my grip on his midsection as we left the parking lot and merged with the busy lunch-hour traffic. Adelaida's men watched as we drove away, cell phones glued to their furious faces as they reported our escape.

Without taking his eyes from the road, Daniel reached around me with his left arm and patted the leather saddle bags strapped to the back of the bike. "You can put your meds in here."

"I'm fine." There was no way I was unlinking my hands and turning around while we were moving.

I gasped when I felt a yank and then a tear as Daniel took the bag from me and stuffed it angrily into the leather satchel. "These damn bottles are playing Chopsticks on my nuts. Put them in the saddle bag. You are the most contrary person I have ever met in my life."

Thoroughly disgusted with Daniel and my current situation in general, I gave in to my childish side and pinched the skin over his ribs. "You aren't exactly a ray of sunshine yourself, buddy."

ABOUT THIRTY MINUTES of mutual huffy silence later, we pulled into the driveway of an old, vine-covered stone building in a quiet neighborhood north of Budapest. Daniel angled his bike into a small parking space and cut the engine.

Taking the helmet off was twice as painful as putting it on, since my last dose of pain medication had been four hours ago. Daniel tried to help me, but gave up, cursing when I yelped at his every movement.

Once off, I handed him the helmet and struggled to dismount from the bike. I groaned as my still-sore muscles protested the experience, and I was forced to use Daniel's shoulder as support while I regained my equilibrium.

Without a word, he retrieved my meds from the travel bag, and looped an arm around my waist.

I'd like to say that I angrily refused his offer of assistance, but I was too exhausted from the pain in my head to care. All I wanted was a flat surface to lie on until the worst of the nausea had passed. I almost cried when I spotted the rickety elevator tucked into the corner of the old lobby. I didn't think I could handle another flight of stairs.

We rode up to the third floor, and then Daniel half carried me down the hall before stopping before a white wooden door. Its human size made me sigh in relief. While the absence of a dragon door wouldn't stop a really determined pursuer, I was sick of staying in places that made it easy for dragons to navigate. At least this floor plan offered me an extra minute or so of protection from any potential dragon visitors.

Daniel finished with the lock and swung open the door, revealing a small studio apartment decorated in decidedly bland colors. He released me and headed for the kitchen.

"I'm getting something to drink. Make yourself at home."

I stayed where I was and took in the living space. A metal-framed futon was pushed against the far wall, opposite a small stand holding a television and telephone.

The telephone wasn't much of a surprise, but the TV was. Since the end of the war, most people didn't bother with television, because they needed a new circuit board about once every six months due to EMP corrosion. With all the massive EMP interference from the tech-jamming weapons we still had floating around in the atmosphere, the upkeep on electronics was expensive—the smaller the circuits, the more often they had to be replaced.

The tech-jammers been placed up there by specialized aircraft during the war, but now we didn't have anyone brave enough to get in a plane to take the weapons down, because the planes equipped with the proper equipment were all military. The dragons had pledged to destroy anything resembling an attack vehicle, and so far no one had figured out how to modify a commercial plane without changing its

appearance, so we were stuck with the things floating around up there and wreaking havoc on our lives.

To each his own, I guess. Some people said my
closet of shoes was an unneeded luxury.

The kitchen consisted of a single countertop and
sink snuggled between a squat yellow fridge and an
ancient gas oven. Daniel must have spent all of his
money on the electronics, because the only other furniture in the room was a large bed near the bathroom
door. The bed was unmade, with a twist of white
sheet in a ratty navy comforter sprawled across its
surface. But it was a bed. I didn't wait for permission. I felt sick, and dizzy, and more than half-dead,
so I simply shrugged out of his jacket, dropped it on
the floor, and collapsed into the welcoming softness.

Except it wasn't soft. Not at all. I hit the mattress
with a crunch and a surprised squeal. When I tried
to roll off of whatever it was I'd landed on, something sharp stabbed me in the side and I yelped. Daniel looked up from the sink in horror, and dropped
the glass of water before rushing across the room.

"No! No, what are you doing?" Completely ignoring the fact that I was being stabbed to death by
his bed, Daniel hefted me up an inch or so to dig his
hands under my back. "Those are my papers. My
notes!" He pulled a rumpled sheet from beneath my
shoulder blade and tried to smooth out the wrinkled
mess before reaching under me again for another.

With no help from Daniel, I finally managed to

sit up. I grabbed one of the papers from Daniel's grip, wondering what had turned him into a raving—and completely rude—lunatic. My name, along with Richard's and Myrna's, was scribbled along the top half, with illegible notes—some circled, some underlined—filling the rest of the white space. Question marks surrounded a section written in dragonscript about troop movement near China's Xinjiang province.

"What is this?" I'd turned the page upside down and was trying to determine whether the marks made more sense in a different order when Daniel snatched it from my hands.

"None of your business. Get up."

I scowled. "Of course. My apologies. It's not like I have a freaking head injury or anything. We can't have your notes wrinkled."

My sarcasm sailed right over his head because he kept on digging through the sheets and blanket, snatching anything he found with the frazzled panic of a guy who'd dropped an entire plate of newly grilled steaks in the middle of a pack of hungry puppies. I opened my mouth for another retort, but Daniel held up a hand.

"Wait. Just give me a second."

He finished gathering the remaining papers, scanning each and shuffling them into some sort of cryptic order before placing them on top of the TV. I sat back down on the bed and heard a muffled snap. When I located the source of the sound, I held it up.

"I broke your pencil."

He frowned but took the pieces and set them on the kitchen counter. "Are you always like this?"

"Like what?"

"A harbinger of death, destruction and dragons everywhere you go?"

I thought back to the last few weeks of my trip. "You know, I wouldn't be surprised if I were."

He snorted and, returning with the glass of water, handed me two tablets. "These are your pain meds. You have a couple of antibiotics you'll need to take before bedtime."

When I eyed him suspiciously, he rolled his eyes and tossed the pill bottle in my direction. "I'm not trying to kill you or anything."

"A girl can't be too careful." I peered into the bottle and compared the pills with the two I held in my hand. They looked exactly the same.

"Thanks." I chased the tablets with a couple of sips from the glass.

"You're welcome."

"So, what do I owe you for all this?" I made gesture meant to encompass everything—the ride, the place to sleep, and ready assistance with my pain medication.

"I'm not that much of a monster. We'll talk about

it later. I need to go out for a while and pick up some things. Will you be okay here?"

"Toothbrush." At his confused expression, I expanded. "I need a toothbrush. It's been over a week since I've brushed my teeth, and it's disgusting."

His nose wrinkled at the thought, but he nodded. "I'll be back soon." Daniel started for the door.

"Oh. I'd appreciate some clothes, if you wouldn't mind." I hated the idea of being in debt to him any further, but it wasn't like I could wear the hospital gown in public and expect no one to take notice.

"Will do."

And with that he was out the door, and I was left to myself for the first time in what felt like ages. I got up and walked the glass of water back to the sink, careful to keep a hand on the counter to prevent myself from falling.

The door opened one more time, and Daniel's head appeared. "Don't try to go anywhere. Those pills will have you stumbling into oncoming traffic, and I can't guarantee I'll be able to rescue you a second time."

He walked in, scooped his leather jacket from the floor, and walked out.

I made a face at the closed door. This man was the most irritating person in the world. But for now, he was also the only thing between me and a hoard of dragons.

SEVEN

"HEY."

His voice came from right behind me and I didn't think, I just reacted, and was surprised when my hand met flesh.

"Owww! What was that for?"

I looked up from the chair I'd been watching television from to find Daniel looming over me, wearing a dark scowl and the perfect imprint of my fingers across his stubble-covered cheek.

I hadn't even heard him come in.

"I was watching television. These pain pills are doing a number on me, for a minute I thought you were a…" I trailed off, my foggy brain a little too slow to explain my slap-first-ask-questions-later greeting.

He continued to glare at me from beside the chair while eying me suspiciously—gauging my honesty.

"I'm sorry. Really. My brain and pain medications don't usually dance well together." I sat up, rubbing my eyes in an attempt to bring the world—the real world—back into focus.

Daniel seemed to take my explanation at face

value, because he turned away and started tossing plastic bags filled with stuff onto the bed on the other side of the room.

I started to ask whether it was really necessary to use the bed as a table, but stopped myself. Somewhere in these bags I hoped there was a toothbrush, and making him angry—again—probably wasn't the best way to get my hands on it.

I wasn't disappointed. When he walked over and slapped the toothbrush into my palm, I immediately headed for the bathroom. I was glad to see my legs were steadier after my hours in the chair, and I was feeling quite cheery at the idea of a clean set of teeth and maybe even a pair of clean underwear to put on after a warm shower. Until I opened the door.

"Oh my God!" I tried to back out of the room, but hit the half-open door instead.

"What? Carol, are you okay?" I heard the thump of Daniel's footsteps. The door opened and Daniel grabbed my arm, pulling me backwards until his body stood between me and the bathroom. He was silent for a moment while he scanned the small space, but then he turned to me in confusion. "I don't understand. What's wrong?"

I couldn't even look at him, I was still trying to process the horror before me. "What's wrong? Look at this place." I pointed to the sink, where an open tube of toothpaste fought for space with a can of aerosol shaving cream, half its contents smeared along the side of the container. In the crevice designed to hold a bar of soap, a man's disposable razor floated in a small pool of water and facial hair. And the sink's faucet hadn't been cleaned in months. I couldn't even tell what color it was under the hard water buildup that caked the surface.

The rest of the bathroom was just as bad. There wasn't a shower. Instead, the bathtub, covered in the same white film as the sink, sulked in the corner near a short shelving unit loaded with frayed towels. And the toilet. I couldn't even make myself look at it. What was I going to do when I needed to relieve my bladder?

Daniel, once he'd figured out that I wasn't in any real danger, released my arm and perched on the edge of the sink. "So you're a neat freak, huh? That actually explains a lot."

Before I could articulate a proper response—I was neat, yes, but that did *not* make me a freak—he pushed past me, only to return moments later with two of the bags.

"For your information, this isn't my apartment. It belongs to a friend of mine who let me crash here while I was on assignment. And I was going to clean it up a bit, until you threw a royal hissy fit. So guess what?" He shoved one of the bags in my arms. "You get to help. These are cleaning supplies. And these," he balanced the other bag on top of the first, "are some clean clothes. Get changed. I'm going to fix us a sandwich."

The first bag clanked a bit when moved, and when I checked, it was indeed a sack full of miscellaneous cans of cleaner, one for every type of known surface.

I wanted to apologize, but Daniel had already left and, judging by the firmness of the click when he closed the bathroom door behind him, he wasn't exactly in the mood to talk. Not that I blamed him.

In this case, at least.

I looked around, trying to find a clean surface to put the bags on. There were none. I put them both on the floor and dug around in the second. He'd bought me a pair of slacks and a white button up shirt, both plain and about a size too large. I sighed. Chanel just wasn't in the cards for this trip.

Before Myrna's project, I'd been ecstatic at the size of the clothing budget we'd been given to ensure we were dressed appropriately for our meetings with the Chinese dragon lord. In retrospect, the new clothes probably weren't needed. The dragon lord was insane and obsessed with waging war against his counterparts all over the world, and could have cared less about what we wore.

But I cared. I loved the clothes I'd chosen. Unlike Myrna's wardrobe—she had terrible luck with keeping things clean in her line of work—mine was still mostly intact. And according to the contract I'd signed with Relobu's offices pre-trip, they were ours to keep. Except mine were likely sitting in the hotel's lost and found, waiting for me to claim them.

And even for all the designer labels in all the land, I wasn't stupid enough to risk my freedom for clothes. I wouldn't put it past the dragons to arrest me as soon as I walked through the front door.

I fumbled with the strings of my hospital gown. Baggy slacks and a shirt were quite a step down from a closet full of designer gowns, but they were better than what I was wearing. I took a moment to silently thank Daniel for getting me a shirt that didn't require scraping over my sore head to put on.

I just finished brushing my teeth—careful not to touch anything that wasn't absolutely necessary—and was slipping into the pair of gray sneakers I'd found in the bottom of the bag when Daniel knocked on the door.

"Lunchtime."

"On my way."

I stopped by the kitchen sink on my way out to rinse my mouth more thoroughly without the danger of accidentally ingesting the grossness that was caked to the bathroom sink. When I finished, I turned to Daniel. He was seated on the futon in front of the television with a plate balanced on his knees. Another sandwich sat beside him on the cushion, and I gathered that I was to join him.

I sat down and studied my food. He'd made us turkey sandwiches, complete with lettuce, tomato, a thin slice of cheese, and layers of both mustard and mayonnaise spread across the bread.

"Sorry about my freak-out in there. I don't think I'm handling my present situation very well. I'll take care of the bathroom as soon as I'm finished eating."

He swallowed. "Don't worry about it. I'd been meaning to tackle the cleaning job myself."

The television was tuned to a news channel, and I listened with interest to the anchorman as he bantered with his co-host.

Hungarian wasn't a language I was overly familiar with, but after the last few hours of staring at the screen, I was able to pick up a most of their conversation. When the anchor made a joke about the current construction on the west side of the city, I laughed.

"You speak Hungarian?" Daniel had stopped eating and turned to watch me.

His interest made me slightly self-conscious, and I had my right hand halfway up to my head before I remembered I didn't have enough hair to tuck behind my ear anymore. I lowered it to my lap with an awkward chuckle.

I risked a quick glance to his face, but Daniel hadn't seemed to notice my gaffe, and was still waiting for a response to his question.

I cleared my throat. "No, not really. But I like languages. You could say they're a hobby of mine. Especially in written form. There's something about the process of communicating thoughts on paper that appeals to me, I guess."

His eyes twinkled. "As a newspaper journalist, I'm glad to hear it."

I wrinkled my nose at the quip, and returned my attention to the news show.

"How are you at dragonscript and Hindi?" The question was asked casually, but I could tell by the way he'd stiffened slightly beside me that the answer was important.

My first inclination was to deny my skills with dragonscript; I'd hidden my ability for so long that it felt weird to share the information with anyone not like Myrna or Richard, who were both involved with dragons on a regular basis. But Daniel waited patiently for my answer with no signs of distrust or judgment, as if he'd simply asked me my favorite color, or what type of wine I liked to have with pasta. Besides, it's not like my name wasn't all over the paperwork in China as the translator on record. It wouldn't take much digging to figure it out.

I decided that shame over something as small as the languages in my repertoire was ridiculous, especially considering I'd just ridden across town with the guy wearing nothing but a thin and drafty hospital gown. I couldn't be more exposed than I already was.

"Fluent in dragonspeak, both oral and written. As for Hindi, I'm better with the written than the spoken form. I haven't exactly had many opportunities to practice in Tulsa. I imagine I'd pick it up a little quicker if I was around someone fluent for a little while. Why?"

"It's what I need your help with. I need a translator for some research on a story I'm chasing."

"That's it? You just want someone to read over some paperwork for you?"

"Well, it's a bit more complicated than that, but yes. I need a reliable dragonspeaker who isn't affiliated with DRACIM." He smiled. "One who's willing to travel. See? You're the perfect woman for the job."

I leaned against the back of the couch and crossed my arms. "Baloney. You weren't at that hospital looking for a translator. You were there trying to harass Richard into admitting he was the guy behind the DRACIM bombing. Which, for the record, he isn't. I just happened to be the easier target, being in a coma and all."

"Isn't a guy allowed to multitask? It's true, my paper sent a lot of us to Budapest to follow the trial of Hian-puo. My colleague Jim had the social angle covered, so when the bomb went off, he stayed for the general public reaction stuff and let me try to run down the source. I was able to track Mr. Green to the hospital, and I fully intended on trying to convince him to allow an interview.

"But I'd also found something at the hotel that my gut told me warranted some investigation. I need a translator to help me. And for now, I need someone that I can hire without causing any flags to raise at

DRACIM. If this story is what I think it is, it'll be the biggest news since the discovery of dragons."

I rubbed at my eyes. The combination of medication, fatigue and a full stomach was starting to make me a bit sleepy, despite the fact that I'd been dozing on the futon for most of the afternoon. I still wasn't completely convinced of Daniel's explanation, but I had to admit that he hadn't once tried to ask me about Richard or the bombing since we'd left the hospital. And maybe it was simple relief talking, but I was inclined to believe him, if only because serving as a translator sounded ten times better than being asked to rat out my friends. "So what's the story that may be bigger than the discovery of dragons?"

"You're exhausted. It can wait." He smiled and glanced down at my plate, frowning when he saw the neat pile of turkey I'd left in the center.

"You didn't like the meat?"

"Vegetarian. Sorry. Again."

He grinned. This time, the expression was natural and without the touch of annoyance I'd seen so often. It suddenly reminded me that Daniel was drop-dead gorgeous when he wasn't scowling.

I stood. "Take your plate?"

"Oh, sure, thanks." I walked them back to the kitchen, and had just started to rummage around in the cleaning supplies bag when Daniel called me back to the television.

"What are they saying?"

I didn't follow his question until the screen filled with a photo of Richard and me from the dragon council gathering. Taken during Hian-puo's trial, it was one of the few times I'd managed to hold Richard's attention while there, and even though we were sitting together, neither of us looked particularly happy about it.

"I'm not sure." The anchorman was fully animated, and speaking so quickly I had a hard time separating the words. "He's saying something about damage to the hotel, and dragons, and…" I stopped, hoping I was wrong about the meaning of *rendõrség.* But when they flashed a photo of a police station on the screen, I knew I wasn't so lucky.

From what I could gather, they'd just announced that I was wanted in connection with the attack at the hotel, and the local police intended to cooperate fully with dragon lords Relobu and Adelaida to help take me and Richard into custody. We'd be immediately deported to Lord Relobu's territory in North America. The brief video of the Hungarian police shaking hands with a man wearing Adelaida's insignia before turning to the woman who must be Relobu's representative pretty much sealed the deal.

I was officially on the lam. Relobu and Adelaida had commissioned the entire world to help track me down.

I looked to Daniel, wondering how much he'd managed to catch. Or how much of this he'd managed to cause.

"Are you happy now?" When he did nothing but raise an eyebrow in question, I continued. "You've managed to get Richard's name attached to this terrorism plot, and now Relobu is after him too."

Daniel laughed. "I didn't have a thing to do with it. Your boy managed to do that all to himself."

Before I had a chance to defend Richard, Daniel dusted bread crumbs from his hands by running his palms along the surface of his jeans. He stood.

"Well, looks like I need to run back to the store. I thought we'd have a couple more days before we had to find a way out of the country, but our timetable has been officially fast-forwarded. You're going to need a makeover."

EIGHT

"THIS IS A bad, bad, bad idea," I muttered as I clutched Daniel's arm like it was the last rope dangling over the Grand Canyon.

We were at the airport, and I was sweating. Shortly after we'd seen the announcement of my outlaw status, Daniel decided we needed to get out of Lady Adelaida's territory and into the territory of a dragon who wasn't Lord Relobu's bosom buddy.

Lady Adelaida and Lord Relobu, the two dragon lords most open to human interaction, were known to seek out experts for their business ventures regardless of the expert's species. Hian-puo had been on the other end of the scale. He'd treated his human employees as slaves, and had been vocal about the fact that he thought we were a bunch of idiots. Most of the other dragon lords fell somewhere in the middle of these two points of view.

My problem was the dragon whose territory Daniel had chosen for our escape. He'd called his office and arranged for us to travel with a couple of journalists on their way to Bangalore, India, to cover a recent earthquake that had caused significant damage to the city. Which put us in the home city of Lady Savitri, Dragon Lord of India, Pakistan, and Nepal.

And where Lady Savitri fell on the scale of human-love was anyone's guess. She was notoriously reclusive, preferring to remain near her home and mate. While I'd never heard a report of human abuse from her territory, I'd also never heard any glowing praise. She rarely left Bangalore, and any official territory business was conducted through dragons she sent to speak on her behalf.

I'd voiced my opinions on the matter but Daniel had, as usual, ignored my protests and insisted this would be our best chance to get out of the country undetected. With Lady Adelaida's police force—both human and dragon—out to find me, I'd had no choice but to agree to Daniel's plan.

He'd told the paper that the trip was an opportunity for his "new wife" to realize her dream of exploring the world.

I hadn't liked the idea at all. And it had nothing to do with having to pretend I was a blushing bride. Heck, I wasn't even worried about being caught with the fake passport Daniel had somehow found someone to manufacture at a moment's notice. No, my fear had everything to do with the fact that we were about to board a plane guarded by a dragon who worked directly under Lord Relobu, the very dragon who'd started this entire mess in the first place.

In a weird twist of fate, the paper Daniel worked

for was based in Tulsa, their main business office just four blocks from my apartment building. I guess it wasn't that weird of a coincidence. Because of the dragon's relative power in our political and economic systems, it was understandable that the population—and their newspapers—would shift toward the cities where powerful dragons resided, whether they liked dragons or not. Half of Tulsa's economy relied directly upon Relobu's business interests.

And naturally, Relobu was the sole source for dragon escorts for a Tulsa-based business.

That didn't mean I had to like it.

Getting on a plane was stupid all by itself. It was simply too dangerous. The same EMP issues that caused television circuits to degrade did the exact same thing to planes, and I wasn't comfortable betting my life on whether the aircraft had been properly maintained. It was one thing to fly over here as we had on a plane owned by Lord Relobu. The dragon lord, like most dragons, had a tendency toward hoarding and financial common sense, so of course he had more money than God. The odds that his planes were equipped with the best and newest circuit boards was a given.

But a newspaper? How did I know they kept their planes in good shape?

Daniel insisted the *Tulsa Times Chronicle* used this contractor all the time for flights, and I had no real reason to doubt they were reliable. The *Chron-*

icle was one of the largest newspapers in the world, and with newsprint being the top source of information for most of the world's population, I had to admit the publishing office likely had enough money to hire a good air transportation provider. Besides, like it or not, I'd have to get on a plane at some point to cross the Atlantic.

If I ever got the chance.

Homesickness hit me hard, and I found myself wishing I was settled into a chair in my boring old office at CreaTV, looking over yet another page proof for graphics errors before sending them off to the printing room. I used to feel sorry for the people who had to work with our dragon clients. Even with the DRACIM agent we brought in for translation purposes, there were still communication issues, and every once in a while, the dragons would get a little irritated and bare their teeth over the color of a model's shirt that wasn't to their taste. I used to think that was a dangerous position. Only now did I understand just how mild mannered those dragons had been.

I wanted to go home, and slip back in to my normal life. But instead, I was about to board a plane heading in the opposite direction.

We wove through what seemed like miles of passenger seating looking for Daniel's colleague. Almost every chair was empty, and the built-in shops and restaurants had long since closed. The Budapest airport looked almost exactly like the one in Tulsa.

Both were designed to accommodate a human capacity ten times its current volume. I wondered whether this terminal's size was a remnant of a time when air travel had been the norm, not the exception, or whether its huge empty spaces were due to some perpetually optimistic politicians who were convinced air travel would return to their pre-war numbers "just as soon as the dragon problem was handled."

Did I mention the current Tulsa government was also criminally fanciful?

"I can't believe you want me to get on a plane surrounded by Relobu dragons."

"Don't worry, now that you look like that, there's no way anyone will recognize you." Daniel caught himself, and turned back to look at me with guarded eyes. "But you look fantastic, really."

I couldn't blame him for the reaction. After we'd seen my picture splashed on the evening news, Daniel had made his second trip to the store. When he'd returned with his purchases, I'd cried. Because this time, instead of ill-fitting clothes, his shopping bag held a pair of scissors and a box of hair color in the worst possible shade of brown. It didn't take a genius to realize what he wanted me to do. It was the proverbial straw on the donkey's back, and it had broken me.

In the last month, I'd been dragged to China, teased by a sociopathic dragon, flown to Hungary, attacked by a different sociopathic dragon, lost all my new clothes, and discovered there was a warrant out for my arrest. The news that I had to cut off what remained of my hair—I'd held out hope that I'd be able to cover the shaved portion with a combover and some cute barrettes until it grew out—had been too much.

At first, I'd avoided the bag altogether, claiming that we could take care of it as soon as I had the bathroom cleaned up. But I'd scrubbed the toilet, tub, and sink until they all shined and I still hadn't worked up the nerve to even look at myself in the mirror.

Daniel had silently taken the scissors from my limp hands and started snipping. I'd sniffled the entire time. Luckily, he was surprisingly competent with haircuts. Before I knew it, the few locks I still had left after my hospital visit were lying on his friend's newly sparkling bathroom floor, and a girl with short, spiky hair stared back at me from the mirror. If I hadn't still had stitches running along the right side of my head, the cut could have been considered edgy and daring.

I cried again when he made me color it. My tears had freaked him out completely, and he'd had to leave the room before he'd finished applying all the dye. I'd tried to finish up the rest, but I'd made a mess of trying to simultaneously avoid the thin strip of tape that we'd added to protect my stitches *and* achieve even coverage everywhere else. Now what could have been a cute and daring haircut looked more like I'd lost the fight against a muddy chainsaw. The tape had managed to keep the hair dye away from my still-healing wound, but the dye had turned the rest of my scalp several shades darker. When Daniel removed the tape—with much whining and complaining from me—the row of stitches stood out like a bolt of lightning in a nighttime sky.

I'd done the best I could to cover my bruises with the foundation Daniel bought, but with my fair complexion and the new hair color, the circles under my eyes were unmistakable. I looked horrible, and both of us knew it.

"What are we going to tell your friend when he sees me?"

"The same thing I told him on the phone. That we're madly in love and looking for a cheap honeymoon."

"Oh, you are a charmer aren't you? What a catch. My friends will never believe I managed to find a guy so great. And when he asks why I don't have any luggage but I do have a gigantic seam in my head?"

Daniel finally stopped scanning the terminal to look at me. He set his small carry-on suitcase on the ground and locked his hands loosely at the small of my back, pulling me closer, until the front of my shirt rubbed at the buttons on his jacket. He leaned his head down until his lips were even with my ear. "He won't ask. Because right now, he's watching us. And I'm making it clear that I like you just the way you are. He'd never dare asking about your stitches, because that would be terribly rude. And Jim doesn't like to be rude."

"Oh yeah, all journalists are models of politeness and refinement. Just like you were at the hospital. Waiting patiently until I actually woke up before hammering me with accusations."

Daniel gave me a droll stare, and I stuck out my tongue. His gaze immediately fell to my mouth, and that dratted attraction started stirring up again. I stepped back a few paces, and watched as his hands dropped from my spine to hang loosely at his side. "We need to find you a girlfriend."

His lips quirked. "And why is that?"

"Because this," I said, gesturing between us, "has got to stop. I'm in a relationship. How would you feel if someone you were dating was running around, having these types of feelings for someone else, and you weren't around to stop it?"

Daniel put his hands in his pockets. "Well, I imagine I wouldn't really like it. But I also don't try to kill dragons and then run off and force my girlfriend to handle the fallout." He shook his head slightly. "With the help of her very sexy reporter friend, of course."

Daniel was obviously trying to soften the blow with his teasing, but I just couldn't enjoy the joke.

"Richard didn't kill those dragons." Until I saw actual proof that Richard was involved, I wouldn't believe that the man I knew to be smart, funny, and caring could be that callous and without conscience. Especially toward the very same dragons he'd spent years working around.

He became serious. "Why do you continue to insist he's innocent?"

"Why are you so convinced he's guilty?"

"Carol. It was all over the news."

I snorted. "According to the news, I helped him. But you're not walking around calling me a murderer."

He threw up his hands. "Because you're not."

"And neither is Richard! I don't understand why everyone I talk to believes he's guilty as sin, while I couldn't possibly be involved." My voice echoed through the empty building, drawing the attention of Daniel's friend, who started in our direction.

Daniel noticed and immediately moved closer to me, leaning in to give me a peck on the cheek. But he wasn't finished arguing. "Carol, I helped you clean the bathroom last night. When you saw a cockroach, you insisted that I pick him up and gently escort him out of the apartment with a tissue. That tiny bug scared the crap out of you, and you still couldn't kill it."

"I know someone I'd like to kill right now," I muttered.

His friend, now only a few feet away, lifted a hand in greeting. Daniel returned the gesture before turning back to look me in the eye. "We can't do this now. Let's just get to Bangalore, and then I'll let you scream at me as much as you want. Deal?"

Still angry, I started to turn, but Daniel held me in place. "Jim is a journalist, and he's a man. All we need to do is act like we like each other for a little longer. He'll notice that we can't keep our hands off each other and assume that what little clothing you're bringing with us is tiny, lacy, and able to fit neatly into my bag. So smile, damn it, and look like you're having a good time."

I smiled, damn it. "So help me, if we were really married, I'd be filing for divorce as soon as I got back to Tulsa."

Daniel laughed. "Can't say that I blame you. If my new husband took me on a honeymoon this terrible, I'd divorce him too." I was startled when he placed a huge smacking kiss on the center of my lips, but I didn't get a chance to react. He released his hold on my waist and stuck a hand out to greet his friend.

"Jim! Good to see you, my man. How's life been treating you?"

The large man pumped Daniel's hand with gusto. Dressed in the full-fledged Okie uniform of jeans, boots, and a belt buckle bigger than his fist, Daniel's friend Jim was tall and built like one of the linebackers playing in the newly re-formed NFL. "I'm good, I'm good. You ever manage to track down Richard Green or his girl? Guess you heard about the big hubbub in Tulsa that had all the dragon security teams roaring back and forth? That bomb that exploded in DRACIM was a doozy. Killed a slew of dragons. Since it went off, Relobu's guys have been swarming every business with even a whiff of a connection to the folks responsible."

Jim turned to look at me. "Well now, you must be Julie."

It took a squeeze from Daniel before I remembered that was the name on my passport.

"Yes, sorry. Nice to meet you, Jim."

"When Daniel called and told me he'd gone and got married, I didn't believe it. But now that I've got a good look at you," Jim's gaze flicked up to my dye-stained and sutured scalp, "I can, eh, see why he was in such a hurry to snap up a good-looking girl like yourself." His words were complimentary, but the end of his statement came out sounding more like a question than fact.

There was a moment of uncomfortable silence while I tried to formulate a response, but Daniel, with a small cough, redirected the conversation.

"I was a little surprised to hear that you weren't already back home. Why'd they decide to reroute you to India? I figured you'd be chasing the DRACIM story."

Obviously relieved to be back on solid conversational ground, Jim shifted his attention back to my "husband."

"Naw. Once most of the fun was back on U.S. soil,

they grabbed one of the eager and hungry to take point. Since I was already in Budapest, the powers that be decided they'd save some cash and send me from here. But I'm interested to see how the Tulsa situation pans out. Pretty crazy stuff."

Daniel nodded. "Yeah, sounds like they're looking for a man and his girlfriend. Everyone's saying they were the masterminds behind the entire plan and the DRACIM manager—Emory something— was just a patsy."

I grabbed Daniel's hand and tried to look like I wasn't guilty as sin. What was he doing? Trying to get me noticed before we even got on the plane?

But Jim didn't seem to register my reaction. Instead, he peered over our shoulders through the glass window overlooking the tarmac. He answered Daniel almost absentmindedly. "Yep. The full story is almost unbelievable. Remind me to fill you in on it later." He gestured to the window. "Looks like our plane is just about ready to get in the air. Y'all ready?"

Daniel took my hand to lead me toward the door, and I winced. The cuts from the dragon attack had healed quite a bit, but my joints still ached at his touch. Jim saw my expression and looked down to where my fingers were linked with Daniel's.

"Looks like you've had a bit of a rough time lately." He pointed to the bruises on my face. "What happened here?"

So much for Jim not commenting on my injuries.

Daniel cleared his throat. "Turns out the horses at the stables we visited a few days ago took exception to my Julie. One of them kicked, and she didn't get out of the way fast enough."

Jim started toward the entrance of the tarmac, and we fell into step behind him.

"Got to be careful with horses. Why, my granddad had his leg broke in two different places when he spooked a nervous mare..." Jim continued telling us all about his grandfather's experiences with the "wild animals" of his childhood as we walked.

I gave Daniel a look that said "I told you so" and pointed to the bruise below my eye. He just shrugged and snaked an arm around my waist.

His mouth was inches from my ear. "You were right," he murmured. "Reporters can be pretty rude sometimes."

"Only sometimes?"

"We're not rude all the time." His mouth tilted in a distinctly flirtatious grin. "Sometimes we just don't understand the word 'no'." Before I had a chance to ask what he meant, Daniel's head dipped and I felt warm lips touch my temple, then nibble their way along my jaw. Before I thought about it too much, I'd angled my head until his lips slid onto mine. Daniel moved back a fraction to meet my gaze, a distinct question lurking behind his eyes. *Are you sure?*

I wasn't. I really wasn't. But his lips felt so good,

and his hand on my waist so right that I had already started to nod when Jim's chuckle interrupted my happy haze. "You two are definitely honeymooners. Sparks practically fly off the both of ya."

Jim's statement had me reluctantly pulling away. Despite the "sparks" Jim was seeing, I had a boyfriend. Guilt flooded through my system at the thought. Richard was out there somewhere, with the entire world literally against him, and what was I doing? Kissing another man.

And liking it.

I deliberately moved out of Daniel's reach.

Daniel tried to get my attention; I could feel him willing me to meet his eyes, but I ignored the request.

He sighed and addressed his friend. "So which plane is the one waiting for us?" His voice was dull, and just a little angry.

I guess I couldn't blame him. My signals were so mixed up even I couldn't tell what I wanted.

Jim was oblivious to our silent exchange. "It's the white twin engine at the end. Nothing but the best for my good buddy. Follow me."

I was careful to stay just out of Daniel's reach as we navigated our way through the seating area and down a hallway before reaching a glass door with access to the runway. A small jet waited on the tarmac for boarding, its propellers twisting lazily in the breeze. At the side of the plane rested a dragon, waiting patiently until we were airborne to join us in flight. The creature was as tall as the plane, and probably weighed just as much. The young woman standing beside it—probably the dragon's translator—looked like an ant in comparison.

I ducked my head behind Daniel's shoulder as we walked, praying the dragon was too bored to care about studying his passengers. Or at the very least hadn't been in a position to catch the news lately.

The dragon adjusted his stance and leaned his head down to speak to the woman. She frowned, and addressed Jim. "Kemoth asked why there are additional passengers. He was informed there would be only two humans aboard in addition to the pilot. Reporter Jim Manning and his camera operator, Jovan Aguilar."

"Oh crap." Daniel said the words so softly I was barely able to make them out.

I stopped, and Daniel followed suit as we waited for Jim to get far enough away that we could talk without fear of being overheard.

I leaned closer, keeping my eyes on the dragon. "What's wrong?"

"Jovan. I thought they'd sent him back to Tulsa. He'd been heading for the airport when I left for the hospital. He's a friend of mine. Was my cameraman for the week leading up to the dragon council. We're pretty close. Close enough for him to know I was dating someone else two weeks ago when I got on the plane in Tulsa."

I had to stop and process the information. Even though I'd teased him about it earlier, it had honestly never occurred to me that Daniel even had a social life. Much less an actual girlfriend.

"Is she...was it serious?"

"No. But I'm not exactly the type to run off and get married to a girl I barely know. As soon as I introduce you, he's going to be suspicious. And he's not nearly as unobservant as Jim."

I ran through all the possible scenarios, the majority of which broke down as soon as Jovan said anything resembling "who is this?"

I turned to Daniel. "Has Jovan met your girlfriend?"

He paused. "No. She wasn't exactly my girlfriend. It was a lot more...casual than that." A light flush crawled up his neck.

"Oh." I was beginning to get the picture. I laughed. "Daniel Wallent, I do believe you're blushing. Embarrassed to admit you're the type to enjoy an occasional friends-with-benefits arrangement?" The idea that Daniel's girlfriend was closer to a semiregular booty call was quite a relief, even if I wasn't ready to investigate the reasons behind my feelings. "If he's never met the other woman, this will be easy. Just let him assume I'm her."

Jim yelled up at the airplane. "Jovan! Get your butt out here. Daniel Wallent got married."

"It's not quite that easy. We've, uh...discussed

some specifics regarding my relationship. Pretty personal specifics." Daniel's hand came up to scrub at his stubbled jaw.

My stomach dropped at the look on his face. "What kind of specifics? Like her name? Occupation?"

"Like the fact that she was a total nymphomaniac, and that I was thinking about breaking it off because of her not-so-subtle enjoyment of very public displays of affection. And the version I relayed to Jovan included specific examples of her more, ah, racy tastes." The flush on his neck grew more prominent, and he didn't seem to be able to meet my eyes.

Jim gestured for us to come closer, his thumbs hooked into the top of his jeans. I gave him a distracted wave that signaled that we'd be there in just a second.

"Daniel. Hurry. Like what?" Visions of full dominatrix gear grappled for purchase in my brain, alongside equally disturbing images of me in a corny sexy-nurse outfit and heels.

Daniel muttered something unintelligible about bumping his leg and wouldn't meet my eyes.

A man, dark skinned and dressed in the same style as Jim, poked his head out the plane's bulkhead door. "I must not have heard you right. I thought you said Daniel Wallent got hitched." The man's eyes scanned the ground until he found us. He raised a hand in greeting.

"Daniel, you need to tell me now. I have to get out of this country. You said she bumped your leg? I don't get it."

"Not bump. Hump. She had a really bad habit of kinda crawling on me, and I told Jovan that I felt like she was always trying to hump my leg."

"Oh geez. Daniel Wallent, I could kill you right now."

THE CAMERAMAN AMBLED down the boarding stairs. "I don't believe it." His words were directed at Daniel, but his eyes were checking me out the entire time. I could almost see the wheels turning circles in his head as his gaze started at my feet and worked its way up. I could tell the instant he got to my head because he jerked, startled, before shooting a quick glance at Daniel.

"I got kicked by a horse."

Daniel stepped in before Jovan had a chance to inspect the damage to my head, and the men shook hands.

"Julie, I'd like you to meet Jovan. Jovan, Julie."

"Well, hello Julie." If his clothing didn't give him away, his accent did. This man was the real deal. Pure Texan. And proud of it.

"Hey. Nice to meet you." I took his offered hand.

When Jovan continued to watch me with unconcealed interest, I leaned closer to Daniel, wrapping an arm around my fake husband's waist in an effort to sell our story. Daniel obliged by draping his arm around my shoulder and giving me a quick squeeze. It was more brotherly than lover-like, but I took what I could get.

"It's great to meet you, too. Daniel had mentioned he had a girlfriend, of course, but I had no idea you guys were thinking about getting married." The latter end of his statement made it clear that he wanted to hear all the details, but Daniel stepped in before I had to come up with a response.

"It was kind of a spur-of-the-moment kinda thing." Daniel pasted a bit of a drawl over his usually crisp speech. But instead of making him seem friendlier, the twang seemed to have the opposite effect on Jovan, especially when Daniel angled his body to hug me even closer. Jovan's eyes narrowed.

"You know, Julie, I feel like I know you from somewhere."

I forced myself not to cringe as Daniel's friend searched my face in an effort to jog his memory. Our story was fraying faster than an old lady's crochet project.

So I took matters into my own hands. I stuck out my bottom lip.

"Daniel, honey, I thought you said we'd get to see India." I wrapped my arms around his neck and did what I was known for. I practically crawled up the front of his body. "What better place to practice the Kama Sutra than in the country where it was invented?"

I saw Daniel's eyes go wide in momentary surprise. Then it was my turn to gasp as he placed both hands on my rear and lifted. "Oh trust me, honey, I haven't forgotten." He pulled me closer, and I couldn't help but tighten my grip on his shoulders.

Balancing my weight on his hips, I leaned back to look him in the eye. He grinned, his smile playful and just a touch mischievous. The familiar heat flared between us, but I fought the urge to back away. If we were going to make this farce believable, I had to be all in. We needed this to be real.

I let out a loud groan and shifted my legs until my core was firmly pressed against his abdomen. I felt the surprised catch of his breath before strong hands tightened on my hips, pulling me down until my face was level with his. The warm hum of attraction spread through my lower stomach like a switch had been flipped. I would have laughed, but I didn't think my reaction was funny right now.

I'd dated at least a dozen men since college, all smart, all handsome. Some of them had even known their way around a woman's body. But this was the first time I'd repeatedly felt the bite of attraction from someone I wasn't even sure I liked. Sure, he'd helped me out of a sticky situation, but he'd made it perfectly clear that he was doing it for his own purposes.

But right now, I couldn't think about it enough to care. Experimentally, I rubbed my lips over the slight dent at the tip of his chin. The spot that had secretly been taunting me for days. I nipped him lightly, playfully, and he growled.

And suddenly, we weren't playing anymore. Daniel's lips devoured mine in a kiss that was so hot, so intimate, I almost forgot where we were. His tongue traced the contours of my teeth, and I'd just opened my mouth wider to give him better access when someone cleared their throat behind us.

"I think y'all better get on the plane before you get much further." Jovan's voice was close, and unmistakably amused. "Kernoth," he said, turning to the dragon, "if it's okay with you, we'll give these two a proper honeymoon."

I heard the translator repeat his words, and with a bored shake of his scaled head, the dragon agreed.

Breathing hard, I scrambled to get my feet back on the pavement. Daniel let me go, and when I worked up enough nerve to actually look at him, he was running a frustrated hand through his hair. Deciding now wasn't the time to talk about our near spontaneous combustion, I tucked my chin and hustled to the plane.

I heard Jovan's laughing voice as he spoke to Daniel. "It looks like you got over that whole leg-humping aversion. Congratulations."

Jim's knowing smirk made me blush as he helped

me aboard, and I scurried for the seat farthest back. Grabbing a magazine from the pouch in front of me, I promptly buried my head within its pages. My chair shifted as Daniel sat beside me, but he didn't speak. He simply handed me my pain medication and a sealed bottle of water, and settled into the chair. Under the guise of opening the pillbox, I sneaked a glance at him through lowered lashes. His eyes were closed, and the back of his head rested against the chair. So he didn't want to talk about it. That was just fine by me.

I swallowed my pills and tucked the bottle of water and medication behind my hip. We'd made it on the plane, and minutes later we were cleared for takeoff.

NINE

SEVEN HOURS LATER, we'd arrived at Bengaluru International Airport. With four and a half hours of time difference between the two cities, we'd arrived in India in the wee hours of the morning, and were greeted by a contingent of sleepy airport staff finishing up the end of their shifts. We'd said a quick goodbye to Jim and Jovan before they headed for the express security line with their press credentials. Daniel hadn't had time to get me anything other than the basic paperwork in Budapest, so he'd left his credentials in his bag and followed me to the immigration lines reserved for the general public. Still fuzzy from my pills, I plodded slowly behind him.

The immigration process took a long time—tourists were rare in India, so the woman at the desk was slow at verifying our documents, but soon we had left the arrivals terminal. The small group of men holding signs for various taxi services was only too glad to see a couple of foreigners, and within minutes we had someone willing to take us to our destination.

"I've have a small apartment rented near Lady Savitri's residence and offices. We'll get settled in tonight, and tomorrow I'll fill you in on the details of what I need you for."

I nodded absently, too busy staring out the window of the car to worry much about tomorrow's plans. The sun was barely peeking over the horizon, and already the roads were filled with people. Motorcycles, cars, and what seemed like hundreds of three-wheeled motorized conveyances Daniel referred to as auto-rickshaws—the traffic was a free for all. Our driver navigated the streets with almost careless skill, obviously familiar with the hustle and bustle as he dipped and dodged other commuters with no discernible use of his brakes, and a total disregard for all traffic lights.

It took us forty minutes of driving to reach the gated community where Daniel had rented a flat. He paid and tipped the driver, and within minutes we were riding the lift up to the sixth floor. We left the elevator and walked down a short hallway, where a young woman looked up from her sweeping to stare at us curiously.

Daniel opened the door and flipped the wall-mounted switch just inside the entrance. I squinted as the fluorescent lights sparked to life. We stepped inside, and when my eyes finally adjusted, I took a look around. This apartment was furnished with more taste than Daniel's Budapest home. The floors were all tile, with a small area rug positioned under a glass coffee table in the living room.

"There are bedrooms here and here," Daniel said, gesturing to the two doors off each side of the living area. "Take your pick. They both have attached bathrooms. There's a switch on the wall next to the light that you'll need to hit for hot water."

I peeked into the nearest room, happy to see the neatly made bed with sheets that were all but begging me to slide between them. I turned back to Daniel. "I'll take this one if that's okay?"

"Sure." He disappeared with the suitcase through the opposite doorway, obviously familiar enough with the place that he had no need to turn on the lights. A moment later he was back, his bare feet padding across the floor as he approached the couch.

And oh God, even his feet were sexy.

I had to get a grip on myself.

"Have you spent much time in India?" During the trip from the airport to the apartment, Daniel had handled everything with a casual ease that spoke of familiarity, and I found myself wondering what his life looked like when he wasn't smuggling women to and from foreign countries.

"A little. The Hian-puo trial was a fluke. There are usually only two of us at the paper covering the international stuff. So I'm in and out of here maybe twice a year. I travel a lot for my job." He propped his feet up on the coffee table and reached for the controls to the wall-mounted air-conditioning unit. When he pushed a button, it came on with a small hum, the blast of cool air welcome in the overly warm room.

I smiled. "I guess you'd have to. Do you like it? The travel?"

He seemed to think about it. "Yeah. Most of the time. Sometimes I get tired of moving around, but for the most part I like collecting new experiences."

I couldn't help but chuckle.

Daniel gave me an odd look. "What's so funny?"

I made my way to the couch and sat on the opposite end, curling my feet under my body before facing him. I wanted to believe that we were just having a normal conversation, like two strangers on the bus, but since some of this information wasn't exactly mine to share, I needed to be sure. "Off the record?"

"Of course."

"I thought I'd enjoy traveling. When Myrna first asked me to help her with the Hian-puo negotiation, it sounded fun. Interesting. I've always liked studying languages, so when she offered to introduce me to Richard Green, I was ecstatic. I mean, the guy created dragonscript. To actually use my language skills for something important, and to get to do it with the very person who created the written version? For a language lover like me, it was a once in a lifetime opportunity. When the project shifted from Tulsa to China, I'll confess I didn't think too much about it. China sounded new and exciting, and I guess I just brushed aside the potential danger of the trip."

"Got in deeper than you expected, huh?"

I gave him a wry smile. "Well, being at the top of Lord Relobu's most wanted list wasn't the plan, for sure." I paused for a moment, unwilling to ruin a relatively peaceful evening, but I didn't feel comfortable pretending Richard hadn't been a big part of my reasons behind joining the team.

"I did it mostly for him, you know."

"Richard?"

"Yeah. A few months before Myrna's assignment, I'd read an article in one of our magazines about how he'd been instrumental in making Relobu Enterprises the go-to company for natural resources. The company had started with zero stake in the region's oil business, and within two years, Relobu owned about seventy-five percent of the pipelines in Texas and eight percent of Oklahoma's. Their growth was simply unprecedented."

"He wouldn't have managed to do it without the help of Relobu's deep pockets."

"True. But many people wouldn't have managed it at all, even with all the money in the world. The article went on to talk about his early career with DRACIM, and how he'd created the entire dragon-script language when he was still a teenager."

"You were dazzled."

I nodded. "Yep. It didn't hurt that he was easy on the eyes, too."

Daniel smiled. "Glass of wine?"

"Sure."

He went into the kitchen, and I stared out the window, lost in my thoughts. Daniel had hit the nail on the head. With only his looks and a biography, Richard had seemed like the perfect man. And when we'd met and it seemed the interest was mutual, I'd jumped at the opportunity to get to know him better. He'd been so different from the men I'd dated before.

For one, he'd had his own money. And even as a dragonspeaker—a career not exactly at the top of the prestige scale—he'd run in circles I'd only just been able to see, much less been a part of. He'd been polite, and polished, and the consummate gentleman. So what if he'd expected me to spend a few minutes alone at a party or two? Or told me, gently of course, that I likely wouldn't understand some of the business dealings he'd wrestled with during the course of his day.

Daniel returned and handed me a glass. "What's on your mind?"

"At the hospital, were you really there just to ask me about this translation project?"

Daniel sighed. "Yes and no. I didn't need you for your part in the events of the dragon council. Lady Adelaida had been pretty open to questions from the human press about exactly why Hian-puo was on trial. And while she didn't just hand us a list of all the people involved with the China trip, she didn't try very hard to hide the information either. It took

Jim and me about three hours to get all the names together.

"The trial gave us more than enough information on the weapon and how Hian-puo had gotten his hands on it. Myrna had been pretty detailed in her testimony on how your team had managed to track down its location and tie possession back to the Chinese dragon lord. But since the point of the trial was to prove Hian-puo's guilt, nobody was asking what the plans were to prevent another bomb being created, or what would ultimately happen to the one that had been confiscated.

"Jim made a formal request to both Relobu and Adelaida's offices for this information, but he was shot down. I approached DRACIM with the same result. I got the feeling that Myrna's Emory was against DRACIM's involvement in the project from the beginning, and he wasn't in the mood to do us any favors."

"Emory's never in the mood to do much, unless it involves eating or sucking up to powerful people. Myrna hated working for him."

"I can totally see why. Anyway, with none of the three agencies willing to speak with us, Jim and I had decided to try to hit you up for information first thing the next morning."

"But instead, Myrna and I were attacked by Hian-puo's dragon, and I ended up in the hospital."

Daniel nodded. "By the time you woke up, the

bomb had gone off in Tulsa, and we had other things to worry about."

"Well, in that case, I guess I should be thanking you for not automatically assuming I had something to do with sneaking it out of the country."

He smiled. "Don't thank me. It's my job to look at people and read between the lines. And while you're not exactly fond of working near dragons, you don't hate them. You don't really fear them either."

"Oh, I'm not sure I would go that far. I seem to be a crazy-dragon magnet. If there's an insane, human-killing dragon within fifty miles, they're sure to head straight for me."

"But you've dealt with other dragons, and you've had no problems. The China team had two dragons as part of the security detail. Plus, your roommate is supposedly dating a dragon, and it doesn't seem to bother you."

"That's…different." I'd first known Trian as a human, so while the thought of him turning into a dragon was more than mildly disturbing from an intellectual standpoint, I couldn't see myself hating him for being something he'd been all along.

"And that's exactly what I mean. Nine times out of ten, humans assume dragons are the bad guys. But you don't. Which is why I can't see you deliberately assisting someone with a weapon that kills dragons indiscriminately."

He had a point. The pair of Relobu's dragons with

us for security purposes on the China trip had been nothing but polite. In fact… "I rode from China to Budapest on dragonback."

Daniel's head came up. "No kidding?"

"No kidding. Richard and Myrna took our only plane to try and intercept the bomb. Myrna's clothes had been royally screwed up from Hian-puo's she-nanigans, and she already had a request from Relobu to testify against Hian-puo at the dragon council. So Richard sent me, express delivery, to hook her up with some court-appropriate outfits. It was actually kind of fun."

"I'll bet." Daniel looked at me with a new glimmer of respect.

"Anyway…" I studied my nails, suddenly uncomfortable with the fact that we were in this apartment alone, especially considering our pre-flight, not-so-pretend make-out session in Budapest. "You were going to tell me about India. And about why you need a translator."

Daniel cleared his throat. "How familiar are you with Lady Savitri?"

"Not very. I know she rules over India, Nepal, and Pakistan but she didn't make it to Hian-puo's trial. I've never even seen a photo of her, but I've heard she's smaller than the other dragon lords, and she's light gray. I understand that she doesn't social-ize with the other dragon nations much, but prefers to stay in Bangalore and tend to her own dragons."

He nodded. "Yes. And it's always been assumed that her relative lack of interest in expanding her territory is what kept Hian-puo from commissioning the bioweapon sooner. Had his territory been closer to one of the more forceful dragon monarchs, I have no doubt we would have seen a scheme like the Tulsa bombing much sooner. Savitri has retaliated viciously when her dragons were attacked while in her own territory, but otherwise, she's ignored Hian-puo's activities in the rest of the world."

I raised an eyebrow. "I bet that doesn't make her very popular with the other dragon lords." From Myrna's work stories, it was clear that a lack of communication was seen as an insult.

"It doesn't. But they respect her. She may be small, but she's one of the most deadly dragons alive. She's a dragon of the venom variety, and her particular brand of poison is just as deadly to dragons as to humans. Even a drop of the stuff can eat straight through their scales. That, coupled with her more than acceptable combat skills, means she could easily defeat most of the reigning dragon lords without blinking."

Daniel shifted on the couch.

"For the most part, they allow Lady Savitri her quirks. Lately, the dragon lords have had their hands full dealing with Hian-puo. He's been crazy for as long as anyone can remember. And his conviction at trial hasn't solved things. The council has removed

Hian-puo from power, but now they have a bunch of dragons with no clear leader, and several high-ranking generals who are already pressing their case to succeed their old ruler."

"Won't the existing dragon council vote on a replacement?" From what little I'd understood at the trial, Lord Relobu and Lady Adelaida had plans for the council to interview the pool of Hian-puo subjects willing and able to take over for their fallen ruler.

"That's what they're telling everyone." Daniel picked up his suitcase and laid it on the bed before unzipping the side pocket and extracting a manila folder filled with the notes I'd crinkled in his friend's apartment in Budapest. He rifled through the mess and pulled out a single sheet. "But look at this."

I leaned closer. "Did you get this out of the garbage or something?" The stained piece of paper was in bad shape, and unidentifiable bits of junk had adhered to the surface. Most of the writing was illegible, but in the far left corner were some words in dragonscript I could make out. "Phase one to commence November 5?" I looked at Daniel. "That's next week. What operation?"

Daniel's expression was excited. "That's what I'm here to find out. For the past few months, Lady Savitri has been expanding the training program for her personal guard, as well as increased the number of dragons she's assigned to military duty. At first,

I'd dismissed the changes as a natural reaction to Hian-puo's recent behavior, since most of the growth has occurred along the border with China." Daniel pulled out another, cleaner, sheet of paper filled with incomprehensible graphs and maps detailing troop movement.

"Okay…" I wasn't following his train of thought. "So she beefed up her army when Hian-puo started acting weirder than normal. I can totally see why. That dragon is crazy. If I was his next-door neighbor, I would have done the same."

"That's what I thought. But look at this." He pointed to a couple of squiggles. "These are the dragons she's moved to northern Pakistan *since* the dragon council."

I stared at Daniel's map. He was right. If I understood Daniel's scribbles, Lady Savitri had been steadily adding to her army along the China-Pakistan border for at least six months before our trip to China, and the numbers hadn't stopped growing since Hian-puo's arrest and removal from power. Along the side of the map, he'd added names, along with lists of numbers, some crossed through, some circled.

"What are these?"

"The names of Savitri's generals, along with troop counts by squadron."

"So, okay." I struggled to get the facts straight in my mind. "Savitri beefs up her army in response to Hian-puo's erratic behavior. We're sent to China, plans of a bioweapon are discovered, and Hian-puo is caught in the act of transporting the thing. He's captured, convicted at trial, but the bomb still makes its way to U.S. soil, and Lady Savitri is still growing her army."

Daniel nodded.

"So what are you thinking?"

Daniel took a large drink from his glass before setting the wine on the table.

"I think she's planning on invading China."

His words made my thoughts stutter inside my head.

"You think she's been biding her time, waiting until Hian-puo did something really stupid and the council came after him so she could take over his territory under the guise of being helpful?"

"I do." Daniel's answer was firm. He was convinced.

And I had to admit I was more than halfway there myself.

Wow. This was huge news. Since the seven dragon lords had announced their presence to the humans and installed themselves in their respective territories, there had never been even a whisper of dominance games between the lords, at least to human knowledge. Which was why Hian-puo's trial had been such a tabloid hit. It was the first time the dragon lords had presented themselves as anything less than a united front.

One out-of-control dragon lord had been enough to cause panic throughout the world. I'd had a little time to catch up on my reading during the flight to Bangalore. Since the details of Hian-puo's bombing plan hit the media, newspapers had printed editorials discussing our own lack of preparation should war break out between the dragon territories.

After the bomb went off in Tulsa, demonstrations had popped up in several cities worldwide calling for renewed focus on our military defenses, despite the fact that the dragons had almost wiped us out the first time we'd attempted to push them out of our countries. If word got out there was instability in another territory, mass panic was a real possibility. Despite our bluster, most humans recognized the fact that we were alive because the dragons chose to keep us that way. If war broke out between the members of the council, humans would end up as the biggest losers, no matter which side emerged the victor.

"Let's assume you're right. The Indian dragon lord has her eye on China. Won't the rest of the dragon council try to stop her before she has an army big enough to make her move?"

"Probably. But they won't be able to. They'd never admit it, but the recent problems with Hian-puo have severely stretched their resources. Lord Relobu and Lady Adelaida put up most of the dragon-power leading to Hian-puo's capture, but they can't afford to spare any many more, or they open their territories to attack from the dragon lords who weren't as vested in the proceedings."

Daniel leaned back into the couch, and I did the same.

"I believe Lord Sandul of Rio de Janeiro is aware of Savitri's actions, because we've tracked an increase in the number of dragons he's training for military service. Right now it's still in the realm of possibility that he's simply being cautious, but it's not going to be pretty if he decides to try for North America while Relobu is distracted with Asia."

"I need to tell Trian about this." If Relobu's security force was about to have trouble with another dragon lord, he needed to know. Even if Lord Sandul had no plans to invade North America, the problem of Savitri remained. With Savitri in control of both India and China's territories, her armies would be unstoppable. If Savitri wanted, she could mount a full-scale attack on any territory she so chose. I remembered Myrna's contemplations during the worst days on the China project, when she said a war between the dragons could quite possibly be the end of humanity because we'd all be caught in the crossfire. Suddenly her worst-case scenario looked all too real.

"Tell Trian what? That the Indian dragon lord has more guards in the air than usual? That you magically found a napkin scribbled with plans for world domination? His dragon lord wants you arrested as a terrorist. Why would they even believe you?"

I let my shoulders slump. "They wouldn't." He was right. Even if I called Myrna instead, we simply didn't have enough solid information to make our case.

"So what did you need me to do?"

"For starters, I need you to go shopping."

I sighed. "Funny, shopping for Myrna was how all my current problems got started."

TEN

AT NINE THE next morning—far too early for my jet-lagged body—Daniel knocked on the door to my bedroom.

"Are you ready?"

I groaned. "I think this is the first time in my life I've been depressed about shopping." I'd been up for an hour already, and had done my best to straighten the wrinkles from my shirt with the steam from my shower.

I swung open the door. "Look at me. Is this really what we want these people to think of Americans?"

Daniel ran his eyes over my rumpled blouse and pants—the same outfit I'd worn for almost two days straight. Without the help of even a comb, I'd been forced to leave my hacked-off hair poking up around my head like tufts of weeds. The only good thing I could say about my appearance was that my bruises had finally reached the point where they only made me look jaundiced instead of beat-up.

He, on the other hand, looked clean, alert and well pressed. "Look on the bright side, the faster we get to the taxi, the faster I can buy you something less wrinkled."

Scowling, I took the cup of coffee he offered and blew on the surface. "Will I also get a hairbrush?"

"I'm sure we can manage it."

Feeling somewhat better about our shopping excursion, I slipped my feet into my shoes and moved to follow him out the door. A young woman, dressed in a pair of loose pants and tunic top with a long scarf thrown over each shoulder, was stepping from her apartment at the same time. She caught sight of Daniel first and let out an excited shout.

"Daniel! You are in the country! Did you get in last night?" I watched wistfully as she tossed a braid of thick dark hair over her shoulder to lay against her spine. I couldn't help but raise a hand to my own head of hair, wishing now more than ever that I'd had just a drop of gel to keep it in place.

He nodded. "Around one in the morning."

She made a scoffing noise and playfully slapped at his shoulder. "You should have called me. I could have brought you some warm chapati and chicken to welcome you back."

Whoa. At one in the morning? A very friendly neighbor Daniel had.

I cleared my throat to remind him of my presence. With an expression of delight that went a long way toward soothing my ruffled feathers at being momentarily forgotten, Daniel captured my arm and pulled me forward. "Girija, may I present my wife, Julie Wallent."

The girl's eyes widened comically at his announcement. "You've been married! When did this happen?"

"Just last week. We're here for our honeymoon."

"That is wonderful news. Very good news." The woman's near constant level of excitement was making me tired, especially since it was clear, at least to me, that she did *not* feel like this was very good news at all.

We said our goodbyes and stepped into the lift.

Daniel and I both raised our heads to stare at the floor numbers as we slowly descended. I gave him a sideways glance. "Nice lady."

He quirked a lip. "Yes. She is."

"She regularly brings you food? Even when it's the middle of the night?"

"Not when I can stop her. I think she's just a little lonely. She moved to Bangalore for her job and about a year ago, her roommate left town. She's been by herself since, and I think the job isn't what she was expecting."

I'd assumed that this was another of Daniel's girlfriends, but his explanation made sense. Myrna and I had been lucky enough to find each other pretty early in our college years, and both of us found jobs in the same town upon graduation, so there'd really been no question about whether we'd continue the arrangement.

Maybe I'd be the type of girl to bring food to a man at one in the morning if I didn't have Myrna. Loneliness can make people do pretty crazy things. I felt like Girija's actions signaled something a little different than a simple need for some company, but it was clear Daniel wasn't interested in that type of relationship. I'd already had plenty of laughs at his expense over the wonderful leg-humping girlfriend and didn't see the point in piling on the humiliation by bringing this to his attention.

In fact, it was almost reassuring that he was well liked by his neighbor. With the exception of his behavior at the hospital, Daniel had been curiously even-tempered, and I'd started to think maybe we'd simply gotten off on the wrong foot.

The night before, Daniel had asked our airport driver if he was available to pick us up this morning, and I was pleased to see the man waving from just outside the security gate. Daniel and I settled into the back seat of the tiny box of a car before he gave instructions for the driver to take us to the shopping district near Mahatma Gandhi Road. The man nodded his understanding and gave the horn a single toot before whipping the vehicle onto the busy street, missing a passing motorcycle by inches.

My hands immediately clenched the handle on the door.

I leaned over to whisper to Daniel. "Is it always like this? The traffic."

He laughed. "For the most part, yeah. You'd be surprised at how rarely there are vehicle accidents. There aren't many traffic laws here, but the worst I've seen wreck-wise is a couple of fender-benders."

"Pretty amazing."

"Yep."

"So tell me about how I'm supposed to help you get enough dirt on Lady Savitri's border movements to write your story."

"With this." He handed me this morning's newspaper and pointed at a small square he'd circled in the classifieds section.

The ad stated that Savitri Enterprises was in the market for someone with experience in dragonscript. My head jerked up. "But Savitri Enterprises is the dragon lord's company!"

"Yeah. They've had this ad running for weeks. I called this morning and the position was still open. The hiring manager confirmed it."

"No. You don't actually expect me to apply?"

"Except for the interview, I doubt you'll even see Lady Savitri. The position requires someone with dragonscript skills, but from the job description, it sounds as if you'll be working in an office with other human servants, not directly with the dragon lord. She has a personal secretary for those sorts of things.

The hiring manager is human, and he'll be the one with whom you'll spend the majority of your time."

"I can't do it."

Daniel regarded me calmly. "You read dragon-script, don't you? And Hindi."

"Yes, but that doesn't mean I'm looking to place myself near another possibly crazy dragon lord."

"With access to her offices, we can find all the records supporting her recent troop movements. And maybe, if we're lucky, you'll run across something that details her future plans. I'm pretty sure she plans to hit China next, but what's after that? Is she happy with just a continent, or is China just the first step before she ends up killing the other dragon lords and achieving total world domination?"

"No way. I won't do it." I'd been so relieved when Daniel said all he'd needed was a translator. It had honestly never occurred to me that we were heading straight for the business owned and operated by the dragon lord he suspected was trying to start a war. "If I wanted to work with dragons, I'd have joined DRACIM." I pointed to the stitches on the side of my head. "This is what happened the last time I took a job opening for a dragonscript expert in a dragon's home territory. That time I did it for a friend I've had for over ten years. And sorry, buddy, but you're not that special to me."

Daniel's eyes narrowed, and then he leaned up

to speak with the driver. "Sir? Can we stop here please?"

The driver looked slightly confused, but obligingly pulled into a narrow alley near a small store selling "fresh chicken." The poor creatures clucked and shifted in their stacked cages as Daniel leaned across my lap and opened the door. The shop's *walla* saw us pull up, and, wiping his hands on his apron, stepped from the booth to greet us.

The driver frowned and pointed to the chickens. "Only in the trunk."

"We aren't purchasing a chicken. The lady wants out." Daniel jerked a chin in the direction of the chicken walla's counter. "I did my part. Enjoy India."

I stared at him in disbelief, then looked out the door. One of the chickens had become a bit too excited at our arrival, and a puddle of white liquid pooled on the ground. He planned to drop me in the middle of a foreign country. And in a pile of chicken shit, no less. I was beginning to develop an abandonment complex. "You're joking!"

Daniel checked his watch. "The story about the Tulsa bombing is already out in the newspapers, and Jim and Jovan have the earthquake more than covered. Right now, I don't have anything to write about except what I *think* is a record of Savitri's military maneuvering written on the back of a napkin. I got you out from under Lady Adelaida's claws, with the understanding that you'd help me with my research."

"You didn't say your research included working for dragons!"

He shrugged his shoulders, his expression bored. "If you won't help, you're not much use to me. And, if you don't mind me using a direct quote, 'you're not that special to me' either." He waved a hand toward the door.

The taxi driver's gaze bounced between us in the rearview mirror. So far, his English had been limited. I wondered how much of the exchange he understood.

I tried appealing to him in Hindi. "Please, sir. Don't let him leave me here. I have no money."

The man shrugged. "No Hindi. Kannada?"

Well, crap. I'd always heard that regional languages were widespread in India, but I'd never had a chance to learn any of them.

Daniel watched me calmly, waiting for my decision. "Listen. I'm not trying to be a dick about this. But I need you. What other option do you have right now?"

I didn't really have one. I had literally the clothes on my back. No money, no apartment, no freaking clue where I was in the city.

"I really, really hate you."

"I know. And I'm sorry. You probably won't believe me, but I'd love to get you back to Tulsa. I just can't right now. You can't. Not without running directly into the arms of Relobu and being locked up next to your boyfriend." Daniel grabbed my hand.

Angry, I yanked it back.

He sighed. "Look. I promise that we'll call your friend as soon as we find some solid proof of Savitri's China plans. She can help Relobu assemble a response to get Savitri under control, and you can take the credit for it. I imagine the intel would go a long way toward getting on Relobu's good side. I'll be able to get the story in the paper before the rest of the news cycle picks it up."

I chewed on my bottom lip. He was right. Without solid evidence, Myrna couldn't take this to Relobu, not without looking like a fool. If I hadn't seen Daniel's research with my own two eyes, or spent enough time with him to realize he wasn't the type to chase conspiracy theories, I'm not sure I would believe the story either. Myrna would listen to me, of that I had no doubt, but right now, Relobu already thought I was a liar. Myrna would need a lot more than a dirty napkin. She'd need incontrovertible proof.

There was another idea that had been percolating since my talk with Daniel last night. What if Richard had already been aware of Savitri's troop movement, and had, like Daniel, assumed she was positioning herself to invade China? What if all his secrecy, all his sneaking around at the hotel hadn't been about the bomb at all?

I know both Myrna and Daniel, along with the

rest of the world, were convinced Richard was guilty.
But I wondered whether Savitri had somehow realized she was being investigated and set Richard up
to get him out of the way, knowing he had elected
to stay in Budapest until I'd recovered. When he'd
been accused of delivering the bomb, Richard had
had to decide between telling Lord Relobu what little he knew about Savitri's plans and the idea being
dismissed as an attempt to exonerate himself, or to
say nothing in his own defense and hope he would
find the proof he needed to make Relobu see reason.

Even I had to admit the idea was a long shot, but
I just wasn't ready to believe that I'd been dating a
terrorist. My distance from Richard and his glamorous lifestyle—well, at least his lifestyle had been
glamorous relative to mine—had made me realize
that maybe we weren't particularly suited for each
other. I tended toward insecurity in relationships,
and Richard's practice of mulling problems in his
head instead of putting them on the table for discussion like Daniel had done wreaked havoc on my
self-esteem.

Why hadn't Richard just *talked* to me about any
of this? In Budapest, when he'd first started avoiding me, I'd tried to ask him what was bothering me.
He'd simply patted my hand absentmindedly and
told me not to wait up for him. Was it any surprise
I'd assumed he was having an affair?

And at the hospital, he'd dodged my questions—

and then me—rather than just tell me what the situation was with Relobu. Maybe I wouldn't have been able to do anything at all to help him, but a simple "heads up, my boss is kinda pissed at me right now" would have gone a long way toward helping me navigate the situation I was in right now. I didn't appreciate being "protected" by being left out of the loop on practically everything.

But it didn't mean I was willing to abandon him altogether. Especially when by luck of the draw my fate had been intertwined with his. Digging through Savitri's paperwork may get Daniel the proof that he needed for his story, but maybe it would also help me when it came time to plead my innocence to a rightfully angry North American dragon lord.

I sighed. "I'll give you two weeks. And then I take my chances with Relobu."

"Fair enough. Let's go buy some clothes."

I closed the car door as Daniel gestured for our driver to resume the trip. The car puttered along for another twenty minutes before sliding into an open parking space along a busy street. We got out, and immediately ducked into a small store offering "western" styles. For a moment I was confused. Living near cattle country in Tulsa caused my idea of western to be similar to Jim and Jovan's cowboy getups on the plane. But the term here simply meant non-ethnic outfits. The store was full of familiar clothing items from basic jeans to spaghetti-strapped sun dresses.

We'd barely made it across the threshold before Daniel found a chair and slid into it.

"Just get what you need. We don't have a lot of time to shop for casual clothes, so this will be the only store you'll see that carries American styles. I'd like to get you to Savitri's as soon as possible, so we need to get all of your things today. I'm more concerned with the work clothes you'll need when you get the job."

So he takes me shopping, and then doesn't want me to shop? I was half tempted to gather up half the store's wares and try them on one at a time just for spite. And then I remembered the chicken scene and did what he asked, grabbing two packs of women's socks, three pairs of jeans, and an assortment of tops. The store's underwear selection was a little on the drab and boring side for me, but I obligingly snagged enough sets to get me through a week without laundry. After two days in the same set of clothes, I was more than happy with the plain cotton variety, as long as it was clean.

From the moment I entered the store, a shop employee had been glued to my side. At first, I assumed it was because my wrinkled clothing and general air of grittiness made me a good suspect for shoplifting. But I'd come to realize she was there to push me to buy more, and assist with retrieving my sizes. Unfortunately she seemed a little uncomfortable speaking to a foreigner, so my initial delight at having my own personal shopping assistant faded to a more general feeling of acceptance.

I followed her back to a small fitting room to make sure I'd properly converted my U.S. sizes to European, and when I was finished she helped me carry my items to the checkout counter. After a little explaining, and Daniel's assurance that we would certainly pay for the items first, the girl agreed to allow me to cut the tags from one of the outfits and wear it from the store.

The rest were carefully cataloged by a smiling young man, who wrote each item on my bill before folding them neatly and placing them in a large plastic shopping bag. When he was finished, the bag was sealed shut with a plastic cable tie, and the bill was added up using an ancient cash register. The total seemed outrageous, so I made a mental note to educate myself on the rupees-to-dollars exchange rate.

Daniel, however, didn't seem fazed by the amount, and after handing over a massive wad of cash, my bags were bundled into our arms and we were out the door. While I slipped back into the rear seat of the car, Daniel took my purchases and stored them in the trunk of the taxi before sliding in next to me.

He directed the driver to a lot only a few blocks away, handed him some cash, and told him to take an hour for lunch. We stepped out of the car and onto the sidewalk.

I had never seen so many people in my life. The crowds were so thick that I was forced to walk a step behind Daniel in order to maintain my place on the narrow pathway. An old man, hobbling with a stick he used as a cane, held out a hand in silent plea as we approached. Without even breaking stride, Daniel dropped a few coins into his palm as we scooted past.

I looked around at the city streets. Bangalore had been one of the few major cities spared from substantial damage during the war and the humans' brief attempt at pushing the dragons back to the Congo where they'd come from. Still, the streets were well-worn and crumbling, partially from the massive crush of people and partially, I assumed, as the result of the earthquake Jim and Jovan were there to cover. It was easy to tell which parts had been affected by the earthquakes, because the breaks in the concrete were cleaner and more jagged than the dust-filled crevices caused by age.

Daniel had told me that the city had been fortunate that the majority of the earthquake's damage had been centered slightly south of Bangalore's city center. Still, the morning's paper had contained pictures of buildings that had been completely flattened by the disaster, including several multi-story apartments typical in the heavily populated capital of Karnataka. Though local authorities had taken swift action to aid those who had lost their homes or loved ones, it was clear that the damage cleanup hadn't even begun, as rescue workers were still trying to locate any remaining survivors.

We'd walked about a block when Daniel stepped onto a stairwell leading to the lower floor of a large shopping center. Here, the walls were filled with colorful stacks of material, some with light reflecting from various jeweled embroidery work sewn onto their surfaces, and others with intricate lace designs along the seams.

Daniel held open the door so I could step through. "Lady Savitri holds a fondness for Indian traditional wear, especially for women. She requires it to be worn by the ladies at all times while in the office. So when you report for the interview, you'll need to be wearing a sari."

Usually I'd be irritated to be told what I could and could not wear, especially when the rules so flagrantly upheld a double standard, and I still wasn't happy about playing dragon bait, but I did have to admit I wouldn't mind wearing some of these fabrics.

"She's a stickler for tradition, huh?" I stepped further into the store and ran a finger along one of the stacks of silk. The fabric was sturdy but soft, and my hands itched to unfold one of the garments to get a look at the entire pattern.

"In some respects, yes." Daniel chuckled. "In fact, it's common knowledge that she employs a British butler. She makes him dress in a formal suit and tails. I've seen some pictures. They guy wears an impressively bushy mustache, so in the tuxedo he looks just like Rich Uncle Pennybags from Monopoly."

I shook my head. I guess it was nice to know even dragons indulged in the occasional harmless-yet-eccentric behavior. Better a compulsion for snazzy dressers than a taste for human flesh, I supposed.

When we'd walked in—I was beginning to learn this was the norm—a shopkeeper hustled to my side and began extolling the virtues of what they had to offer. Between his accent and my unfamiliarity with Indian clothing, my head was soon spilling with all the options available for purchase.

I could get used to the attention. Back in Tulsa, even with my relatively healthy salary from CreaTV, I couldn't afford to frequent the high-end stores that hired enough salespeople for one-on-one service. But here, especially now that I was dressed in something *not* resembling a crinkled paper sack, I no longer felt like a criminal on the verge of a shoplifting citation. With all the sumptuous fabrics on display, this shop felt more like a bridal suite than a department store, and it was actually kind of nice to be treated like a queen. I'd barely touched one of the saris before the man removed it from the stack and unfolded it with flare. The material, at least five yards' worth, now stretched in a long ribbon along a counter built just for that purpose.

"I'm not sure how this works." I'd seen women dressed in saris before, but I'd never had the opportunity to try one myself. The cloth was a gorgeous pale blue, with elaborate navy embroidery along one side. At one end, sewn loosely to the rest of the fabric, was about three feet of cloth in the same navy as the embroidery.

The salesman beckoned a woman from behind the counter. She rummaged around for a moment, then approached with something in her hand. "Try *choli*?" She held out a small blouse, similar in style to her own, and pointed to the fitting room built in to the far wall. I nodded and gathered a bundle of the skirt in my hand to avoid stepping on it, and followed.

"Thank you. I'm Carol."

"Vijayalakshmi." She chuckled when she saw my face. "Lakshmi will do."

I grinned. "Thank you. Very nice to meet you, Lakshmi."

In an absurdly short amount of time, she had me strapped into a basic cropped shirt called a *choli* and a thin cotton skirt that I understood to serve as a slip. With a series of deft flicks of her wrist and a good amount of folding, I soon had the majority of the sari wrapped around my waist. The most decorative side of the cloth was left free to hang over my shoulder—a *pallu*, Lakshmi called it—like a long scarf. In the front, she'd created neat folds to form an accordion-like ruffle effect from waist to feet.

I studied my appearance in the mirror mounted just outside my dressing room. The skirt portion started at my navel and stopped maybe a half-inch above the floor, covering my legs entirely.

The *choli* material ended just under my breasts, leaving about four inches of skin showing from my ribs to my waist. My blouse was a sleeveless version while Lakshmi, wearing a sari herself, stood beside me in a *choli* with tight three inch sleeves.

Still, it was a surprisingly modest outfit, while at the same time it was very clear that there was a woman's body under all that material. A large swath of cloth ran directly across my chest, leaving no amount of cleavage visible. But the folds at my hips accentuated the curve of my waist, giving the illusion of a distinctly voluptuous form. Even with my hair sticking up in product-less abandon, I didn't look half bad.

Sensing a sale, Lakshmi hurried to hand me a length of red cloth with gold embroidery, and I hurried back to the small changing room, feeling like a Barbie doll opening her closet for the very first time to find rows upon rows of fabulous outfits. I loved red. But before, when I still wore my long, natural auburn locks, red had been the one color that I'd been forced to avoid. But now, with my hair gone and what little was left dyed a dark brown, I wanted to see if I could pull it off.

My earlier cotton slip was exchanged for another in the same color as the sari, and then I was able to begin wrapping and arranging the sari fabric around my hips. It was a soft and decadent silk, and with Lakshmi's help the skirt was soon hanging in graceful waves to the floor. The top portion of fabric lay neatly against my chest with strategic folds to mimic the rippled effect of the skirt. A brooch in the shape of a peacock's feather secured the cloth to my shoulder, ensuring everything stayed in place.

Gathering the skirt in one hand and padding out to the communal mirror, I admired the completed outfit. I felt like a princess, and for the first time in a while, I wanted to giggle like a schoolgirl. It was gorgeous. I was gorgeous.

"You should always wear red. It's my favorite color." I looked up to see a reflection of Daniel standing just behind me. Our eyes met in the mirror, and I flashed back to the runway in Budapest. There, his eyes had held the same mixture of heat.

I swallowed. "I think I'll pass on this. Can I take the blue one instead?" I broke eye contact with Daniel, and stepped toward the shelves for the folded cloth. At any other time, I'd have killed to find an outfit that looked that great on me. But when Daniel looked at me like that?

My head stopped working, and I couldn't afford to go there.

I turned to Lakshmi. "The blue one is fine." But my fingers couldn't help but pause against the crimson material as I took one last look at myself in the mirror. The deep red of the cloth, combined with the exotic style of the dress made me feel incredibly daring and provocative.

Daniel gave me a look that made me shiver. A look that said, *I know what you're thinking, and I like it. A lot.*

But he didn't speak. Instead, he turned back to the counter where the man who'd been displaying the fabrics was waiting. "Do you have a tailor on staff?"

The man nodded, and while Daniel explained our time constraints to the shopkeeper, Lakshmi pulled out a cloth measuring tape and wrapped it around my upper arm. She did the same around my ribcage, explaining that the short navy cloth attached to the pale blue fabric was the material reserved for the *choli*. It would be separated from the main bolt of material and sewn specifically to my measurements in whatever style I chose.

Lakshmi smiled as she handed me a design book filled with the available *choli* styles. "He is your new husband? A fine choice."

"Oh, no. We're not—" I stopped myself. Daniel had explained that the Indian culture was largely more conservative than the one I was raised in. I didn't want to offend the woman by telling her the man I was allowing to buy me clothing was not my husband, so I gave her a small smile and nodded.

I chose a blouse style for the navy *choli*, and with her help I picked out three more bolts of fabric that went well with my coloring. Even though I wouldn't need it for the office, Lakshmi managed to also talk me in to a *shalwar kameez*, which I now knew was the name of the clothing Daniel's neighbor had been wearing, only mine was decorated with bold strokes of green and gold. Daniel managed to get the shopkeeper to agree that one *choli* would be delivered to the apartment early tomorrow morning in time for my interview, and the rest we'd pick up as soon as they were ready.

At the shopkeeper's urging, I took the bolts of fabric with me, leaving only the short portions of *choli* material behind for sewing.

With gratuitous input from Lakshmi—she seemed to be having as much fun as I was—we chose a variety of styles for the remaining blouses from wired catalogs she'd given me, along with a good selection of the cotton skirts required to be worn under the wrapped fabric.

It was well past noon when we were finished, and I was quick to agree when Daniel suggested we take a break for lunch before embarking on the adventure of shoe shopping. I could tell this wasn't his favorite of pastimes, but he was surprisingly gracious in the face of my enjoyment, especially when I caught sight of a store dedicated primarily to fancy women's shoes. Nothing got me more excited than the promise of new shoes after a successful shopping excursion.

The food was spicy but good, and two hours later

I was shocked when we had to rearrange the items in the trunk of our taxi to make room for the last of my purchases. "Good grief. I just cost you a fortune!"

He gave me an answering grin. "Don't worry about it. I'll charge most of it to the newspaper when we get back to Relobu's territory. Provided I deliver on this project, they'll be delighted to pay. Besides, I felt bad that you were forced to leave all your stuff in Budapest."

I studied Daniel's face, looking for a sign that he was joking. Most men I knew wouldn't have remembered—or cared—about the new clothes I'd left behind. One of my ex-boyfriends had called me shallow for my love of fashion, while at the same time he spent more money than he made fixing up an old car he'd bought from an auto shop. We'd broken up when he started asking me for money to help him pay rent because he'd blown it all on a new muffler.

But Daniel seemed perfectly serious. He may be rough, and direct, and even more than slightly mercenary, but he'd never once been judgmental about another person's interests.

"I appreciate it."

"It was a pleasure. Truly."

ELEVEN

IT WAS MONDAY afternoon, and I had a meeting with a dragon. I'd worried about it all morning, and now my stomach was a bundled mass of nerves. If my purse were human, it would have died of strangulation before we'd left the flat. For some stupid reason, I thought making the decision to go through with Daniel's plan would take care of the terror I felt every time I thought about coming face-to-face with another power-hungry dragon lord.

Daniel watched me flex my hand as I tried to loosen the muscles that were cramping from the constant tension. "Don't worry, you'll be fine. The position has been open for months, and you're a shoo-in for the job."

I managed a weak laugh. "I appreciate the pep talk, but you're forgetting that I don't want the job. It's not like I have a great track record with dragons, you know." I bit my lip nervously as Lady Savitri's place of business grew larger as we approached.

The building was an imposing sight, standing easily several hundred feet taller than anything on the surrounding landscape. The structure had obviously been put together specifically for dragons, because every few floors there were flat landing platforms jutting from the side of the building in almost every direction.

Why did all dragons insist on living and working in enormous castles? I mean, I understood that they were big, and buildings built with dragons in mind had to be larger than the human-sized office space, but I would never understand why the architecture had to scream "I'm big, scary and dangerous!"

Daniel shot me a smile and patted me on the knee.

We'd turned off the main road and, after a brief stop at a security booth, our auto-rickshaw sped through the gates and up the driveway to the main entrance of Savitri Enterprises.

Daniel—probably in an effort to brighten my bad mood—had stopped at a street vendor offering fresh coconut milk for breakfast. It was fun watching the man open a hole in the husk with a machete, and the milk had been sweet and strangely filling. Now, even that small amount of food was raising complaint in my stomach, unwilling to co-exist peacefully with the nerves running through my system.

Now more than ever I wished I'd been in a position to turn down Daniel's offer. I didn't need another excuse to throw up on a dragon lord.

The driver stopped before the grand double doors and cut the engine. Daniel offered me a hand as I stepped down from the small, yellow-roofed rickshaw, my movements still tentative in the unfamiliar sari.

"According to the guy I spoke with yesterday, there's a reception desk just inside. Oh, and don't forget—" Daniel handed me my passport, "—you're Julie Wallent. Not Carol Jenski. Carol blows up dragons. Julie helps them. Savitri wants the girl who helps dragons."

I stuck out my tongue. "Ha-ha. Very funny." I glanced down at my freshly printed CV. "Jeez, everyone's embellished a bit on a resume, but this is the first time I've gone to an interview and lied about my actual name."

He laughed, and placed a hand on each of my shoulders. "Don't worry. You'll be fine. And I'll be right here when you're finished. Tonight, we'll relax. Do a little sightseeing."

I took a deep breath and nodded. Daniel's words gave me the push I needed, and made me realize I was probably overreacting. Myrna worked with dragons all the time. And it was possible Savitri didn't make a habit of killing or otherwise injuring her staff. Otherwise the smiling woman manning the reception desk wouldn't be smiling, right?

Julie Wallent. Recently married. Former hotel manager looking for work closer to her husband. Dragonspeaker. And of no relation to notorious terrorist Carol Jenski. Got it.

I smiled. I could do this.

I informed the receptionist of my appointment, and she asked me to have a seat in one of the over-stuffed, human style couches near the window. About five minutes later, a tall Indian man with a distinctly British accent walked out and shook my hand, introducing himself as Krishnan Venkat and urged me to follow him back to his office for my interview. With me on his heels, Krishnan pushed through the door into Savitri Enterprises business central.

The office area was huge, the rows of cubicles separated by wide corridors designed to accommodate dragons. My nervousness came back when I got a good look at the fifty-foot ceilings, but I brushed it away and followed my guide to a small office.

Krishnan was polite, and the interview questions easy. He started by handed me a single sheet of paper, followed by a thin spiral notebook and pen. "Please copy this into English and Hindi." The page contained a brief passage on wheat and rice prices, written in dragonscript. I made short work of the English version, and while I struggled a bit with the Hindi numbers, I felt that my version was a close approximation of the basic meaning of the original text.

My interviewer seemed to agree, because he smiled widely and peppered me with a few questions in the same Indian tongue. When he was satisfied my language skills were passable, if not fluent, he leaned back.

"I'll be completely honest. This has been a difficult position to fill. The DRACIM office here in Bangalore has only recently started offering classes in dragonscript, and with the written language being so new, the hiring pool has been virtually nonexistent. I was delighted to receive your CV. Your Hindi needs a little work, but that's to be expected. Can I assume that since you read and write dragonscript, you are also a dragonspeaker?"

I nodded. "I've never been officially tested, but my roommate—" I stopped, forgetting for a moment that I was supposed to be married, "—I'm sorry, my former roommate worked for DRACIM in a translating capacity, and she said I was pretty good."

"How are you with the Indian dragonspeak dialect?"

I smiled. "It's about as good as my Hindi. But I'm a fast learner. I can pick it up relatively quickly."

My answer seemed to satisfy him, because he moved on.

"How is it that you aren't affiliated with a DRACIM office? Isn't that a little unusual?"

It was. In fact, in North America, a non-affiliated dragonspeaker was almost unheard of. The dragons used DRACIM exclusively for their translating needs, so if you weren't affiliated, you were most likely unemployed. Luckily, Daniel and I had expected the question and had a valid, if a little vague, answer. "My interest in dragonspeaking developed after college. By the time I realized this is what I wanted to do for a living, I had already been in the workforce for several years, and I'll confess that it felt odd to attend screening events with applicants who were several years younger than I. I decided to stay in the hotel business where I had already proven myself in real-life, so to speak. But recently, that life started to feel a little less fulfilling than it had in the past. So I took the plunge, and here I am."

"What brings you to India?"

Oh, you know. The usual. A dragon-killing bomb, a sexy but stubborn reporter, and the fact that an entire army of North American and European dragons were ready to hunt me down and kill me like a cockroach in a cake store.

I coughed. Daniel and I had decided to stick to the story of our recent marriage, adjusting the details as necessary until our honeymoon became a long-term job assignment for my "husband." I gave Krishnan a brief version of our fake wedding and the trip over, and eliminated the fun bits about bombs and cockroaches.

He nodded. "Well, Julie. If you want the job, it's yours."

I did my best to look appropriately pleased at the opportunity. "I'm delighted. Thank you."

"I hate to do this to you, but we've had a contractor from the India DRACIM office who's been giving us as much time as he's able around his other projects. Unfortunately, he was called on to attend the trial in Budapest, and he isn't scheduled to be back until next week at the earliest. If at all possible, I'd like to have you in here before his return, so we can look into moving him on to other projects."

I froze when he mentioned Budapest, and I had to force myself to keep a calm expression. I had no idea what would happen if Savitri discovered I was the woman wanted by Lord Relobu. The announcement of my terrorist status had gone out after Hian-puo's trial had wrapped up, so Savitri's representatives had likely already left Budapest. But surely the dragon lord at least paid cursory attention to the world news, if only to make sure *she* wasn't the one about to be attacked.

Daniel was confident that even if she surmised I had entered her territory, the dragon lord wouldn't expend the energy and manpower Adelaida had trying to apprehend me. But I also didn't hold out much hope that she would look the other way with an accused dragon killer under her very snout.

Krishnan was still speaking, and I struggled to catch up. "…and so we're getting rather behind on some of our work. I know you and your husband are still settling in, but we'd love you to begin with us as early as possible."

"I can start tomorrow."

Krishnan seemed surprised, but he nodded. "Tomorrow it is."

We killed the next few minutes making small talk

about the local restaurants I should try to get a true taste of India. He'd just finished extolling the virtues of the chicken tikka at the Sahib Sindh Sultan when he looked up and scrambled to his feet.

"Lady Savitri. I'd like you to meet Julie Wallent. She's just accepted the dragonscript position."

I was certain my heart had stopped the moment I realized he was speaking to the dragon lord. I turned to find a gray dragon standing directly behind me, the points of her spiny wings peeping above muscled shoulder blades as they rested demurely against her back. The large claws on her feet scraped audibly on the floor as she shifted her weight, and fear jolted through me like a spear through the chest. I sprang out of my chair.

Even as the smallest of the dragon lords, Lady Savitri still towered over me by at least a foot. If compared to the bright colors of Lady Adelaida and most of Lord Relobu's kin, Savitri's uninterrupted gray scales would have seemed plain. But their color complemented her relatively slender body and long neck. Dragons had been genetically engineered from a mixture of different animal DNA samples, and if I had to guess, Lady Savitri's petri dish had received an extra dose of lizard or amphibian. Her scales were tiny and arranged in a very fishlike pattern, their gleaming surfaces reflecting the light from the fixtures above.

She angled her head to look at me, and I had to

suppress a shudder. Hian-puo's dragons had shared the sensuous movements and unnatural stillness of their Indian sister. The memory of being taunted by a massive dragon who had killed and eaten a goat in the grossest way possible, right in front of me—for the fun of it—made my skin crawl.

Unaware or unconcerned with of my rising discomfort, Lady Savitri stared closely at me for several moments. I had to clamp my lips together to keep a scream from escaping from my throat when she leaned closer, her nostrils flaring as she took in my scent.

"She is American?"

Dragons could guess my nationality from how I smelled? I was creeped-out all over again.

Krishnan cleared his throat in preparation for his answer, but I stepped forward and gave the dragon lord a slight bow. I'd accepted the position, so like it or not I needed to act like I could handle the job. And part of the job was speaking with dragons.

"I am. My husband and I only recently arrived in Bangalore."

She studied me once again. The silence stretched beyond the comfortable, and I was half afraid she'd somehow recognized me from reports coming out of Budapest.

"You worked for Relobu?"

"No, ma'am. I did not. I am a civilian. With a love of languages. Both spoken and written."

Her eyes flashed with emotion. I'd almost have called it disappointment, but before I could consider why, the dragon nodded curtly and waddled off to attend to other business. I watched as she lumbered along the wide corridor, bending her slender neck over the cubicle walls to speak with the various humans within. I watched the employees I could see carefully, but while they all treated the dragon lord with respect and caution, none of them wore the terrified look that had been a staple among Hian-puo's human staff.

So she wasn't as obviously bloodthirsty or sociopathic as Hian-puo. Then again, Myrna had always spoken of Lord Relobu as a levelheaded dragon specimen, and he was currently holding a jail sentence over my head for simply being in the wrong place at the wrong time. Massive mood swings seemed to be a common thread among dragon royalty.

I guess now that I was an employee, I'd get the chance to find out whether mood swings were a regular part of Lady Savitri's day as well.

DANIEL WAS WAITING for me just outside the door. I called his name and he looked up, a question in his eyes.

"I got the job. I'm supposed to be here at nine tomorrow morning."

I expected him to congratulate me, or at least give

me one of his familiar self-satisfied smiles, but instead he reached for my hand.

"You're okay?"

"I'm fine. A little shell-shocked." I filled him in on my encounter with Lady Savitri. "She wasn't actually *nice*, per se, but she wasn't slicing human bodies into pieces and hanging them from chandeliers either."

Together we walked back to the street, his hand still wrapped around mine. I tried to ignore the feel of his fingers against my palm, and the unwelcome jolt of attraction at the casual touch. I was so keyed up from the interview that my libido was more than a little confused.

When my brain started replaying how nice his hands had felt as they held me against him before our plane trip, I pulled free of his grip and scratched lightly at my head. My gaze drifted to the outline of his broad shoulders under the thin cotton of his T-shirt, and I felt my face grow warm at the thought of following the path of muscle from the bottom of his neck to the base of his spine.

Daniel twisted to flag down an auto-rickshaw, and the muscles in his back flexed.

Down girl.

Oblivious to the thoughts playing through my head, Daniel motioned for me to get inside. "Did they tell you what they needed a dragonscript specialist for?"

I shook my head, trying to dislodge the adrenaline-fueled fantasy and focus on his question. "Not really, but it sounds as if I'll be going through a ton of paperwork they had assigned to a DRACIM employee who was reassigned to the Budapest event."

I waved off his alarmed look. "Don't worry, I met almost no one in Budapest. I spent most of my time either shopping for clothes or crying because I thought my boyfriend was sleeping with my best friend."

Daniel's eyes grew even wider, and I gave him a wry smile. "Don't even think about teasing me. It's a long story, and it's nothing compared to your leg-humping booty-call buddy. For the record, Richard wasn't sleeping with my best friend. He was just ignoring me in favor of Relobu business."

At least I hoped it had been Relobu business. I pushed the disloyal thought from my mind.

Daniel laughed. "You haven't had a very good time lately, have you?"

My smile faded. "Not exactly, no."

Daniel reached up and smoothed down a strand of my spiky hair. "Let's see if we can do something about that. At least for tonight."

"Krishnan said the Sahib Sindh Sultan had a mean vegetable biryani."

He grinned and nudged me good-naturedly. "You want to know the best part? The restaurant's in the mall." He held out a hand. "Come on. I'll buy you another pair of shoes."

"Be still my heart."

TWELVE

OUR MEAL WAS surprisingly pleasant. Krishnan had been right about the vegetable biryani, and Daniel was an excellent dinner partner. With the news stream filled with the stories of DRACIM's trip to China—Myrna and the gang were doing a great job of pushing the trip as proof that the dragon council was enthusiastic about cooperation with humans— I was officially free to share stories from my visit, on or off the record. I told him about Cai, a young girl who we'd rescued along with her mother, from a horrible situation as servants to Hian-puo and his human-hating generals. He laughed when I told him Myrna's experience with a scientist who hadn't taken well to flight by dragonback, and had spent most of his time in China trying not to heave up his latest meal.

It appeared that Daniel had been serious about giving me a break from stress, because he followed my lead and kept the conversation in neutral territory, with us sharing stories of work experiences, childhood memories, and the occasional good-natured tease. In short, it was the perfect date.

He took my hand as we browsed our way through the mall shops, stopping occasionally to read the labels on things we didn't recognize. Soon, we'd tired of the retail scene, so we stepped outside. The night was warm, but there was a breeze, so we eschewed help from our auto-driver to walk to the nearby public garden, chatting about nothing in general and enjoying some time breathing relatively fresh air.

With the help of a hit to the worldwide economy, Bangalore was slowly regaining its status as the Garden City of India, as less of the city's citizens could afford a gasoline-powered vehicle. The sizable reduction of cars on the road—to imagine Bangalore holding more vehicles than its present amount was mind-boggling to me—had led to a healthier population of flora.

The park had quite a display tonight, and we weren't the only ones enjoying the peaceful surroundings. A path had been created to allow better access to the sights, and it stretched in a wide circle through the well-cared-for lawn and flowering plants.

We strolled in comfortable silence, each of us lost in our own thoughts, until we heard music playing several feet ahead of us. With wordless agreement, Daniel and I started to make our way toward the sound. Turning a corner, we discovered a small band, consisting of only a set of speakers, a guitar player, and a man holding a tambourine. The band had set up in a small clearing near the center of the garden. The song list was surprisingly familiar, with hits from back home cropping up at a semi-regular pace. A street vendor was busy taking advantage of the gathering, and sold hot tea from a rickety cart made for the purpose. Daniel got us each a cup and, after finding a small patch of grass to sit, we settled in for the show.

The singer's voice was surprisingly good, and soon I was humming along to the music, the stress from earlier today a long-forgotten memory. After the band finished a particularly energetic number, they slid into a soft rendition of an old favorite of mine.

"Would you like to dance?" Daniel looked at me over the rim of his cup, and nodded toward the band. Several couples, some dressed in traditional Indian saris, and others in jeans and T-shirts, had already created a space a few feet away from the music. He helped me up when I nodded my assent, and soon I was swaying back and forth to the rhythm, eyes closed, pressed against a warm male body, and breathing in the flowery scent of India.

This is what I had wanted from Richard. From the beginning, he'd dutifully showered me with flowers and small gifts, and I'd been a willing companion when he wanted to try out the latest upscale restaurant on opening night. But his attention had been just that. Dutiful. As if paying attention to me was one line of a very long checklist of activities he'd needed to complete within a twenty-four-hour time frame.

I'd simply wanted to have a man I could hold close, without worrying whether my eye makeup had run, or my hair had gone frizzy, or whether my hips were slightly too large for my jeans. With Richard, I'd always had the vague feeling that we'd somehow been keeping score, and every time I asked him for something, he'd write it down in a mental accounting list, and I'd be expected to do something for him to even out the ledger.

With Daniel, there was no doubt I'd be severely in the red if we were keeping score. He'd put himself in danger, pulled several strings, and spent an enormous amount of money—even if it wasn't his— making sure I was taken care of. Granted, he had his moments of supreme jerkery—the scene at the chicken *walla* was proof of that. But in general, when he wasn't dead set on uncovering dragon plots of world domination, he was a pretty decent guy. Tonight proved it.

No wonder he had girls humping his leg and offering to make him chapati in the middle of the night. He had a way of making a woman feel like she was the only one who mattered.

I shifted when his hand touched my bare waist, and I turned my face into the crook of his neck and breathed deep. I could certainly get used to this.

"Carol, look." I opened my eyes and followed the

tilt of his head. Far above, shadows circled in the sky, making lazy patterns against the starry night. One by one the other couples stopped to stare, pointing at the magnificent creatures that had joined the festivities.

The air was filled with a mixture of music and dragon song as the massive beasts called to each other in the air.

Daniel pulled me closer, wrapping his arms around me and touching his nose to my temple. "We're dancing with dragons."

IT WAS AROUND eleven when we made it back to the apartment. I waited at his side as Daniel keyed us in, and then I slid out of my shoes just inside the door. He walked past me toward the refrigerator.

"I had the apartment manager stock the kitchen. Do you want something to eat, drink?"

"I had way too much to eat at dinner, but I'd take a glass of wine if you still have any."

"Red or white?"

"White. Thanks."

I headed toward my room, anxious to change out of my sari before it wrinkled further. I was beginning to get the hang of wearing the garment, but I'd managed to crush the skirt by sitting on it during the auto-rickshaw travel from the restaurant to the apartment, and then later in the grass. I wasn't sure whether I'd have a chance to have it ironed before I needed it for work.

My other sari blouses should be ready for pick up tomorrow morning according to our discussion with the shopkeeper, but just in case, I unfolded the other length of cloth that matched the green top I'd worn today. Pulling on a long T-shirt and pair of leggings from yesterday's purchases, I re-entered the living room.

Daniel sat at the sofa, two glasses of wine resting on the coffee table, along with a pair of tiny scissors, some cotton balls, and a massive jug of hydrogen peroxide.

I raised an eyebrow. "Are we having a party?"

The corner of his lip twitched. "Something like that. It's time to take your stitches out."

My hand immediately flew to my head. The injury was practically invisible unless someone knew where to look, and with careful styling I'd managed to hide the shaved portion of my scalp from view.

In fact, today's excitement combined with Daniel's charming conversation over dinner had made me actually forget about the change in my looks. His words reminded me of my fall from redheaded temptress to scruffy refugee, and my mood plummeted.

But he was right, the stitches needed to come out. The itching around them was so distracting there were times I could swear I'd contracted head lice. If it got much worse, I'd end up tearing them out with my fingernails.

No, Daniel's way was better.

I sighed and approached the sofa, placing my rear on the floor between it and the coffee table. Grabbing my glass, I drained the wine in four quick gulps.

"I'm not really a fan of blood. Or surgery. Or basically anything that requires cotton balls and peroxide."

Daniel stared at my now-empty glass in surprise. "I can see that." Without another word, he pushed off the couch and went back to the kitchen. Returning moments later with the opened bottle of wine, he sat and pushed his glass—still full—in my direction. "Here. It's probably best if I wait until after for a drink."

"I'd appreciate that." I shot him a sideways glance before repeating the gulping process with his wine, daring him to comment.

He wisely refrained, instead tipping my head down for better access to my wound. The wine was quickly working its way through my system, and despite the horrible snick of the scissors as Daniel opened them for use, I was able to stay relatively still.

I winced when I felt the pull on my skin, and as soon as he took his hands from my head I poured myself another glass. Soon we developed a rhythm. Each time he'd pause, I'd take a sip of my drink.

I let out a small yip of pain as he slowly worked the nylon threads free.

"Tell me a little more about your life in Tulsa. You

work for CreaTV, you've got to have other stories about crazy artistic people in your past."

"None that I can come up with right now." It was as if the metal scissors had short-circuited my brain. They were all I could think about.

"You told me you're a manager at CreaTV. For which magazine?"

"I uh," the knuckles of my left hand tightened on Daniel's knee as I felt another pinch, "I'm the art director for *American Style*. I'm basically responsible for making sure the magazine looks good before it's ready for the racks. Contracts, photography, editorial content…you name it, and I have a hand in the pot."

"That's great." The scissors snicked. "What do you like about it?"

Daniel didn't actually care about the answer. I knew he was only trying to keep me still by taking my mind off the Frankenstein project above my forehead. But I answered because I needed the distraction, or else I might put a hole completely through his leg with my nails.

"The variety, I guess. Though after this past month, I have a new appreciation for the control I have over the finished product. Myrna gets a kick out of dealing with the unknown. I get ulcers."

"I think I got them all." Daniel laid the scissors on the table and opened the bottle of peroxide. I breathed a sigh of relief. Until the saturated cotton touched my head.

"Ow! That freaking stings!"

"I'm almost done."

He'd stopped asking me questions, too focused on pouring acid onto my poor skin, so I decided to see if the distraction worked both ways.

"So tell me a little bit about being a newspaper reporter. What do you have to be good at?"

"Research. And people. You have to be able to drill down to the truth in an instant. To have an instinct for what a person means instead of what they're saying. More often than not, it's not the same thing."

I laughed. "I would be a terrible reporter. I can't read people at all. Case in point, I'm the idiot who jumped on a plane with a guy I'd never met before."

He chuckled. "I'd say you did pretty well, but I'm probably a little biased."

I struggled into a standing position, but three glasses of wine in rather quick succession had left me less than steady on my feet. I tilted, windmilled, and would have fallen flat on my face had Daniel not sprung up from his seat to catch me. My nose flattened against his chest, and I turned my head to the side, resting my cheek against the warm fabric of his shirt while I listened to the steady thump of his heart.

"You're not. Biased that is. You've been incredibly kind to me."

He brushed a strand of hair back from my face. "Carol, look at me."

Placing a hand against his chest, I drew back to meet his eyes. They'd gone dark with emotion.

"I have not been incredibly kind to you. In fact, I've spent the last several days mentally berating myself for blackmailing you into doing something you really, really don't want to do. I owe you an apology."

I touched his cheek with the palm of my hand. "Apology accepted."

"No. You shouldn't let me off that easy." He pulled on my fingers as if to dislodge them, but he seemed to change his mind at the last second. Instead of dropping my hand, he brought it to his mouth, running his lips from wrist to elbow.

And that's all it took. Even through the haze of alcohol I felt the familiar jolt of attraction, and suddenly the steady pressure of skin on skin seemed to drive the increasing heat pooling low in my belly. I snuggled closer, wanting to feel the touch of his solid form against the parts of my body that were rapidly coming alive in his presence.

I felt him pause for an instant before strong arms crept around my waist.

"Chemistry is an odd thing, isn't it?"

I felt the vibration deep in his chest when he laughed. "Wine can do a number on your balance, that's for sure."

I leaned back to meet his eyes. "I'm not talking about my balance." I placed my hand against his heart, gratified to feel the skin on his chest contract at my touch. I wasn't the only one who felt the thick pull of seduction tonight. Slowly, without breaking eye contact, I ran my palm up to his shoulder and over the thick muscles along his left arm.

Taking my time, I traced the path my eyes had taken earlier in the day, stepping free of his embrace to follow the curve of his spine. He twisted slightly to track my movement and I sighed, leaning once more against the hard contour of his back.

"I wanted to do this earlier today, at Savitri's."

"Oh yeah?" His voice was husky, and I smiled at the sound of breath hissing through his teeth as I ran a hand under his shirt for a touch of bare skin. He tensed when I lifted the hem and placed my lips against that same patch of bare skin. He smelled wonderful—all warmth, and strength, and with just a hint of something uniquely Daniel.

"Carol." His words were ragged. "You have to stop."

"Why? Because I'm really bad at reading people?"

"No. Because you've had a lot to drink, and when you touch me like that, it makes me want to forget that fact and kiss you senseless."

I pouted a bit, pulling the shirt even higher and nibbling at the spot just below his shoulder blade. But then I stopped, and dropped the T-shirt. "I know. I want to kiss you senseless too."

I felt his heartbeat kick up a notch more.

He stepped forward and then turned to face me.

I had to smile. His eyes were wide, and a little wild, and I couldn't help but feel just a little powerful to be the thing that finally caused the always-collected Daniel Wallent to panic.

I let him flounder for a moment, enjoying the fact that while he tried to form the words to tell me I was far too drunk for sexual decisions, his eyes kept dropping to stare at my breasts, which were no doubt standing at attention through the thin cotton shirt.

"You know, since I'm such a bad judge of character anyway, I don't see why a few glasses of wine would change that. Kiss me, Daniel."

He lasted a single beat before his lips were on mine, his tongue coaxing me to open for him.

I did, and had to gasp at the pleasure. Daniel in a teasing mood was one thing, but Daniel aroused was something totally different.

And totally delicious.

I moved closer to his hard body, rubbing against the hard ridge of his erection.

Daniel groaned and pulled me even tighter. "Carol, honey, you're killing me."

I pulled back from his grasp just long enough to help him lift his T-shirt. Soon my blouse hit the floor next to his, and I was kissing him like there was nothing better in the world.

His skin was smooth, and warm, and just different enough from mine to make my body sing. I reveled in the feel of a calloused hand as it traced the outline of my waist.

"You are so beautiful." His voice was mere inches from my ear, and I sighed when I felt the tips of his fingers slide under the waistband of my pants and push down. "If you want me to stop, I need you to tell me now."

"Daniel Wallent."

His breath was a hiss of sound as I returned the favor and loosened his zipper. "Yeah?"

This was going to be the most painful thing I'd done in a while.

"Remember when you told me I let you off too easy?"

An unintelligible groan was his only response.

"You were wrong. I'm just as vindictive as every other woman. The good news is, once you've accepted your punishment, I consider the slate wiped completely clean."

I pulled my hands from his body and stepped back. "Consider this your punishment. Goodnight, Daniel."

THIRTEEN

I WASN'T EXACTLY skipping to work the next morning, but my mood had nothing to do with the dread surrounding my new job. Instead it was a mixture of acute guilt and a not-so-slight hangover that had me simultaneously tiptoeing out the front door of the apartment and recoiling in horror at the bright sunshine awaiting me outside.

From the moment I woke, my mind had been replaying the moments where I'd slowly run my hand up the front of Daniel's jeans and he'd looked right at me, his face a mask of desire and confusion as I stepped back and left him with barely a word.

When we first met, I'd accused him of playing games to get me into bed. That exchange had turned out to be a misunderstanding. But now, I was the one playing games, only what I had done was worse. Because what I'd done was real, and it was done deliberately.

I could feel my face heat at the memory. Just outside the gates of the apartment complex, I paced back and forth along the road, trying to come up with some way I could face Daniel and explain that I really wasn't the angry, pathetic excuse for a human being that I'd been last night. While Daniel had been patiently dealing with my physical injuries, I'd drunkenly attempted to deal with my emotional ones. And there, on the floor, I'd realized that I couldn't remember the last time I'd actually felt in control of my own future. China, the Tulsa bombing, and now Bangalore, I was still dangling like a puppet for whoever was around to pull my strings.

I'd suddenly decided that I didn't want to be that person anymore. I wanted to strike back at the events that had lead up to my current situation. Unfortunately, the alcohol I'd consumed to settle my nerves had ensured that my attack was fully directed at the only other person in the room. And now all I wanted to do was apologize and make it right.

But just as it was when I'd first opened gritty eyes to face the day, my brain was completely empty of ideas. How did you explain to someone that you were mad at fate?

"Oh Lord, what am I going to do?" I didn't notice that I'd spoken aloud until a young man, maybe twenty years of age, stepped into the path I was wearing into the ground.

"Ma'am? You require an auto?" He gestured to the small green-and-yellow vehicle parked a few feet away.

I couldn't help but look toward the top floor of the apartment complex, where I knew Daniel was sleeping. He probably hated me now.

"Um, yes. Yes, thank you." I gave the man the address of the sari shop on MG Road, as we'd received word that the rest of my *choli* tops were available for pickup.

It was cowardly for me to use the clothing as a reason to leave before Daniel was awake, but after last night's performance, it was a welcome excuse to give me some time to think. I'd left Daniel a note on the kitchen counter, telling him not to expect me until later in the evening, as I planned to go straight to work after my errand. I'd initialed it with an elaborate *J*, just in case the super decided to stop by with more groceries.

Soon, we'd pulled up to the small shop, and I circled around to the side entrance as instructed, since they weren't open for another hour or so.

Lakshmi, the same woman who'd assisted me during my shopping spree, met me at the door, and I gave her a distracted hello.

She grinned widely and hustled me in, muttering something about clasps and embroidery. One by one, I tried on all the blouses, and Lakshmi made minute adjustments to the fit when needed. I'd brought the pale blue sari with me, so I saved that blouse for last.

"Your husband did not join you today?" She peered around me, as if Daniel would suddenly materialize from the corner.

"No."

She gave me a curious look but said nothing, instead concentrating on helping me into the sari's matching petticoat. I glanced at the clock mounted on the wall. I had fifteen minutes before Krishnan expected me to report to my new job.

"Lakshmi, thank you so much. It's beautiful. They are all beautiful."

I admired the blue silk in the mirror, and marveled at the intricate details on the *choli*. They'd definitely done a lot in a small amount of time. Tiny pale blue flowers were hand-embroidered along the cuffs of the navy blouse in the exact color of main sari material.

When I got back to Tulsa, and if I still had a job, I wanted to do a magazine spread on India. Specifically their fashions.

"Do you have paper?" I took the scraps of an old bill from Lakshmi and scribbled a number across the surface. "I'd love for you to call this office. A friend of mine would be very eager to view your work." I gestured to my sari.

Lakshmi took the paper with a confused smile, and walked with me to the door.

It was time for my first day at work. And since I couldn't think of a good way to apologize for last night, I had a puritanical urge to make up for it.

KRISHNAN WAS ALL smiles when I walked through the door, and after filling out the usual employment forms, he quickly escorted me to a small cubicle in the busy ground floor of Savitri Enterprises. My eyes widened at the boxes of paper stacked chest-high in every available space.

Krishnan winced at my expression. "I might have underestimated the amount of work we had waiting for you."

I stared at the boxes. This paperwork could take weeks to go through, and that's assuming it was legible, organized, and I could simply skim it. But judging from the way most of the box lids sat unevenly along the tops and edges of paper poked through the handles on the sides of almost every box, I was guessing organization hadn't been the top priority.

It would take a hundred years to find military records in here, and that's assuming there were any.

Nevertheless, I gave him a bright smile. "Not a problem. That's why I'm here." I might not have fun while doing it, but if reading through these papers was the fastest way I could get the proof of Savitri's growing army Daniel was looking for, reading was what I'd do.

But I really, really hoped there was an easier way. However, I had a hard time coming up with a question that didn't sound in any way similar to "so, Krishnan, can you tell me where you've filed all your military secrets?"

I decided to start small. "Any place in particular you want me to start?"

Krishnan jerked forward, apparently happy to

have something to do. He picked up a box from the floor, set it on my desk, and rifled through the first few pages. "Yes, this is it. This one should contain some details on dairy and petrol agreements we've made with Adelaida's territory. They need to be read, summarized, and bundled so I can get Savitri's signature on them as soon as possible. For now, just translate them to English."

"What do dragons want with dairy agreements? Is it for Savitri's household staff?" I'd never heard of a dragon eating anything but a meat-heavy diet. They could eat cheese and milk, sure, but generally if given a choice they gravitated toward pork and beef—the rarer, the better.

I assumed the dairy was intended as food supply for the dragon lord's human servants. Based on what Myrna told me, the arrangements between personal servants included room and full board in addition to a salary. But it seemed odd to me that out of all of this paper, Krishnan wanted me to start on food arrangements for only a handful of people.

"The agreements aren't just for her house staff. It's for everyone. All of India. The petrol too."

"Lady Savitri negotiates on behalf of humans?" I was fairly certain Lord Relobu didn't do that for North America. We had a human government in place for that. Since the war, their meetings didn't happen in stuffy offices like those of their forebearers since most of the national buildings had been bombed, but the newspapers still reported on their activities. And we still voted for our representatives.

Lord Relobu wasn't involved with anything the American government did. Well, at least not directly. Obviously the dragon lord's feelings were taken into consideration—he could pretty much put an end to any laws the humans developed simply by ignoring them, or attacking if someone was stupid enough to try and enforce them. But for the most part Relobu maintained a separate authority over his dragons, and left the humans to their own devices.

I guess that wasn't the case with Lady Savitri. Maybe, like Daniel had said, she really was power hungry. She'd taken full control of the humans in her territory, and now she was turning her attention to expanding her rule into China. The usurping of the Indian government must have happened very recently, otherwise we would have heard about it.

But it didn't make sense. How had the human citizens of India not realized their government was no longer functioning autonomously from Lady Savitri? Wouldn't the politicians complain at their loss of power? My mind was racing with questions. I had to get this information to Daniel.

"Prime Minister Kapoor asked for her help with this matter. Since Lady Adelaida owns the major oil and dairy production companies in the Middle Eastern and European territory, he thought it best to have Lady Savitri and her staff handle the negotiations. India has the highest human population in the world, you know. It's important that we get the very best price from Lady Adelaida."

I nodded. Before humans had even realized dragons had been genetically "born," China had been one of the first countries to enter World War III. Because of the country's size, it was obviously seen as one of the larger threats to the guys on the other side of the disagreement, and had suffered quite a few attacks as a result. The war stopped—at least between the humans—when the dragons started claiming territory, but the Chinese had strenuously objected to Hianpuo's arrival, and had lost millions of their population trying to force him from their land.

In contrast, Lady Savitri's settlement into India had been much less violent, with the Indian people quickly recognizing there wasn't an upside to fighting her claim. As a result, India had officially overtaken China as the most populous country in the world.

Suddenly, my wild suppositions seemed ridiculous. Lady Savitri hadn't overthrown the Indian government. She was helping them.

"I see." I cleared my throat, embarrassed about the place my mind had jumped. Daniel's military conjectures were turning me into a conspiracy theorist. "I'll get right on these."

Krishnan smiled and bid me farewell.

I sat in the chair and sighed. I hadn't even been

here an hour and already had a headache. Picking up the first bound set of papers and a fresh notebook, I started taking notes on the agreement between Adelaida and India, making sure to note all the important dates, numbers, and addresses. But after only about twenty minutes, I'd finished with the petrol contract, and I hadn't seen a single mention of troop movement near China. Which wasn't surprising, of course. This room was a mess. No one in their right mind would have routed high priority troop commands into this black hole. There had to be another room with all the good stuff in it.

Because I hadn't the slightest idea where to start on Daniel's project, I was a model employee for Savitri. At this rate, I'd have all her normal, non-secret business cleaned up within a couple of days. And I'd know more than I ever wanted to about petrol and dairy products.

It was time to change my approach.

My behavior last night had me itching to find whatever proof I could in hopes that Lord Relobu might accept the information in exchange for leniency on my arrest order. I'd be delighted to go home immediately and never have to face Daniel—or my feelings—again.

I scanned the room, trying to determine where I should start digging. But alas, not one of the boxes was labeled "super-secret invasion plans."

I was just about to leave my cube and wander the

halls, hoping that I'd run across, I don't know, a room that looked suspicious or something, when something caught my eye. It was a small white envelope, unopened, dangling precariously between a stack of old bank statements on the top of the desk, and another stack of random files that had been half shoved into the desk's open single file-drawer. Addressed only to "The Dragon Lord of India," the envelope caught my eye because of the very un-banklike pattern of embossing that ran along the back flap. It matched the stylized logo from the hotel in Budapest. I was almost certain. I remembered admiring the elegant illustration of alternating dragon heads and tails in a deep gold.

I snatched it up, tearing through the paper with a ragged nail. When I'd finished reading the short note, I slammed my palms on the desk. "That rat bastard."

I'd read too many notes written by Richard Green to mistake the sender as anyone else. The note was typed, but the phrasing, the sentence length…I was an expert at written languages, after all, and absolutely everything about it pointed to my boyfriend as the author of this letter.

Furious, I ran my gaze along the neat rows of pencils, notebooks, and paper clips. And stopped at the phone.

I hesitated for only a moment before picking up the receiver and dialing my apartment. When there was no answer, I crossed my fingers and dialed

Myrna's work number. Based on the last time I spoke with Myrna, odds were good she was holed up at DRACIM.

"DRACIM Reparations, this is Myrna."

"Hey. Whatever you're doing, I want you to stop, find Richard and kill him."

"Carol? Is that really you? Wait just a sec."

There was a slight rattle as she settled back at her desk and adjusted the receiver. "Sorry, there are a couple of interns still here helping me sort through the backlog. I had to kick them out of my office. I've been so worried. There've been reports that they came looking for you at the hospital, but no one knew where you'd gone."

"I'm fine. Safe. Richard on the other hand, isn't going to be so lucky. You will never guess what I have in my hand right now." I was so furious I didn't give her enough time to respond. "It's a letter. Addressed to Lady Savitri. And judging by its contents, I'm betting every other dragon lord received a note exactly like it. He signed my name to it, Myrna! He sent an invitation to a "private demonstration" of another of Hian-puo's bioweapon on the thirteenth of December. And he put my name on it. While we were running around trying to stop Hian-puo's bomb, Richard was busy commissioning another one!"

Myrna sighed. "I know. Lord Relobu's copy arrived in the mail last week. That's what was behind his announcement that you were to be apprehended.

Lady Adelaida got her letter about the same time as Relobu. When the Shui-Tech scientists who'd worked on the bomb suddenly resigned without telling anyone where they were going, the two dragon lords got together and decided to try and find you before any of the other dragons could make contact, just in case you really did manage to get another bomb built and intended on selling it to the highest bidder." Myrna paused. "I am so sorry. I feel awful. I dragged you in to this mess. If I hadn't introduced you to Richard, Relobu wouldn't be out for your head and you could come home."

My shoulders drooped. I guess that answered my question about whether Relobu still planned to arrest me as soon as my feet hit American soil. I'd half hoped Myrna had worked a miracle and convinced Lord Relobu that I'd had nothing whatsoever to do with Richard's plans for the bomb. But obviously that wasn't the case.

"So it sounds like I'm still unwelcome in Tulsa, huh? Have you heard from Richard? Did he get out of Budapest?"

Myrna's pause did not make me feel good about her answer. "Unfortunately, Relobu still wants your head on a platter. Richard, on the other hand, is already back home."

"They caught him? What did they do to him?" My mind suddenly flashed back to some pictures I'd seen of a general who'd displeased the former

Chinese dragon lord. The general was a dragon, and he'd still managed to have almost every bone in his body broken before Hian-puo had sliced him neck to hindquarters and ended his life. The way I felt right now, I almost hoped they'd given Richard the same treatment.

Myrna made a noise, half snort, half snarl. "He's still alive, but only because they won't let me near enough to kill him myself. Relobu sent Trian on an out of town project, so I'm getting my information from spotty sources. They don't exactly trust me much at the moment. But they all tell me Richard is holed up at Relobu's house and in perfect health. He turned himself in. Pretended like he'd had no idea anyone was looking for him, and said he'd been trying to track you down after he'd realized that you'd sent out those letters, and probably had another bio-weapon, or at least a copy of the device schematics.

"He acted like he'd been working in Relobu's best interests the entire time."

I was quiet for a moment, absorbing the information. "That doesn't make any sense. And Relobu believed him?" Before the question was even out of my mouth I knew the answer. Of course Relobu believed him. Richard had worked for the dragon for years. I was the new girl who'd asked to be on the team, even though she'd never had any real experience dealing with dragons.

There was another long pause, and for a moment I thought I'd lost the connection.

Myrna's voice was hesitant. "I've tried getting information from some of my contacts in Relobu's house, but mum's the word on the Richard situation. All I know is that Richard spent a couple of hours in a holding cell downtown before Relobu sent some guys to pick him up. Richard and the dragon lord were in a closed-door meeting for about two hours, and when they emerged, Lord Relobu said Richard was not to be harmed.

"I'm only hearing this stuff through the grapevine, but it looks as if Richard will be taking back some of his responsibilities with the company."

"What?" Of all the fates I'd imagined for Richard, being reinstated as Relobu's chief operations officer had not been on the short list.

"Crazy, right?"

"Well what happened to Emory? I mean, if Richard was welcomed back with open arms, did Relobu give Emory the same benefit of the doubt?"

Myrna snorted. "Of course not. Emory was taken into custody the day the bomb went off at DRACIM, and Relobu hasn't wavered in his belief that Emory was involved. The only difference is, Relobu thinks he was working for *you*."

"And Emory didn't call Richard a liar?" If Myrna's old boss did anything well, it was blaming other people for his shortcomings. Frankly I was surprised Emory hadn't started talking before they'd even managed to get him in cuffs.

"That's the problem. At the time of the bombing, Relobu was so furious he sent a contingent of dragons to the DRACIM base for Emory instead of allowing the Tulsa police department to pick him up. It's possible Relobu might have calmed down enough to allow Emory a chance to explain himself as Richard did. But a group of humans heard we'd let a dragon take custody of a DRACIM employee. While the cleanup crew was making certain we'd cleared all traces of the biomaterial from our building, the humans formed a small militia and tried to shoot down Relobu's contingent, claiming humans weren't subject to dragon law, and therefore could not be tried for killing them. One sec—"

There was a loud click and then a groan as the spring mechanism used to open the two enormous, dragon-sized doors in her office engaged. I waited while Myrna spoke to one of her interns about organizing food for tomorrow's safety meeting about train accidents and low-flying dragons.

"I'm back. Sorry about that. Anyway, Relobu's team made it to DRACIM, but when they were leaving, the dragon carrying Emory was almost shot down. She lost her hold on Emory and dropped him from about twenty feet in the air. It broke several bones, one of the main ones being his jaw."

"Oh crap. Emory wasn't in a saddle?" For my dragonback trip from Beijing to Budapest, I'd sat in a seat designed to strap tight around the dragon's belly, placing me near the dragon's neck, just above the wings. The saddle had a pretty intricate seatbelt that kept me anchored even if the dragon decided to fly upside down.

Which I'm happy to confirm he did not.

Myrna snorted. "Nope. They'd brought him a saddle, but somehow the dragons incorrectly assumed Emory was a delicate flower of a man, and not the three-hundred-and-fifty-pound candy lover that he actually is. The seatbelt didn't fit him. The dragons were in a hurry, so it was decided that one of them would simply carry him clasped between his lower claws."

"Ouch." The flight itself in that position couldn't have been comfortable. And to be dropped? Just the thought made me rub at the wound on my head in sympathy.

"Yep. Anyway, he's still not able to speak—the doctors are keeping him pretty drugged up because of the pain and to ease the use of his feeding tube—but when he's well enough, Relobu has demanded an audience. We can always hope that at that point Emory will point the finger at Richard, but as of right now, Relobu has not lifted the bounty on your head. The doctors say it will be at least two weeks before he'll be in any condition to have guests."

I wasn't happy about my situation, of course, but I was pleasantly surprised to hear that I had potential support for my story, even if it was just Emory. "Well, that bodes well for my triumphant return."

"Exactly. But until then, I think you ought to stay where you are for now. Just to be safe. And I'd rather not hear the details. Right now, Relobu hasn't quite forgiven DRACIM for allowing the deaths of his dragons, regardless of who specifically caused the deaths. We've been asked, through a politely worded memo, not to approach the Relobu properties until this blows over. But just in case he decides to lift his moratorium on DRACIM employees, I'd rather be in the dark on your whereabouts. How're you holding up?"

Her question was cheery, but I could hear the exhaustion in her voice. It sounded as if Myrna had taken over most of the Tulsa DRACIM office when Emory had been arrested. I'd dialed Myrna with the intention of sharing Daniel's theories about the trouble brewing in India, but I didn't feel comfortable heaping on to her worry. Myrna never worked this late unless there were severe problems. And if humans forming militias and shooting down dragons weren't severe problems, I didn't know what would qualify.

And Relobu refusing DRACIM interference? That was unheard of. She had enough to deal with. Until I had proof, I didn't want to make Myrna's day worse than it already was.

"I'm doing fine. Really. A—" I wasn't sure how to describe my relationship with Daniel, "—a friend helped smuggle me out of Budapest on a plane. I'm currently stretched out in a hammock in Cancun, soaking up the sun, right under Relobu's snout."

"Uh huh, sure you are." Myrna knew better than anyone that I turned into a roasted tomato when I was in the sun for more than five seconds, and the idea of sand between my toes gave me the creeps. Her voice turned serious. "Wherever you are, I'm glad you're okay. I'll do my best to get you home."

"Thanks."

I hung up the phone and looked around. I'd decided that my next move was to start thinking outside the box in order to locate Savitri's military records, but after my talk with Myrna, I couldn't get my brain to do anything but replay the letter Richard had sent over and over.

Lady Savitri of India,
Hian-puo isn't the only one with dragon-killing bioweapons. For the right price, you too can obtain the ultimate tool for ensuring your territory's continued dominance. Appointments for product inspection can be made by calling the number printed on the back. I look forward to making your acquaintance, and hope that this is the beginning of a mutually beneficial relationship.
—Carol Jenski

There, right on the page, was unquestionable proof that I was a complete idiot for trusting Richard, and that Richard was the vilest human on the planet.

I'd be useless doing anything that required more than the minimum of thought. So I guess it was time to translate some dairy contracts.

FOURTEEN

IT TOOK ME the rest of the day to read through the second contract. I was still brooding over the news that Richard had used me as a scapegoat for his stupid plan. If the evidence had been any less straightforward, I wouldn't have believed my own eyes.

And if anyone other than Myrna had filled me in on Richard's return to Relobu's good graces, I'd have called them a liar. But her pitying tone, the letters, and memories of Richard's almost casual dismissal of my well-being after I'd woken at the hospital in Budapest made his actions sadly plausible.

I was furious. But I was also very, very hurt. It was one thing to simply decide a person wasn't the one for you, it was quite another to realize they'd played you for a fool in a stunt that was as far from a game as you could possibly get. The last time I'd felt this lost and hopeless, I'd wanted Myrna with me. But now all I could think was how much I wanted Daniel to wrap his arms around me and remind me that there were good people still left in the world.

I'd wondered whether my repeated contact with ugly surprises—be they dragon attacks or unwanted haircuts—had somehow dulled my emotions. Two months ago, the news that my boyfriend wanted to break off our relationship would have left me in prime form for a gallon of ice cream and a sob-fest once I got back home. Richard had gone further than a simple break up: I'd just found out that he'd deliberately placed my life in danger to save his own.

I didn't feel like bursting into tears. Or crying. Or even eating a gallon of ice cream.

Well, okay. I always felt like eating a gallon of ice cream, but that was beside the point.

No. I didn't want to cry. I wanted to hit something. Preferably Richard's perfect face. Before I'd even found the letter, I'd already decided to break things off with him when I got back in the country. I still wanted to break things off, but now it was in a very literal sense. As in, break his limbs off his body. Especially when I thought back to all of my guilt-ridden regrets about leaving him to fend for himself in Budapest. Or for acting on my attraction to another man.

For once in my life, I felt like I might actually do the crazy ex-girlfriend thing and try to stab him to death with a shoe. Only this time I would *not* feel guilty about it the next morning.

I was guilt-free with regard to my relationship with Richard. But that didn't mean I was off the hook regarding my behavior with Daniel the night before.

I still halfway hoped the ground would swallow me so I could stop replaying his dumbfounded reaction.

I was becoming a little more anxious by the minute. I was still completely at a loss for what I would tell Daniel when I saw him. It was almost five in the afternoon, and I'd finished up the translation on the second contract for Krishnan's review. I was walking it over to his office, mentally preparing the mother-of-all forgive-me speeches when the wide double doors at the far side of the room opened and an enormous dragon stepped through.

Based on the long beard of flesh that dangled from his chin, this dragon was male, and well past puberty. His scales were a dark red, nearly the color of rust, and I could tell from the way he entered the room that he both knew he was scary and enjoyed it. With his large bones and blunt snout—not to mention the ugly scar across the right side of his neck— he looked nothing like Lady Savitri, and everything like a dragon-sized gladiator.

I wasn't the only one who thought so. Though no one screamed or passed out in fright, a hush fell over the entire office and all heads turned in the dragon's direction, eyes watching warily as he stalked into the room.

The human-sized office equipment only made him look bigger, and I saw a couple of humans cower involuntarily as his head swung over the tops of their flimsy cubicle walls.

But other than the self-satisfied gleam in his eye, the dragon didn't pay any attention to the silent work staff. After a scan of the room, he headed directly for the doors to Lady Savitri's private work quarters.

One by one, my new colleagues returned to their previous tasks as he passed them with his lumbering gait. Conversation gradually returned to normal.

I let out a little squeak when a hand unexpectedly touched my arm.

"Sorry, didn't mean to startle. Were you looking for me?" Krishnan gestured to the stack of papers I'd been unconsciously hugging to my chest.

I took a deep breath. My jumpiness around scary dragons hadn't disappeared quite yet. "Yes. The dairy contract." I handed him my notes. "I had a little trouble with some of the language in the middle. It wasn't the dragonscript. I think you should have someone look at the terms, because it's not really clear when delivery should occur in relation to when the payment is made." I still hadn't managed to look away from the door the dragon had walked through. The giant reptile had given me the shivers, just like the dragon who'd teased me in China. Both of should be required to wear a sign that read: DANGER: HALF-CRAZY DRAGON around their necks.

"Wonderful, thank you."

"Who was that?" I nodded in the direction of Savitri's office.

"Shal Benaki. One of Savitri's generals. He was

originally from Pontal's territory, but migrated to Savitri's territory with permission from the African dragon lord." Krishnan frowned as he stared at the closed doors. "She keeps him around because he's an excellent strategist. But he's not exactly the friendly sort."

"Has he ever hurt a human?" Benaki hadn't touched anyone here, but when the entire office quietly retreated to their cubes at his arrival, the dragon's eyes had held the same fierce amusement that I'd witnessed in the worst human-abusers of Hianpuo's dragons. Specifically the dragons who'd taken great pleasure in tormenting two human slaves, Cai and Jia, who worked his castle. Myrna and Trian had eventually convinced Lord Relobu to offer the mother and daughter sanctuary in North America after they helped with the recovery of Relobu's imprisoned team. But both seven-year-old Cai and her mother would wear physical and emotional scars from the experience for the rest of their lives.

Krishnan shook his head. "Once. He swore it was an accident, that the man tripped over his tail and fell into the desk, breaking his arm. But Savitri knows Benaki too well, and publicly punished him for the 'accident.' Since then, he's never been friendly, but he's resisted the urge to cause mayhem.

"Usually Savitri is careful not to let Benaki near her human employees when she isn't present. But it doesn't stop him from making everyone uncomfortable."

"I haven't worked around dragons much, so excuse me if this is a stupid question, but how does Savitri keep her generals in line? Don't get me wrong, if she were attacking me, I'd be suitably terrified. But Benaki is over twice her size. You said Pontal was Benaki's original dragon lord. Doesn't he owe allegiance only to the lord of his birth?"

"You're thinking of the birthright custom?"

"I think so."

Myrna had tried to explain the system of dragon rule before, but I admit I hadn't paid that much attention. From what little I could remember, dragons were somehow predisposed to follow the lord of their birth territory. Some scientists speculated that it was built into their genetic make-up. The fluke medical procedure that had created dragons had been aimed at eradicating cancer, and each mixture had been created to combat specific forms of the disease. Each of the seven original dragon lords had been spawned from a different mixture.

The medical team's main goal had been to ensure the cancer-curing cells replicated consistently within the body without mutation, to increase the odds that the injected DNA continued to attack the proper cancerous cells they'd been designed to eradicate. Because of this, when dragons had been accidentally created, all dragons had essentially been programmed to replicate the appearance and behavior of their parents as closely as possible. This caused the dragons to feel an almost overwhelming need to work with members of their birth family.

Of course, some of the older, original offspring of the dragon lords—the ones who had one of the petri-dish-created dragons for both mother and father—shared equal amounts of DNA from both parents and had more choice in which lord they more closely identified. But Benaki looked far too much like the African dragon lord to be anything other than the child of two Pontal-descended dragons.

"Some people speculate that Benaki's distance from his birth dragon has caused…issues in his thought processes."

That may be, but I was quickly learning that some people—and dragons too—simply chose to be a certain way, and no one would be able to persuade them differently.

Speaking of persuasion…

"You said Savitri punished him publicly for his 'accident' with the human. He allowed it? He seems like the type of dragon who would be humiliated by something like that."

"Savitri might be small in size, but she is a skilled fighter. You forget she's successfully maintained a border between Pakistan and China for many years. Even those under Savitri's rule by birth are not mindless followers. She's had a few subjects who made the mistake of thinking they could easily take her throne. Every one of them is dead. She holds her possessions like a true dragon lord. With a vicious temper and an absolute belief in the superiority of her claim."

I thought back to the growing number of dragons on the Pakistani border. Dragons, especially dragon lords, were not only possessive of the things they already owned, but were historically greedy about things they did not.

I gave Krishnan a small smile. "I think I'm finished for the day. I'll see you tomorrow."

Eyes already scanning my notes, he gave me a distracted wave and wished me a good evening.

FIFTEEN

I LEFT THE office as soon as I gathered my things, my head pounding from the hours I'd spent hunched over scribbles of dragonscript. I rubbed the back of my neck absently as I walked to the gate, my other hand holding the sack that held my newly completed *cholis*.

Someone yelled "Julie" several times before I remembered that was my name while at work, and I looked up to see Daniel waving at me as he approached from the street. My muscles tightened as he walked up the hill, his long legs and broad shoulders covered in a perfectly fitted pair of slacks and a short-sleeved polo. As always, he looked calm, professional, and incredibly hot.

I remembered being impressed with his sense of style when we first met in the hospital, and it appeared that it hadn't just been a part of his "doctor" persona. Reminding myself that my attraction to men who dressed well hadn't exactly worked out well for me in the past, I mustered a smile.

"Sorry. I forget I have a different name," I told him when he was close enough for me to whisper.

"I figured. Sorry I missed you this morning. You didn't have to go to the tailor on your own."

I gave an uncomfortable chuckle, and then decided it would be easier for both of us if I went ahead and brought up the reason for my quick departure.

"Daniel. I just wanted to apologize for last night. I had a little too much to drink, and with the whole stitches thing—I guess the relief of it being over made me act a little crazy. I solemnly swear it will never, ever happen again."

Because of his sunglasses, I couldn't see his eyes, but I was glad to see the corner of his mouth lift into a brief smile.

"Don't worry about it. Like I seem to remember mentioning to you earlier, I totally deserved it. Besides, what's a little bit of drunken groping between husband and wife?"

I smiled, glad to see I hadn't made our live-in arrangement unbearably awkward for both of us. Daniel succeeded in hailing an auto-rickshaw, and we climbed inside.

"How was your first day of work?"

I laughed, but without humor. "Work was good if you consider the fact that I found overwhelming evidence that Richard set me up to be the fall guy in his plans for the bioweapon." I filled Daniel in on the details of Richard's note.

"No. He didn't. That bastard."

I shook my head. "Oh, he did. And I share your

sentiments on his parentage. I talked to Myrna, and she's not sure whether he was truly planning on selling another bioweapon or whether it was a ploy to get the dragon lords all in one place so he could set one off and kill them all at once."

"Good Lord. I'm speechless. I'll admit I never saw that coming."

"Heh. You and me both." I looked out the opening in the auto. "I didn't get a chance to dig around for anything specific on the troop movements today. Sorry."

He put his arm around my shoulders. "Carol, it's fine, really." He waved away my apology. "Not a problem. I didn't manage to track down my contact until this afternoon anyway."

Daniel had told me about a source he had that might be able to narrow down the location of the things we were looking for on the possible invasion of China. "Did he know anything?"

"Yeah. He says all military correspondence is delivered directly to Savitri's personal assistant, Nipa. She's human, looks about a hundred years old, and guards the file cabinet we need access to like a hawk."

"Of course she does. Why can't anything be easy?"

"Why indeed?"

"I think I've seen this Nipa woman in the break room. I'll see what I can do to make myself invaluable."

"Well, no need to worry about it now, we'll deal with that hurdle tomorrow. Tell me what else you managed to get your claws into."

I told him about the cubicle full of paperwork, Savitri's negotiations with Adelaida on behalf of India, and the unnerving visit from Benaki.

"Benaki...big dragon, maroon, with a scar about here?" Daniel ran his hand along his neck.

"That's the one. Krishnan said he used to be Pontal's dragon, until he requested a transfer to Lady Savitri's service."

Daniel grunted. "I'll bet he regrets that now. Rumor is he got that scar when he tried to assume control of a dinner party Savitri was hosting. She told him to step down, he got surly, and she reacted."

"Really? Wow." Krishnan hadn't been kidding when he said Savitri could take care of herself. I found myself wishing I'd been around to see the fight. Benaki's scar was rough-edged, ragged. It had been clearly made by a sharp tooth or claw, not by any type of blade. Savitri didn't seem big enough to cause that amount of damage.

"Yep. Every year or so there's a young dragon who mistakenly assumes Savitri is an easy target because she's small, and because she chose to settle down with a single mate instead of the usual dragon lord practice of multiple sex partners." He gave me a playful smile. "Sexist assumptions aren't restricted to only the human race."

"I have to admit, it never occurred to me that she would have a single mate." The idea of mating for life wasn't unheard of in the dragon community, in fact one of Lord Relobu's nieces life-mated last year. The two dragons were so obviously in love that the human newspapers had done a couple of stories on them. The public had been so fascinated by the pair that much of North America had been waiting for her to give birth to her "royal" twins for months now.

But marriage, if you could call it that, wasn't the norm. With only seven original dragons, the lords generally did whatever it took to increase their territory's dragon population to a size sufficient for defense of the homeland. The fact that Savitri had mated with a single male dragon meant she either felt confident in the size of her dragon armies, or decided to leave the churning out of dragonlings to someone else.

I wasn't sure which option I preferred. The talk of dragon armies reminded me of my conversation with Myrna. "I called DRACIM Tulsa. I figured since the guy who used my office worked for the Bangalore branch, it wouldn't seem completely out of the ordinary for the Tulsa number to pop up."

I caught Daniel up on the recent Tulsa events, including the formation of human militias, Emory's injuries, and Myrna's frantic work schedule. By the time I was finished, we'd reached the apartment.

"Now, if you don't mind, I'm going to go upstairs,

make a sandwich and try to seduce you. Only this time, we're not stopping until we're both so tired we can't move."

Daniel stopped and stared. I could feel his eyes on my back as I walked to the elevator, and moments later, I heard the crunch of his shoes on gravel as he followed me.

THAT ELEVATOR RIDE was the longest I'd had in my life.

Daniel had already managed to get the brooch holding up my *pallu* unpinned from my shoulder by the time we hit the apartment, and as soon as he'd keyed us in and the door was closed, I helped him free the sari from my waistband and drop the material to the floor. Daniel watched as it fell, and his hand went still against my hip.

Wearing only the cropped blouse and underskirt, I had a momentary urge to cover myself, afraid that Daniel's initial enthusiasm stemmed from a need to give me a taste of the same medicine I'd fed him the night before, and that any second he'd back away, leaving my desire burning white hot with no way to quench it.

I'd known, intellectually, that my actions last night had been cruel. But now, with my hands practically itching to touch him somewhere, anywhere, I realized just how heartless I'd been.

I placed a tentative hand against his chest. "I'm sorry. For last night."

Daniel pulled back, his eyes locked to mine as he considered my words. "You're not planning on doing it again, are you?"

The horror in his voice caused me to choke back a laugh. "No. Absolutely not."

The weight of his body pressed me back against the wall and he chuckled. "Then you're forgiven."

He grabbed my leg just above the knee and went to hook it around his waist, but the sari's cotton underskirt severely hampered my movement, and the sudden shift in my center of gravity without full motion of my legs nearly knocked me—and him—to the floor. Daniel managed to steady us both with a palm to the wall, but by then, we'd both dissolved into laughter.

I put both feet firmly on the floor, and stood on my tiptoes to place a chaste kiss against his closed lips.

"Maybe the entryway isn't the best place to do this. We should try this somewhere less hazardous to our health," I said as I slipped the buttons loose on his shirt one by one, taking time to run my knuckles against his skin with every movement.

When I was finished, I took a moment to admire his broad chest, running my fingers along the slight dip down the center where pectorals met sternum. For a reporter, he was in surprisingly good shape, and I was delighted to find that my touch caused his muscles to tighten in anticipation.

Feeling a bit more confident that we were both under the same crazy spell, I placed my hand, palm down, right over his heart, loving the unique sensation of soft skin over hard muscle. There was something about touching him that managed to make me feel safe and fearful all at the same time. And I loved it.

Daniel had grown a bit impatient with my exploration, because suddenly I felt his hands tug on the drawstring of my skirt. The knot held true, and the second jerk was slightly more insistent. By the third, he'd pulled so hard I was sure I heard the material rip.

Breathing hard, Daniel made a sound somewhere between a grunt and a curse. "What the hell do they make these drawstrings out of? Titanium? Are there special chastity knots they teach you in dressing rooms or something?"

I matched his mock serious expression. "It's a sign. The Hindu gods refuse to allow us sexual satisfaction until we find a proper place to partake. Come on." I pulled his hand from my skirt and led him toward my bedroom, walking with a deliberate twist of my hips to give him something nice to look at. When I felt his hands cup my ass, I knew I'd been successful.

The feeling of power evaporated, however, when I happened to glance in the mirror installed on the back of the room's closet door. The reflection caused me to stop short. It was crazy to me that I could forget about my appearance for hours at a time. But now, after a long exhausting day, my hair was a mess, my eyes ringed in dark circles, and my skin blotchy from the heat. The image was shocking, and not in a good way.

"Hey."

Daniel put a hand on each side of my jaw and gently turned my face until all I could see were his deep brown eyes. "I don't like it when you get sad."

"I'm not sad. I'm just…wistful. I really did have a nice head of hair."

He leaned down to place a kiss on the tip of my nose. "Don't you dare do that to yourself. What you have here," he moved a lock of my hair with his index finger, "on the outside? It's temporary. Your hair is not at all why I'm attracted to you."

He put his hand on my head, and very carefully, very gently ran his fingers through my short locks, taking care to avoid the worst of my injuries. "In fact, I love your hair short like this because it allows me to see more of your face, and gives me access to trace your ear, like this."

He bent down and touched the tip of his tongue to my lobe, then used his lips to trace a path up.

"Gahhh…" I tried to speak, but my brain had short-circuited. Daniel's breath vibrated across my ear as he laughed.

"I love your lips."

"And I love yours." He ran a finger lightly along

my upper lip, grinning when I pretended to bite. "I love them, not because they're full and red and infinitely kissable…"

He stopped talking for a moment to show me just how kissable those lips could be, and by the time we both came up for air I was out of breath, gripping his arm and leaning closer for more.

"I don't like your lips just because they're pretty. I like them because of the words that slide past them, and how they can make me laugh, sometimes even when you don't speak."

I'd never been with a man that could make me melt and laugh at the same time, and I told him so.

"I like the sound of that."

I stepped from his reach for just a moment and cocked a brow as I slid the knot of my skirt's drawstring free. "See, it's not as hard as you think it is."

His eyes didn't quite manage to return to my face, his gaze causing warmth to pool in my belly. Daniel's face was flushed as he took in the sight of me wearing a crop top and panties. The shirt suddenly felt far too restrictive, and I decided that it needed to go. With Daniel's help, I made short work of the row of metal hooks. Once released, Daniel and I shrugged off our shirts at the same time. We drank in the sight of each other for a moment more, before Daniel moved a hand to his jeans, nimbly popping the top button free.

It wasn't long before we were both surrounded

with discarded clothing, and wrapped around each other skin to skin. Daniel kissed me again, deep, and I wondered how I'd never noticed all my other partners had been doing it wrong. I nipped at his tongue when he slowed to explore my lower lip, and he answered by wrapping me tight and falling onto the bed.

And then, with me straddled on top of his stomach, the laughter left both of us, leaving only heat and desire behind.

It was a long time before either of us managed to sleep.

SIXTEEN

THE NEXT DAY came far too soon for my comfort, except for the pleasure of waking up next to Daniel. My eyes opened slowly, and I took a moment to study his sleeping face, brushing back a stray lock of hair that had fallen against his forehead. I knew the second he woke, because his mouth twisted slowly into a sexy smile.

I let out the unconscious breath I'd been holding. Last night had been earth-shattering for me, and not just because of the sex. This morning, I felt a thousand pounds lighter. Even though all the problems from yesterday still remained, they didn't seem to weigh on me like they had before my time with Daniel. Whether that had been his intention or not, I was glad that he'd managed to help me feel a little less alone in the midst of my situation.

"Good morning." His voice was rough with sleep, and it took all my willpower not to snuggle back against him and simply enjoy a lazy day tucked into the bed of a gorgeous man.

If only I could always wake up to this.

The thought was sudden and rather startling, but

when I prodded at it, I found that I didn't mind it taking up space in my head.

I smiled down at his face. "Good morning, yourself."

He shifted, propping his head up with his elbow on the pillow. "So. I've come to a decision."

"Oh yeah? What's that?" I could tell by the twinkle in his eye that the playful Daniel was up bright and early.

"I think that it's rather wasteful of us to be using twice as many sheets as we need, especially when washing them will strain Bangalore's water supply. What d'ya say? Wanna go green?"

"I've got a better idea," I said as I gave in to temptation and touched the warm expanse of skin peeping out from beneath the bedding.

"Hmm…" Daniel stretched and rolled over, allowing me access to another part of his body that was up bright and early. I obliged, and leaned closer to his ear.

"If we're trying to save water, I really think we should concentrate on our bathing habits. It seems to me that if we showered together—" I paused as his hand reached up to cup my breast, "that would save us both water *and* time. You can't go much more green than that."

"Carol Jenski, you may just be the smartest woman I've ever met." I groaned as his hand left my nipple to trace the curve of my waist, but I stopped complaining when he pushed me back onto the bed and rose above me.

Daniel made certain that by the time we hit the shower, we'd sweat enough to make it worth the trouble.

BY EIGHT-THIRTY, I was headed back to the Savitri office complex, Daniel at my side. With a promise to meet me around noon for lunch, he left to speak with a contact who claimed to have a possible connection to one of Savitri's war generals. While I tried to find a way into Nipa's file cabinet, Daniel was trying to trace some of the dragon lord's orders from a different angle, starting with the generals who would have most likely been privy to the most confidential strategies.

I stepped through the office doors and was surprised to note there were very few people milling about. After glancing at my watch to confirm it was, in fact, nine in the morning, I stopped by Krishnan's office. Relieved to see him sitting at his desk—I'll admit that even though I had no good reason, there was a moment during which I'd expected to hear that he'd been eaten—I gave Krishnan's door a light tap and he gestured for me to enter.

"Did I accidentally get my days confused and come to work on a Saturday? There's hardly anyone here."

He laughed. "No. You just haven't been properly

introduced to Indian work days. They generally begin a little later than in the United States. But no worries, I just returned from a trip to visit my family for the holiday season in the U.K., and I'm still not fully adjusted either."

Krishnan picked up a file from his desk and handed it to me. "These arrived direct from Lady Savitri just this morning. She would like to have them translated to dragonscript and delivered to her office as soon as they're complete. It's urgent, so she asks that you work as quickly as possible."

Well. I'd expected getting access to Savitri—and her inner office—was going to be much harder than this. I'd planned to volunteer my time to Savitri's assistant for anything the dragon lord needed, but it had never occurred to me that I'd be taken up on the offer before I'd even gotten around to making it.

I barely managed to keep my hand from trembling as I took the manila folder, and it took all my will to school my features into a calm expression. It was one thing to work for the dragon lord with Nipa as my human buffer, but quite another to report directly to the dragon herself. "Of course. I'll start immediately."

On the way back to my cubicle, I opened the folder and started to read. Shock had me stopping in my tracks, startling a young woman who'd been trailing me down the hall. I gave her a distracted apology and practically ran back to my desk.

The first letter—written in old-school shorthand by Nipa—was only two paragraphs long and addressed to one of the generals Daniel had identified as a member of the Indian military who'd shifted his forces to the Pakistani border. The tone of the note was tense and almost angry. Lady Savitri had skipped any sort of formal greeting, no small slight in the dragon world.

Return your contingent to previous post near Delhi. Do so immediately. I insist upon an explanation for your move to the Pakistan border within twenty-four hours. That explanation will be given in person, as you are formally relieved of duty. Ignoring this missive will be viewed as treason, and will result in your execution.
Lady Savitri

I flipped through the folder and found other notes nearly identical to the first, each addressed to the same list of dragons Daniel had scribbled along his map. Lifting my head from the paper to stare blankly at the wall, I tried to process the information.

Lady Savitri hadn't ordered the troop movement. In fact, since these letters hadn't yet been mailed, it appeared that the dragon lord had not even been aware of her generals' movements until very recently.

Had they banded together and decided to start a war without her?

Based on Daniel's last count, there were six Indian military companies gathered at the border, led by six different generals. Another two contingents were stationed on the borders of China and Nepal. Every single one of them were less than a day's dragon-flight away from Lhasa, a main city in the southwest corner of China. From there, it was another day before those dragons could reach Hian-puo's capital city, and if that happened, China would be officially under the dragons' control.

Did Savitri realize she was forty-eight hours away from an international disaster?

I nibbled on my lower lip, trying to decide what to do. I was terrible at unraveling conspiracies, and I hadn't a clue where to start to get the rest of the story. Looking at the clock attached to my wall, I could see that there were still three hours until I met Daniel for lunch. If he'd been at our apartment, I could have called him, but he was out tracking down leads, and he hadn't given me the name or number of the contact he planned to visit.

I briefly considered calling Myrna, but she was likely asleep, or still busy trying to handle the recent dragon-human eruptions plaguing Tulsa. Calling Trian would be a good choice, since he was the most experienced with combat-related stratagem. But he was also Lord Relobu's hunter of choice to track me down and drag me back to face trial for something I didn't do, and I wasn't quite ready to go that route.

No, until I got more information, or Savitri's troops actually attacked, there wasn't much I could do.

No, the only option I had was to do as Lady Savitri asked and convert the letters into dragonscript and deliver them to her office.

I'd just bent over the first with notebook and pen in hand when Benaki slammed through the double doors, a large leather satchel slung across his wide chest. He didn't even pause to look over the office. Instead he headed directly toward Savitri's door, passing my cubicle in a flash of maroon.

That dragon scared the crap out of me. I hunched back over my desk with the pen and started praying he'd be gone by the time I had to deliver the letters.

Unfortunately, I wasn't that lucky. I finished up the final missive and Benaki still hadn't reappeared.

Cursing my rotten luck, I briefly considered handing the pages back to Krishnan for delivery. But my curiosity about what was going on behind those closed doors was stronger than my fear of ugly looks from Benaki. I hoped that seeing Savitri's face when I handed her the letters would give me a clue as to her part in this mess.

Was she worried? Or simply furious? Did she have a plan in place to stop the armies if they did indeed try to invade? Or was she actually just having me write these notes so she'd have plausible deniability if the other dragon lords managed to put together a defense before she had enough dragon-power to take over their territories as well?

My head was spinning with possibilities as I walked down the hall. Where was Daniel? My calm, rational, take charge...whatever he was...when I needed him?

And to top it all off, we had to add Benaki into the mix? The dragon who had once "accidentally" broken a guy's arm and then tried to pretend the man had just tripped.

Great. Just fantastic.

I forced myself to remember Benaki's scar. The one Lady Savitri had given him as punishment for his "accident." Savitri wouldn't let me be hurt.

I shivered. Actually, the only guarantee I had was that Benaki would be punished after the fact, not that he wouldn't hurt me in the first place. Not exactly the same thing.

Regardless, I needed to suck it up and do what I needed to do. If I could learn something that would help stop a war, then to me, it was worth a broken arm.

My decision didn't stop me from being terrified. I was half afraid people could hear the sound of my knees knocking together. But I clutched the letters to my chest and headed to the enormous closed door at the end of the room, pressing the button to activate the door opener. The thick wooden panels swung open with a groan.

As I stepped into Lady Savitri's private work space, I had to stop and gape. It was nothing like the dank, dark dungeon I'd expected. Hian-puo's castle had been full of old statues, weaponry, and hanging tapestries embroidered with gold thread that matched his gold-plated everything else. If he'd been going for feudal King Midas, he'd hit the nail on the head with the gaudy ornaments.

But Savitri's private workspace was surprisingly sparse and open. There wasn't a desk or furniture of any kind, except for a small human-sized chair—likely for Nipa—placed directly across from a wooden beam that served as the dragon lord's perch.

The ceilings were so high that I could barely see them, and the entire office was lit only by sunlight from outside. I'd heard that dragons as a rule possessed excellent night vision, and I briefly wondered what Nipa did if she ever had to work late.

With potted plants tucked into every other corner, the room felt more like a football-field-sized outdoor patio than a business office. In fact, there were no panes of glass in the windows at all, and I felt a warm breeze ruffle what little hair was left on the crown of my head. Lady Savitri took full advantage of the tropical Bangalore climate.

Based on the curling ivy hugging wide stone

columns, and the bushes of flowers peeking over the window frames, it appeared there was a garden just outside. A wide, dragon-sized opening, paved in stone and leading into the jungle confirmed my suspicions.

As I moved closer, I could hear the voices of Savitri and Benaki. I wasn't near enough to understand their words, but based on her tone, the dragon lord was furious. They argued for another minute or so, and I'd almost worked up the courage to step fully outside and interrupt when Benaki appeared in the garden doorway as if he were heading back to the human office space.

Savitri appeared behind him immediately, and I was shocked at her next words. "You will die for this. No one ignores my orders."

She caught sight of me. "Julie, fetch the dragon guards at the front gate."

I looked back and forth between the two dragons, and decided leaving the room was an excellent idea. I bobbed my head to show her I'd understood, and had half turned for the door when Benaki stepped toward me, claws out.

"No."

I froze. Without a choice of furniture to cower behind, I felt terribly exposed. Trust my luck to plunk me right down in the middle of a deadly dragon argument. I looked to Savitri, unsure of what to do. Benaki was close enough to slice me open with his claws if I made a move toward the door.

At Benaki's word, Savitri had growled, and now her teeth were in full view. I could hear the rug beneath her feet rip as her exposed claws dug into the thick weave when she shifted.

But she wasn't looking at me. Her voice was low and guttural when she addressed the general. "You dare to override my instructions?"

Moving almost faster than I could follow, Savitri lunged, swiping a claw in the direction of the much larger maroon dragon. Almost a full second later, purple blood gushed from a deep cut on Benaki's side. The general looked down at the gash in his scales, and then to the liquid splashing onto the same carpet destroyed by Savitri's feet. He raised his head to look the dragon lord in the eye.

And he laughed.

The sound seemed to vibrate through the room. But that wasn't what had goose bumps breaking out on my arm. Sane dragons didn't laugh like that. No, only the mentally unsound goaded dragon lords into stabbing holes through them.

And crazy dragons certainly didn't worry themselves with the health of their human audience.

Benaki shifted when Lady Savitri started to move, the big dragons resembling wrestlers as they slowly circled each other, looking for an opportunity to strike.

I used their preoccupation to put some distance between myself and their very sharp claws and teeth. After I'd entered the room, the door mechanism had engaged, closing the wooden panels. There was no way I could leave the room without drawing Benaki's attention.

So when Savitri growled and gathered herself for another attack, I pressed myself against the wall.

"I don't think you want to do that." Benaki used the claws on his right hand to pull a box from the satchel at his side. He tossed the box in my direction, and I yelped in surprise as it skidded along the floor.

"Open the box."

With Savitri's eyes still on the general, I didn't feel that I had another choice. An odd plastic material, it was similar in size to a shoebox and held together with a single piece of ribbon. Keeping my eye on the general, I approached the container cautiously. With eyes squinted half-shut with trepidation, I pulled the string and slowly lifted the lid from the box, half afraid a shoe-sized dragon would leap from the interior and try to rip off my face.

When the contents failed to jump free of their prison and attack me, I opened my eyes fully and peered into the silk-lined space.

Inside, nestled on a bed of crushed black velvet, lay a tightly curled obsidian talon. The talon's surface was polished to a shine, and could have been beautiful. Except for what it was attached to—wilted scales the color of a ripe orange covered a fat knuckle at the base. My body knew what it was before my mind could process the sight, and I slung the box and its contents as far away as I could manage.

The container bounced across the floor, landing in a small heap right at the dragon lord's feet. Time seemed to slow as Savitri glanced down at the amputated claw, and her eyes widened in horror.

Benaki rewarded her expression with a chuckle. "As you can see, it isn't in your best interests—or should I say, your husband's interests—for you to deny my requests."

Savitri's ferocious growl morphed into a whimper. "Eriel…" Her eyes stayed locked on the floor. "What have you done?"

"What have I done?" Benaki let out another rumbling laugh. "I've taken what should have been mine the instant Hian-puo imprisoned Relobu's dragons. I left my birth country and have served you faithfully for three years. And now, when China's dragon lord falls and his territory is open for possession, you order a retreat instead of claiming the land?" Benaki's snout lifted into a sneer and he pointed to the grotesque claw. "Human emotion has no place in our society. Your love for this dragon? That is what makes you weak."

Savitri finally looked her general in the eye. "You killed my mate? I will show you who is weak!" I cringed as the dragon lord primed her muscles to pounce, spikes I hadn't even noticed on her tail lifting in preparation for attack.

I finally understood how this tiny dragon managed to maintain her throne. Savitri in a killing mood was a sight to see. The flesh just behind her jaws had fanned out around her face, and deadly venom dripped from her top incisors, hissing as it hit the stone floor. She rose to full height on her back legs, her neck weaving in a deceptively lazy pattern as she prepared herself to strike like a snake. Her irises had shrunk to tiny slits.

Benaki tensed, but he didn't move out of her range. "Eriel is not dead."

His words caused the dragon lord to pause, her words slurring as her tongue danced around dripping fangs. "You lie."

"I do not. Your precious mate is safely ensconced in your palace, guarded by a team of dragons under my command. And by my honor—"

Savitri hissed. "You have no honor!"

The general barely reacted to her interruption, only pausing briefly to glare at the female dragon. "By my honor he will remain alive and well, as long as you are smart."

The maroon dragon turned, leisurely scanning the room as he detailed his demands. "You will not attempt to attack me again. You will do exactly as I say, with no arguments, and no tricks, or I will kill you and your mate immediately."

"And how will this end? Weeks from now, will I still be a puppet in your play for power? Am I simply expected to live the rest of my life under the threat of your teeth? I think I would rather die." Savitri's dark gray scales were glistening with sweat, the stress of the situation causing the muscles near her spine to quiver.

Benaki sneered. "I can arrange that, should it be your wish. However, my wish is for control of China. Nothing more. Representatives of the dragon council are due to arrive here in Bangalore later this week to collect your recommendation for Lord Hian-puo's replacement as dragon lord of China. As soon as I garner the votes needed for my claim to his throne, I will leave you and your worthless territory."

Lady Savitri huffed out a laugh. "If you believe staging a coup d'état on my rule will garner respect with the council, you are more naive than I ever imagined. China's ruler will be culled from its citizens. They will never accept an outside leader, much less a dragon who has already defected from his homeland once before. They will not stand for it. *I* will not stand for it."

Benaki gave Savitri a hard look. "As you say, your territory is the closest to Hian-puo's domain, and therefore your vote will hold sway over the other lords. They will not chance installing a leader you do not support, as they cannot afford to help defend China should you invade. You alone will have final say over the new leader of China. So, Lady Savitri—" Benaki gave her a mocking bow. "—the council will accept me upon your recommendation, or you won't have enough boxes for the pieces of your beloved Eriel."

His demands communicated, Benaki turned for the door, banging a fist against the opening mechanism.

I huddled closer to the wall as the general swept past me out of the office. Startled exclamations from the office staff erupted before the sound was immediately cut off by the thick double doors swinging shut.

I took a moment to ponder what I'd just heard.

I had one important question answered. Lady Savitri had never planned on taking over China. She'd placed her dragons on the border for protection from Hian-puo's increasingly hostile behavior. By his own confession—boasting, more like—Benaki was the dragon with plans to invade China. He'd seen Hian-puo's trial and the Chinese lord's likely execution as an opportunity to become a dragon lord himself.

But how had he convinced Savitri's generals to join in his scheme?

The dragon lord's voice pulled me from my thoughts. It was a moment before my faculties returned to the point that I could translate her words to English.

"Julie, I need you to find Nipa."

I nodded, turned, and was halfway out the door before I realized I still held the letters intended for her generals. The ones demanding that they fall back from the borders of Pakistan.

"Ma'am? Did you still want these posted?" I held up the folder.

The dragon lord's face tightened. "No. I'm not certain which of my generals have defected to Benaki. Hold them until I can identify my true friends. Or until I can assure Eriel's safety."

Wondering how I always managed to find myself in the middle of all the international dragon crises, I nodded. "I'll go find your assistant."

SEVENTEEN

SADLY, FINDING NIPA was far easier than I imagined.

Upon opening the doors of Lady Savitri's office, I was confronted by complete pandemonium. Mangled remains of cubicle walls were strewn throughout the room, interspersed with puddles of blood, both human and dragon. The office had been transformed into a war zone. Savitri's old assistant lay in the middle of the tile floor, cradled in the arms of Neetha, a young woman who worked in a cube next door to mine. Or *had* worked in a cube next door to mine. Our cubicles were nowhere to be found.

A circle of people stood around the two women, most of them either panicked or crying as they watched Neetha attempt to wake the limp woman from her unconscious state.

Judging from the amount of blood dripping from Nipa's temple, she wasn't waking up anytime soon. If she ever woke again.

I looked around the office and grabbed a sweater from the back of a tipped-over chair. Pushing through the crowd of people—all yelling at one another in a frantic mix of English and various local dialects—I pushed the sweater into Neetha's hands and told her to keep it firm on Nipa's head.

I'd just turned to one of the other ladies in an effort to find out exactly what had happened when Lady Savitri stepped out of her office.

"I smell human blood. Who's been injured?" The dragon's gaze quickly settled on the fallen woman, and Lady Savitri drew in a shocked breath. The humans, still affected by their recent trauma, backed away as her fleshy collar began to rise in anger.

Neetha babbled through her tears. "We didn't expect... He gave us no warning. Nipa took offense at the way Benaki addressed one of her copy girls and demanded he apologize immediately or she would report his lack of courtesy to you, my Queen. He picked up a file cabinet and he...he hit her with it!"

Unable to continue her story, the poor girl tried yet again to wake the older woman. Nipa's face was pale from blood loss, and one of the other office employees tried and failed to find a pulse. She wasn't going to make it.

Lady Savitri seemed to come to the same conclusion. The dragon scanned the room, and I felt myself tense involuntarily when her furious eyes met mine.

"Julie, I need you in my office, now!"

With the combination of anger and the natural tendency of a dragon's voice to be growly, her order echoed through the room like the roar of a cannon. All heads turned in my direction as most of the office, unversed in dragonspeak, tried to follow what was happening. The people who had been standing beside me seemed to disappear, sinking back as they determined that I was the center of the dragon's attention. Threading my hands together behind my back to keep them from shaking, I nodded once and headed back into her office.

It was Savitri's turn to viciously slap the button on the door as I stepped through the entrance. I buried my urge to run as Savitri began to pace, her spiked tail and fully extended claws causing me to cringe every time the dragon lord got within three feet of me.

"Find out how many dragons Benaki has guarding my mate." In her fury, Savitri's words literally shook the room. I must not have done a good job of hiding my fear—perhaps she could smell the beads of sweat trickling down my back—because, after a quick glance in my direction, she made a conscious effort to lower her voice.

"I'm sorry. I know this isn't what you signed up for, but I'm going to need someone I can trust."

"Excuse me?" As the new girl in town, I didn't understand why in the world Savitri would trust me over the people who'd been with her for years. I struggled for a polite way to ask my question without trying to convince the dragon lord I was untrustworthy. "I appreciate your willingness to rely on me. And rest assured, I will do anything in my power to help you. But why am I the only person you can trust? I've only been here two days."

"Exactly. At this point, I have no idea who Benaki has persuaded into his service. If he has my husband, one of my guards must have let him into the palace. And my generals? Those letters you hold will be the third message I've sent to my commanders. I don't know whether my company leaders have ignored my orders, or if Benaki has ensured they never received them."

Savitri's explanation of why she considered me trustworthy made sense. But did I really want to be involved? Was there any way I could avoid it at this point?

I know what Daniel would say.

News of the coup would give him plenty of fodder for a career-making story for the *Tulsa Times Chronicle*. Sure, he'd love to have someone on the inside feeding him information as events unfolded, but I wasn't sure I was the person for the job. Tracking troop movements from a cubicle? While danger had always been a possibility, the odds of me actually getting hurt gathering information from paperwork had been relatively low. But front and center of a coup d'état? This project seemed to push the limits of what was sane, even for an investigative reporter.

If Daniel broke the story before Savitri rescued her husband, there would be no way Benaki would allow him to live. Which left me the most important question. Could *I* live with myself if I knowingly left someone to die? Even if it was a dragon I'd never met?

"Please, Julie. I need your help." Savitri bowed her head in respect, almost as if she could see that I was waffling. "I need to find out whether Eriel is safe."

I looked at the dragon. For all her strength, and yes, sometimes ruthlessness—as evidenced by those dragons who had been stupid enough to challenge for her position—she was still a creature with the capacity for kindness. And since I'd started this job, I'd seen Savitri treat her employees with nothing but respect, even if it was an aloof sort of courtesy.

Was she difficult to work for? Maybe. I hadn't been here long enough to tell. But she didn't seem unfair. And right now, she needed my help.

I straightened my shoulders and met the dragon's pleading eyes, shoving my fear aside and concentrating on the problem at hand. "What do you need me to do?"

Savitri sagged in relief. "Thank you."

EIGHTEEN

"MRS. GREEN?"

I was standing in the footprint of my cube, trying in vain to get the telephone line to make a connection so I could call the police, the hospital, anybody, when there was a tap on my shoulder. I jumped about a mile in the air, and couldn't help the small squeak of alarm that escaped before I realized it was the young woman from the front desk.

Her mouth was a small *O* of terror, and it probably made me a bad person, but I was glad to hear an answering yip of fear come from her mouth. She might not have been in the room when the carnage started, but it didn't take a genius to figure out that something really bad had just happened.

Almost nothing in the room was still standing, and there was a literal hole in the wall where a printer had landed when Benaki had it sailing through the room.

I sighed. "What can I help you with?"

My words pulled her gaze from the carnage back to my face, and she paused while she seemed to retrieve the reason for her visit.

"Mrs. Green. Your husband has left several messages. He seems slightly alarmed. He said you were supposed to meet him at noon."

After the events of this morning, it took me a moment to figure out that she was talking about Daniel, and that I'd promised to meet up with him for lunch. I glanced at the cheap plastic clock that had miraculously continued ticking despite its sudden relocation from my cube wall to its current position in the center of the tiled floor. It was almost three in the afternoon.

Funny how time flies when dragons are throwing hissy fits and slinging bodies around.

"Did he leave a phone number?"

"Yes ma'am. But the dragons at the door…" she paused, chewing at her nail as she decided how to explain, "they've ordered me not to return any calls until they give me notice to do so."

Figures.

I thanked her and headed for the reception area at one speed above a brisk walk. If there was one thing I knew I wanted, it was to get out of this building.

The girl turned and followed me, albeit with a more decorous rate of acceleration. "What's going on?"

Without having any idea where to start—I really had no idea what was going on, or what would happen in the next five minutes, even—I ignored her question and sailed through the office doors, fully expecting to see a very worried or very angry Daniel sitting on the room's plush leather sofa, but instead I was faced with an empty room.

Empty of humans, that is. A pair of stern-faced dragons stood on each side of the building's main entrance.

The receptionist noticed my disappointment.

"They are allowing no visitors past the front gate."

I sighed, and turned to study my jailers. The dragons were of the smaller variety, which serves to say they were only a foot taller than me instead of six. Their scales were the exact same shade of sand brown, and I couldn't help but wonder whether they were related, or if they'd been chosen to guard the front entrance because they presented a pretty picture to the outside world.

Based on my limited experience with Benaki, and his total disregard for order—the mangled furniture and broken printers standing as testament to that fact—I guessed it was a mere coincidence.

"How long have they been here?" I was pretty certain I hadn't been so distracted this morning that I'd missed seeing them upon my arrival. Even with the events of the last few weeks, I wasn't so jaded that I'd stopped noticing the creatures.

The girl swallowed. "General Benaki ordered them to make sure no one entered or left the building." Her eyes were wide and frightened as she realized the guards and the mess in the office were almost certainly connected. "What's going on?" She repeated her question, this time with a hand placed on my arm to prevent me from ignoring her once again.

I gave her honesty. "I'm not entirely sure."

But I needed to at least try and find out. I approached the dragons cautiously, unsure exactly what Benaki's plans were for all the human employees. Had he just dismissed us, or were we being corralled until he had the chance to get rid of us all?

The dragon on the left waited until I was within ten feet of the door before he spoke. "By order of my lord, the great General Benaki, no one is to leave this building."

Well. It was always hard to tell with dragons—their voices were always terrifying—but the creature didn't sound overly excited or gleeful about his announcement. In fact, he sounded like any other run-of-the-mill security guard bored half to death. He hadn't even bothered turning his head in my direction.

I took that as a good sign. At least they weren't planning on slaughtering us yet. That's not to say I was happy about being held prisoner. It was like the time the generators in the CreaTV building back home had run out of juice while I was on the elevator with two other people. We were nearly certain that the elevator wouldn't actually fall and kill us all, but it didn't mean we wanted to spend our entire day in a four-by-four box.

This box was substantially bigger, but I still felt my pulse rate rise at the thought of being held here indefinitely.

If Benaki had managed to somehow convince Savitri's dragons to hold their own dragon lord in the building, then it was clear this wasn't just a self-centered whim. He'd made actual, detailed plans for this takeover.

Somehow, I needed to talk to Daniel. Maybe he could help me figure out just how far Benaki's influence stretched within the ranks of Savitri's army. Or at least he would have an idea of how to get me out of here. I took a couple of steps back from the pair of reptiles before I spoke, just in case I'd misjudged the situation or one of these dragons had a hair-trigger temper like Benaki. I pointed past them to the front parking lot.

"My husband is out there. I was supposed to meet him for lunch. If I could just step outside for a moment, let him know—"

"No." This time, both dragons turned to peer at me curiously, as if they were trying to determine the depth of my stupidity. The one on the right opened his mouth for the first time. "Benaki said no one leaves the building." His speech was slow and deliberate, and his teeth flashed as he attempted to enunciate.

I fought the urge to roll my eyes. Unused to my American accent, they thought I hadn't understood the order. "No, no, I understand Benaki's orders, but my husband has been waiting for me for hours. I just need to speak with him for a moment."

When the dragons made no move to open the door—in fact, the slightly crankier one on the left snorted a not-so-subtle poof of smoke from his nostrils in response—I clenched my hands behind my back and tried again.

It seemed my fear of being trapped overruled my fear of being eaten. Or maybe Benaki had finally pushed me over the crazy line right along with him. I'd certainly dealt with enough stress lately to justify a mental breakdown.

"Can I assume you are aware General Benaki has seized Lady Savitri's mate, and is currently using him as a bargaining chip in his plan to take over as dragon lord of China?"

There was a gasp behind me from the young receptionist, but neither of the dragon guards so much as twitched at my news. Which meant it wasn't news to them. They were definitely General Benaki's dragons.

Crap. I'd been carrying a small hope that maybe all these dragons needed was to hear the full story, and they'd be falling all over themselves trying to get back into the dragon lord's good graces before she sliced them to bits.

Then again, if they were loyal little soldiers,

they'd have Benaki's best interests at heart. Maybe I could use that.

"How well do you think Benaki's plan will work if news gets out that he's acted against a ruling member of the council?"

The dragon on my right twitched first, so I addressed my next question to him. "And how do you think the dragon council will treat those who facilitated Benaki's attack on Lady Savitri?"

The dragon snorted, his pupils narrowing to slits. "The dragon council will never know of Benaki's actions. Lady Savitri and her mate won't live long enough to share it."

"Shut up, you stupid frog-spawn." The other dragon swiped a clawed hand toward his partner, and I waited a moment while they scuffled. Today might not be my lucky day, exactly, but Benaki had given one good thing today. He'd chosen two idiots to guard the door. And after eight years of dealing with upper management as part of my job with CreaTV, I knew I could work with idiots.

When the dragons had settled a bit, I raised my hands in a placating gesture. "It's fine. Don't worry. I have no intention of calling up the dragon lords. Why would they listen to me anyway?"

The dragons cocked their heads, partly confused, and partly interested at where I was taking this conversation. Forcing my shoulders to relax, I ran a hand nonchalantly along the surface of the desk as I spoke, as if I were thinking aloud.

"You see, *I* won't be calling the dragon council, but I feel I should mention that my husband won't feel the same."

The dragon on my left—the one I'd gathered actually had a brain in his head—stilled, and watched me closely. He'd begun to connect the dots.

General Benaki's plan hinged on Lady Savitri caring more about her mate's safety than about who ruled the territory next door. But it also hinged on the dragon council taking Savitri's recommendation. Which they wouldn't do if they realized her judgment had been severely compromised. Or that she no longer had control of the army they were loath to face. Without her dragons, Savitri was no threat at all, either to China, or to the dragon council. I believed that Benaki fully intended on killing both Savitri and her mate, just as soon as the dragon council had voted him onto the Chinese throne, but for now, the general needed the Indian dragon lord alive.

He also needed the rest of the world to think that Savitri was still in full control of her territory.

I looked the smart dragon straight in the eye. "My husband is a reporter for the *Tulsa Times Chronicle*."

The dragon's eyes widened. Apparently reporters didn't gain any likeability points in translation.

"And yes, just in case you're not familiar with the North American media, the *Tulsa Times Chronicle* is *the* premier newspaper in Relobu's territory, and yes, I have it on good authority that Lord Nir Relobu is a regular subscriber. So you see, it's very important that I let my husband know that I'm okay. Because if I don't, he'll start digging around in Savitri's business, and by extension, General Benaki's."

"So—" still hiding my shaking hands, I took a deep breath and tried to look confident as I marched toward the front door, "—I think it's in your best interest to let me pass."

I'd managed to touch the glass before the dragon's arm blocked my vision—and my escape.

"Benaki said no one leaves the building."

I opened my mouth to argue, but closed it when a clawed hand gripped my shoulder.

Damn. I really thought I'd had him.

"However…"

The dragon's next words were music to my ears.

"I will allow you to write a short note to your husband. Tell him you've been asked to work late, and will contact him as soon as you're free."

I stepped away from the door, and back to the relative safety of the receptionist's desk, where the actual receptionist stood, wide-eyed.

"My note will have to be in English. He doesn't read dragonscript." I prayed I'd get lucky for once and these dragons wouldn't be able to read the note.

The dragons looked at one another, and engaged in a quiet conversation before turning back to me.

The girl beside me jumped when the dragon on the left—I'd started mentally referring to him as Smart Dragon—addressed her.

"You there. Girl. Do you read and write English?"

The dragon growled when she tried to sneak a glance in my direction. Instead, she swallowed audibly and nodded. "Yes." The word came out so quietly that I barely heard her.

He looked back to me. "You write your letter." And to the girl, "And you will verify that it says exactly what it should say. No mention of Benaki, Savitri, or anything other than her plans to work late."

The receptionist and I looked at each other.

Well, crap. I wouldn't be surprised if the poor girl fainted in fear. I'm not sure she would be able to remember her name right now, much less have the presence of mind to help me fudge a letter to get us some help.

So I had to hope Daniel was smart enough to read between the lines.

"I need a piece of paper."

My request snapped the receptionist out of her fog and she opened a drawer to dig for a pen.

"What's your name?" I asked the girl when I saw tears trickling down her cheek.

"Prita." She swiped at her face with a silk-encased forearm.

I gave her shoulder a reassuring squeeze. "Well,

Prita. It's nice to meet you, despite the circumstances."

I scrawled a quick note across the back of a telephone memo pad and pushed it across the desk to Prita, glaring at the dragons by the door the entire time. The Stupid One grinned back at me. Or snarled. It was hard to tell.

Prita took the piece of paper, and spoke my words aloud, translating to dragonspeak as she read. "Daniel, I'll be stuck at work for a while. Krishnan has me looking hard at the Moneybags acquisitions, and there are a lot of legal traps we have to get around. Don't worry about bringing me clothes; I can pick up the red sari being held at the cleaners if I'm in a bind."

"Happy?"

I addressed my question to the smarter of the two dragons, praying that the note didn't trip any of his subconscious triggers. My fingers itched for an eraser. The "in a bind" line had probably been a bit too much, but I'd had to think fast. My only choice at this point was to brazen it out.

The dragon stared right back, and I had to grip the bottom of the desk to keep from cheering when he nodded. "Give me the note, and I'll deliver it."

NINETEEN

I SPENT THE next couple of hours fighting off a panic attack.

What had I done? There was nothing Daniel could do about a group of dragons loyal to General Benaki and trained in military maneuvers. Without fancy dragon-killing bio-material, humans didn't exactly fare well against dragons, and I seriously doubted Daniel could get his hands on any of that stuff with the entire dragon population on high alert.

When we first realized they existed, but before we realized they were intelligent beings, humans tried to band together and exterminate their entire race. I'm not even sure the dragons noticed. Our weapons, even the huge, armor-piercing variety, had simply been an annoyance to the flying reptiles. The bio-material was only thing that seemed to harm them at all. Unfortunately, the weapon didn't allow you to choose your targets.

Even if by some miracle Daniel could find a dragon-killing device, he wouldn't be able to use it at Savitri's palace without also killing the dragon lord's mate.

I almost hoped Daniel hadn't understood my message. His comment about the butler at Savitri's house had been a passing observation; it was possible he'd written off my Monopoly reference as a lame attempt at a joke. As for the red sari, days had passed since he'd first mentioned that he'd liked the color, and I'd passed on the outfit as a result. Would he even remember that I didn't actually buy a red one?

I wandered around the office, speaking quietly with some of the other employees. The mood was hovering between panic and grief as Nipa's friends mourned her passing, and others realized we would all likely share her fate in the near future. While I'd been arguing with the dragons at the front door, Benaki had installed other dragons to guard the main work area. The phone lines had been severed— whether during Benaki's printer-throwing temper tantrum or later by damaging the central control box at the corner of the block—and everyone was trying to come to terms with the situation.

Shortly after Benaki hand-delivered her mate's finger, Savitri had been "asked" to share a release with the local press. It was announced that there had been a chemical accident at Savitri Enterprises, and that we were all being kept here under quarantine, until they could be "assured the contamination was appropriately neutralized." Delivery boys were asked to leave their packages near the front gate, and family and friends were instructed not to worry.

Those dragons openly loyal to Savitri had been promptly beheaded, and we'd all had to watch as their bodies were lifted between two or more of Benaki's dragons, depending on the body's size, and flown to the building's waste-processing unit for disposal.

I wondered what the garbage company would think when they were finally allowed to pick up our trash. Especially given the relentless Indian heat.

The dragon lord had made a brief visit to assure herself of the relative safety of her human employees, but she'd quickly retreated back to the confines of her office. Krishnan had quietly explained that dragons, on a good day, were only slightly temperamental. But Lady Savitri, forced to endure the stress of a murdered assistant, her slaughtered dragons, and the capture of her mate, wasn't exactly fit for company. Stressed dragons forgot to sheathe their claws.

After all the "troublesome" dragons had been disposed of, Benaki's guards lined up all of the humans and forced Krishnan and I to translate as they read us the riot act. No contact with the outside world and no leaving this room without permission. Anyone who ignored these rules would be killed.

After the "staff meeting," one of Benaki's dragons had enlisted Krishnan to facilitate the planning of a reception for the visiting dragon council delegates. I sat in the floor near the wall and listened as the dragon dictated exactly what the mood of the reception would be. Basically, he'd demanded that we all appear completely delighted with our jobs to anyone and everyone who so much as glanced at us, and to feign confusion should someone actually try to speak with us.

When the amount of translation between humans and dragons had become too much for Krishnan to handle on his own, I'd been drafted to assist with the domestic side of the delegation's stay. Guest rooms were prepared for our human visitors in the attached palace, and perches were moved onto the building's multiple flight decks for the dragon contingent so they could enjoy the hot weather that was well-suited to the dragons' reptile-based tastes.

By the end of the day, I was exhausted, my recent injuries and the unexpected physical labor sapping what little strength I had left.

"How are you holding up?" My boss appeared at my side as I stared, unseeing, at the spot where Nipa had taken her last breath. The body had been removed and stored in one of the empty walk-in kitchen freezers until further arrangements could be made, but it was clear from the way my colleagues walked wide circles around that specific portion of tile that she was still very much on everyone's mind.

We were all very aware of the possibility that no one would be around long enough to make those arrangements.

I twisted my hands together to burn some of the anxious energy building as our confinement stretched on. "I'm doing okay. Did I hear Benaki finally consented to allowing you to get us some food?"

Krishnan nodded. "I ordered pizza. It seemed like the easiest thing."

"Delivery?"

"Yeah. We have an account with the vendor, so they're leaving the food just outside the door." His tone was defeated, probably because he too had carried a vague hope of using the need for food as an excuse to make contact with someone who could get help, or help us spin this situation into our favor.

"Hey, look on the bright side. Benaki could have just starved us to death. In fact, I'm pretty surprised he acquiesced to your request. I didn't peg him as a dragon who put worth on the life—or usefulness—of humans."

Krishnan huffed out a humorless laugh. "He isn't. But the dragon council reps would notice if there were no humans to receive them upon their arrival."

"Good point." My mind raced. We had to get word to one of the dragon council that Lady Savitri was compromised. "How much contact will the humans have with the dragon council?"

Krishnan sighed. "Plenty. But it won't matter. With Nipa gone, we're the only employees in the building who are dragonspeakers, and they won't even let me out of their sight to pick up some pizza."

Shocked, I jerked my head to look at him. "We're

the only dragonspeakers?" I'd figured out that the majority of my office mates didn't understand dragonspeak, but I'd honestly never given any thought to why Krishnan and I had been the only ones drafted to translate this afternoon. This particular Savitri Enterprises building had thirteen floors. Granted, I'd been told that many of them were used only on the rare occasions that Savitri had guests she wanted to entertain—the kitchens, the apartments and the conference rooms took up a good six of those floors— but that still left seven floors of employees.

Krishnan noticed my look of confusion. "This is the only floor built for human use. Savitri's office was placed on this floor to allow the second and third stories to remain open for flying space."

I thought back to the hugely tall ceilings in her office. No wonder I'd felt so small.

"The receptionist is also a dragonspeaker, but she's fallen ill from the stress of the situation. While they refuse to let her out to see a doctor, they did allow us to make a place for her to lie down in one of the empty office spaces. There have been several that are similarly afflicted, and a great many more with physical injuries. Though we have very few supplies, we've have managed to set up a makeshift infirmary, should you require any assistance."

Krishnan's eyes landed briefly on my scalp, which had, until yesterday, housed a row of stitches. My hand automatically touched the wound. "Oh, thanks. But I'm fine." His gaze was curious, but he didn't push.

"So we're it, huh? The stars of the show once the dragon council representatives arrive."

I got a wry smile in return. "Now you know why we were so excited to find you for the job. Your job skills are rare. Very rare. Only a small percentage of the population even gets the opportunity to attend school at all, much less study something as specialized as dragonspeak. Considering Savitri Enterprises is the only corporate employer of dragonspeakers in the country, it's not exactly a large job market. But we don't see many people who can read and write the dragon language, especially with your level of skill. I can assure you, there are always projects needing your type of expertise."

So Savitri Enterprises thought I was an irreplaceable resource, and basically promised me lifelong job security. That would make me feel a lot better if I thought I had any chance of surviving my current position. Maybe I should have asked about the life insurance policy.

Krishnan must have been following the same line of thought. "We're not getting out of here, are we?"

I met his eyes. "No. No we're not."

With Benaki blocking all communication with the outside world, and the odds of notifying the dragon council representatives of our plight without drawing the attention of Benaki's dragons close to nil, I didn't see an option where Savitri's humans, myself included, would be allowed to go back to our homes. We knew too much. And when Savitri died in a convenient accident—as she inevitably would—we would be the only proof left of his treason. So it was inevitable we'd find our own accidents shortly thereafter.

Krishnan sighed.

"Mr. Venkat?" A slim man touched Krishnan on the shoulder, and peered nervously toward the main office doors. "I believe that dragon needs something."

I turned toward the exit and located the dragon in question. He was indeed gesturing in our direction.

Krishnan patted his sweating temple with an already damp handkerchief. "I hope that's the pizza."

"Me too." Though I knew I wouldn't be able to eat a bite. My stomach hadn't stopped churning since this morning. We were all feeling the stress.

Krishnan disappeared through the doors, only to reappear moments later balancing a large stack of greasy cardboard boxes. I walked over and took them.

He murmured his thanks, and then waved over a male coworker to help him go back and get the remaining food. We cobbled together a buffet station using half a conference table and some torn cubicle walls. After a few minutes, most of the humans had gathered loosely around the dinner. A few even grabbed a slice or two of pizza, but it appeared to be less about hunger and more about keeping their hands busy.

Krishnan gently escorted a still shell-shocked Neetha into a waiting chair. He whispered something in her ear, and she nodded. He must have been persuading her to eat something, because he straightened and snagged a plate before striding with purpose toward the vegetarian offerings at the far end of the spread.

I'd already adjusted my attention, and was engaged in conversation with one of the men who'd shared a cube wall with me, pre-dragon, when Krishnan called my name.

"Julie." He stood, looking just as stunned as Neetha. I hurried over. "I believe this is for you."

A small white envelope had been taped to the inside lid of the box containing a mushroom and spinach pie. My name—my fake name—was scrawled across the face, and I felt my heart thud hard in my chest when I recognized Daniel's familiar scribbles.

"Keep an eye on the dragons, will you?" I asked Krishnan as I stepped as far out of their line of sight as possible without arousing undue suspicion. I slid the note out and started to read.

I've seen the press release, and I received your message. Planning a visit to Uncle Moneybags tomorrow morning with some friends of mine.

If all goes well, I'll be up one significant other. Tell your dragon to play along, and I'll get word to you on the outcome as soon as possible.

Stay safe, or I'll think of something worse than chicken poop to drop you in.

BTW, There's a red sari here I'm dying to see you wear.
—*Daniel*

TWENTY

"KRISHNAN?" THOUGH I was striving to stay calm, I couldn't help the small tremor in my voice. "Can you get me in to see Lady Savitri?"

His eyes sharpened as he glanced at the paper in my hand. "I think so. Since they have her mate, she's not really a threat. They haven't restricted access to her."

"Good. We need to see her, now. I might possibly have some good news."

With a quick glance to the guards—after a full day's worth of watching us do nothing but mill about the building's rooms aimlessly, we barely got a head turned in our direction—Krishnan and I made our way to Savitri's office door, and pushed the button to engage the pulley system that helped lift the thick wood.

I waited for a roar from one of the dragons, but they stayed silent.

"Lady Savitri?" Krishnan stepped into the room.

We found the dragon lord outside in her garden, curled up near a copse of sandalwood trees.

She scowled when she saw us approach.

"Leave me. I am in no condition for company." Her words were punctuated by a low growl, and the flesh collar just under her jaw trembled in warning.

Krishnan hadn't been kidding about the danger of cranky dragons.

I couldn't just blurt out the fact that a super-secret rescue mission was being mounted to obtain her mate, so I cautiously approached. I heard a snap and a crack just before one of the sandalwoods came crashing to the ground only inches from where I stood.

Okay, then. This would be close enough.

I took a quick glance around the garden to make sure Benaki didn't have dragons listening in on our conversation. But apparently Savitri's current state didn't just scare humans, because the only soldiers I could see flew a hundred feet above us. They were watching, but they weren't stupid enough to come near the dragon lord.

My gaze moved back to Savitri. I wasn't exactly sure where to start. The news that Daniel planned a rescue attempt wouldn't make sense unless I told her how Daniel had contacts willing and able to suc-cessfully attack a hoard of dragons. But revealing to the dragon lord that my "husband" was, in fact, not my husband but a reporter who'd sneaked a wanted criminal into her country to spy on her activities might not be the best approach either, considering Savitri's mood. At this point, announcing I had lied to her would cause her to assume I'd been in cahoots with Benaki all along.

When we'd been in China trying to negotiate a deal with Hian-puo, Trian had warned me that some dragons could smell lies. I'd never gotten a chance to ask him how humans could tell the difference between dragons with this talent and those without.

Odds were good that Savitri did not possess this particular skill. I'd told her my name was Julie when we first met, and she'd barely blinked.

But if Richard had taught me one thing, it was how easily lies got ugly. I sucked in a deep breath. It was time to tell the truth.

That didn't mean I couldn't start with the good news first.

"Lady Savitri, there's a chance we can rescue your mate."

The dragon's head rose from the ground and swiveled in my direction. I fought the urge to turn tail and run. Her pupils had contracted to slits, and she bared her teeth.

"Tell me."

Stumbling a bit over my words, I started from the beginning, telling the dragon lord of my involvement with Tulsa's DRACIM team in China, how my less than stellar choice in men had directly contributed to my outlaw status, and the reasons behind my acceptance of the job with Savitri Enterprises. Only after I'd bared my soul did I explain the note I'd managed to sneak to Daniel and the message we'd just received with our dinner.

The dragon listened silently while I finished my story. Krishnan, too, remained silent. I wasn't brave enough to face him and see his reaction. Instead, I fiddled with the *pallu* of my sari, adjusting the cloth across my chest and shoulders to avoid meeting his eyes.

Savitri rolled to her feet, and I tried not to cringe as she placed her snout directly in front of my face. "Can you get a message to your reporter?" The dragon lord's eyes were clear and sharp with intent, and while she didn't look happy, she also hadn't ripped me to shreds.

In my book, that was a very good sign.

I shook my head. "I don't think so. I'm not even sure what the plan is. This is all I have."

Pulling the note from my skirt, I unfolded the paper and read back the message. When I was finished, I looked to the dragon. It was her mate. Her territory.

"What do you want us to do?"

Savitri looked to the sky. "We'll do the only thing we can do. Be ready for a fight when the proper time comes." She looked to me, a clear warning in her eyes. "But until then, we will not try to contact anyone else. Not DRACIM, and not the press. I will not put my husband in further danger. Is that understood?"

I wanted to balk at her order—what if I had another chance to reach Daniel—but couldn't drum up the courage for the attempt. "Understood."

Even if I didn't like it.

WITH SAVITRI RE-ENERGIZED by new hope that her mate may survive his kidnapping, the dragon lord asked us to communicate her wishes with the rest of the staff. We were to do everything Benaki asked of us. We were to be docile, eager-to-please humans with no real personalities. We were to make Benaki believe he'd won our loyalty with his show of force. If there were any guards watching, we were to disregard Savitri's orders completely.

For her part, the dragon lord planned to be disagreeable and unnerved by her staff's sudden abandonment. She planned to rant and rail enough to keep Benaki convinced of her fury, but ultimately allow him to do as he wished. Until, of course, her mate was safe. I doubted Benaki would be alive much past that point.

But for now, we were to wait. And none of us were doing it very well at all.

With the help of the men, the cubicle walls that were still somewhat functional had been rearranged into sleeping quarters, and cardboard boxes we'd found in a closet spread on the floor for bedding. I lay on the women's side of the divider, trying to force myself to sleep.

There was plenty of pizza left from lunch, though Krishnan had managed to hide most of it for an excuse to order more. The dragons probably thought we were starving from the way we ripped open every single box. But there had been no note. I had no way of knowing whether Daniel even managed to confirm the position of Savitri's mate, or if he had, whether whatever plan he'd had for freeing the dragon had been successful. Or even if he survived.

Benaki announced that the dragon council representatives would arrive tomorrow shortly before noon. Which left Daniel and his "friends" very little time before Savitri would have to select Benaki for China's new dragon lord, or call the general's bluff and hope her mate was still alive when the dust settled.

The first thing I'd done after speaking to Savitri was to address the guards about our clothing. Granted, we'd only been detained one day so far, but with the stress and constant Bangalore heat, I was less than my best in the smell department. I assumed the others felt the same way.

I'd made my case to the dragons at the door, telling them that if Benaki hoped to pull off the appearance of normalcy in Savitri's territory, it wouldn't do for us to look tired, bruised and bloody when the dragon council arrived. The guards had shrugged at my request and shooed me away from the exits, but they must have taken it to someone in charge, because folded stacks of clothing appeared a few hours later. Pressed slacks and dress shirts for the men, and color-coordinated saris for the women. Our new Savitri Enterprises uniforms, I guess.

I wasn't fond of the idea of clean clothes on a not-so-clean body. Krishnan and I had again managed to get the dragons to see our point of view, and we were allowed to visit the guest floors in groups of five at a time to use the showers. The announcement came with a great deal of rejoicing, and soon there were even some quiet giggles from my female companions as the elevator slowly climbed to the proper floor.

My coworkers seemed to have acclimated relatively well to their newfound captivity. With each hour the dragons stuck to their promise of no harm, Savitri's human employees relaxed just a fraction more. By the time we'd all bathed and congregated down on the main office floor, most of my bunk mates were either whispering quietly to each other, or were already sound asleep.

But I couldn't seem to do the same. I rearranged the wad of clothing that served as my pillow and stared at the ceiling while I mentally recited Daniel's message word for word.

Why hadn't he sent another note? If Daniel had contacts powerful enough to rescue Savitri's mate, certainly he could manage to sneak in another status update.

Unless, of course, they had failed, and he was injured. Or dead.

The thought made my heart stutter. If Daniel failed, we had no hope of survival. We'd be chopped up and thrown away, just like Savitri's dragons.

But that wasn't what was really bothering me.

My entire life, I'd been attracted to jerks. The boyfriend in high school who'd left me at a convenience store when the scantily dressed senior was suddenly single. The guy in college who lived in my dorm room for five months because he couldn't be bothered to pay his own rent. Or Richard Green, who'd tried to kill a city full of dragons, and put the blame on me when it didn't work out.

That last one was a doozy. And now, here I was, realizing that I'd finally managed to find a man that wasn't a jerk. Daniel was kind and caring, and possessed sense of humor that perfectly matched mine. I thought back to our lovemaking. When had I ever laughed so hard with a man, while feeling incredibly cherished at the same time?

In my mind, I saw Daniel's easy smile, and the twinkle in his eyes the day he'd threatened to toss me from the car. So he was brusque. And focused. And more than a little annoying at times. But he was also patient, and loyal, and a truly magnificent kisser.

He was the first man that cared for me not because of my looks, or for what I could do for him, but because he clicked with the real me. Not just the spiky-haired, fashion-loving linguaphile parts of me, but the insecure and sarcastic sides as well.

Daniel had seen all my flaws—some I hadn't even realized I possessed—and liked me anyway.

And there, in the middle of a cold tile floor, I admitted I loved him.

And that I might have been the one to lead him to his death.

A sob tore from my chest before I even realized I'd started crying.

In the dark, I saw Neetha's head came up from her place on the floor. "Julie?"

I waved her back, sniffling. "Go back to sleep. I'm fine." I tried to wipe the tears from my face, but they kept running down my cheeks. So when Neetha rose silently and wrapped her arms around my shoulders, I hugged her back as we both cried for lost loved ones.

TWENTY-ONE

I MUST HAVE fallen asleep at some point, because I woke to a thin stream of moonlight shining through the un-shuttered window. For a brief moment, I forgot where I was, and spent a precious few seconds admiring the beauty of an Indian night sky. And then reality came crashing back. I closed my eyes, wishing I could fall back into oblivion if only for a few more seconds.

But there would be no more sleep for me. I checked the door, as if our guards might have miraculously disappeared and I'd find Daniel and the white horse brigade riding in with trumpets.

I had no such luck. In fact, I found the source of my midnight wake-up call. A sandy-scaled dragon leaned against the wall near the main entrance, snoring like a freight train. On second thought, I'm not even sure a freight train could achieve the sheer earth-shaking volume of the dragon's inhalations.

Deep vibrations echoed through the room with each breath he took, sending the desks and chairs we'd piled in a spare corner skittering across the floor from the vibrations. Dear Lord, the dragon was loud.

His partner was one of the more fashion forward of Benaki's dragons. In a practice usually associated with those of Adelaida's ilk—she was widely recognized as the world's first dragon fashionista—this dragon wore almost an entire bolt of red silk draped around his ample neck. He, unlike his partner, was fully awake. And amused. When he noticed my attention, he laughed—short huffing snorts that added to the room's relentless clamor.

Most of the staff had given up on sleeping. More than a few women sat against the wall staring blindly at the floor. I checked to make sure none of them were frightened—I imagine it would be an even more terrifying experience to be surrounded by dragons and not understand their words.

When I was sure they were merely irritated, I rolled over and moved to lie back on my cardboard pallet. Instead, my gaze was drawn to a blinking red light in a nearby executive office. I shot into a sitting position.

It was a telephone! And it was working! I swung my gaze back to the guards. Mr. Sandman was still asleep, and Mr. Cape had lost interest in our misery and was busy…whistling, I think?

Lady Savitri's orders—no contact with anyone outside these walls—rang in my ears. But when I'd made the promise, it had never occurred to me that I would have a chance to speak with someone directly, without fear that a note would be intercepted before it even left the building.

I scooted slowly across the floor, until I was blocked from their view by the cubicle walls. Only then did I dart into the office and grab the receiver.

"Hello?" I kept my voice at a low whisper.

The connection was filled with static, and there was a slight pause before I heard a woman speak.

"Yes, hello? Is this Savitri Enterprises?" The girl's voice was terribly young and uncertain in response to my less-than-professional greeting, but before I could answer, she pushed on. "My name is Fatima and I'm calling from Bangalore Telecommunications Customer Service department. We wanted you to know that we discovered a massive break in your line and have taken steps to repair the issue. Would you be willing to participate in a brief survey about your recent experience with Bangalore Telecommunications? Also, we'd like to fill you in on some of the new offerings for our platinum level customers."

Thank the Lord, it was a sales call! I didn't know who'd reported the outage, but I could kiss them right now.

"Listen, Fatima, we've got a bit of a situation here. I need you to get on the phone and call the Tulsa office of DRACIM. Better yet, it'd be great if you could connect me." I rattled off my roommate's number before the poor girl could interrupt.

"Um, ma'am, I don't believe I can—"

"Don't worry about it. Just dial the number and ask for Myrna Banks. Tell her we have a rogue general doing a pretty good job of taking over the entire Indian Territory. She needs to notify Lord Nir Relobu to get his army in the air to help us out."

"Ma'am, I'm sorry. This isn't—" papers rattled as Fatima struggled to keep up. "I'm afraid I do not understand. Can you repeat your request?"

I realized the excitement had thickened my native drawl and I forced myself to speak slowly and enunciate. "I need you to call Myrna Banks at the Tulsa DRACIM office. This is her number."

I'd barely managed to get out the first two digits before the line went dead.

"Fatima. Fatima? Crap." I pushed the hook mechanism three or four times, but it was no use. I'd lost the dial tone.

When the phone still didn't work after a few minutes, I slammed it down and headed for the office next door. In the back of my mind, I knew the odds of the problem being with the equipment itself were infinitesimal, but it didn't matter. I'd just found someone who could help me get word to…well, anybody, and I just couldn't accept that a dead phone was the end of all hope.

I took another peek at the dragon guards—the snoring one was still snoring and the fat one was still fat. When he looked in my direction, I waved and held up the empty mug I'd found on the office desk near the telephone. A lone woman with a dry throat must not have been high on the danger list, because the dragon, now that it was clear I'd given up trying to sleep, ignored me completely and looked toward a group of men who were huddled near the remaining copy machines and talking quietly.

I took that as tacit permission to go on about my business. Convinced that all it would take was a new telephone handset, I kept my eye on the guard as I rushed into the office. But I hadn't made it more than a few steps before I bounced off of something hard, rough, and scaly.

Savitri peered down at me from the dark corner she'd been curled into. "Julie? Whatever are you doing?"

"I, uh…" I held up the empty coffee cup. "I was just getting something to drink."

"I see." Savitri dropped her head back to the floor and closed her eyes. The dragon lord looked terribly ill. Her scales had faded from their usual dark gray to a color that was more suited to ashy fireplace leftovers. Around her eyes and mouth, small fissures had formed between the plates of her skin, and if I hadn't seen her drinking from the fountain in her garden earlier this morning, I would have said she was severely dehydrated.

"Lady Savitri?"

The dragon's eyelids fluttered slightly, but she didn't move from her prone position.

I stepped closer and put a hand on her winged shoulder, and then gasped. The dragon lord's body was emanating heat. I suddenly wondered whether Benaki was smarter than I gave him credit for.

"Lady Savitri, have you eaten lately? Had anything to drink?"

"I was provided meat for lunch. I have my own water supply." Her words were so faint I had to put my ear right next to her mouth to hear her words.

"Was the meal provided still living?" I didn't remember hearing any of the icky animal sounds that usually accompanied a live meal.

My question drew an angry, if tired, snort. "Of course not. They fed me a goat, fully cooked and stringy as an overworked racehorse. It tasted terrible."

Masking my grimace at the thought that Savitri would know how a racehorse tasted, I ran to the nearest supply cabinet and rummaged around for a bowl. Filling the container with water from our cooler, I placed it on the floor near Savitri's head.

"You need to drink this. I think you've been poisoned." I'd remembered a story that ran in the paper a few years ago. A group of humans, tired of being the victims of frequent cattle thefts from dragons flying overhead, had decided that instead of contacting DRACIM to negotiate a settlement, they would take matters into their own hands. They'd done so by injecting copious amounts of rat poison into freshly killed cattle, leaving the meat out for the dragons while their live cattle were kept safely inside their barns.

The rat poison hadn't done much but cause the dragons mild indigestion, but DRACIM had been called in, just in case the dragons decided to retaliate against the farmers for their discomfort. Myrna had been assigned the case—who at the time served as Emory's assistant and catchall for the worst DRACIM cases. It had taken a week to soothe ruffled feathers on both sides of the incident. After convincing the humans it was in their best interest to manage the thefts through the official channels provided by DRACIM and Lord Relobu, the farmers were allowed to return to their jobs. As for the dragons, they'd been up and flying around within the week, albeit over different pastureland and under the close watch of their dragon lord.

But what if Benaki had found an additive more dangerous for dragons than simple rat poison? It would certainly be the easiest way to get rid of the dragon lord. Her entire staff had witnessed her declining energy levels, but we'd all just assumed it was due to worry for her infirm mate. But it was clear to me that her affliction was almost certainly designed to be fatal, and Benaki almost certainly to blame. He couldn't kill her outright, and yes, her death immediately after Benaki's confirmation as China's dragon lord would be suspicious, but his involvement would be very hard to prove.

Savitri had perked up enough to drink the water, but the very fact that she wasn't roaring with claws out was testament to just how sick she was.

"Here. Let me get more. You need to flush whatever it is from your system." All I could do was get her to drink, and hope the poison required multiple doses.

I headed back to the water cooler, only to notice that the telephone was blinking—again. Water forgotten, I skidded across the tile floor in my haste to reach the line before it was again disconnected.

"Hello!" At two in the morning, I must have sounded like the most cheerful person on planet earth. "Fatima?" I prayed it was the same caller as before, so I didn't have to start over with my panicked instructions.

"Yes. This is Fatima." I could tell by her tone of voice that she was *not* happy about who she was speaking with. "I apologize that we were disconnected. I wanted to tell you that Bangalore Telecommunications values your—"

"Oh, please. Just stop!" Exasperated, I held up an angry hand, as if I could physically stop Fatima's dogged determination to finish her employer's preapproved script. "Fatima, this is a matter of life and death. Like I told you before, it is imperative that you get in contact with the Tulsa DRACIM office—"

I screamed in frustration when the line once again went dead, the need to avoid the attention of Benaki's dragon guards momentarily forgotten.

But the focus of their attention didn't actually matter. Because I had another dragon to deal with.

"Julie, what are you doing?" Savitri, her body bowed as if she were in enormous pain, stood just outside the door. Her question was asked in a soft tone—for a dragon—but I couldn't mistake the simmering anger in her voice. "Why are you attempting to contact DRACIM? Was I not clear in my instructions earlier today?"

I opened my mouth to speak, but no words came out. Just hours earlier, she'd expressly forbade any attempts at communication with the outside world, for fear Benaki would become aware and further damage her already maimed mate.

She must have seen the answer in my eyes, because she shuffled forward, claws extended. "What did you tell them?"

"Lady Savitri, with all due respect—" I gasped when the telephone in question hit the wall and exploded into a thousand pieces. The low hum of Savitri's staff chatting just outside the office came to an abrupt halt.

I looked beyond the dragon lord's shoulder. The guards must have started this way when they noticed Savitri rising from her resting place, because they stood right beside her.

Three angry dragons. All staring directly at me. I looked to Savitri. "I didn't tell them anything. I didn't get a chance."

TWENTY-TWO

THE DRAGON COUNCIL representatives arrived right on schedule. Per Benaki's orders, the rest of the mangled furniture and cardboard, which we'd been attempting to clean in small bits, had been cleared from our makeshift living area. The furniture and pieces of cubicle walls that were still standing had been converted into a similar, but much sparser, office space once more. Now all of Savitri's humans stood in a loose semi-circle in the small meadow to the west of the building that served as a landing space for the dragons.

Including me.

Savitri had been furious about what she viewed as a betrayal on my part, and had barely been able to look at me without snarling. I'd pleaded with the dragon lord to see reason, and to realize that Benaki would never allow her to live, no matter her actions. I told her in no uncertain terms that her mate wouldn't last the week.

I'd been convinced that I'd gone too far when Savitri lunged toward me, teeth bared, but she'd pulled back at the last moment, turning her back to me in an unmistakable signal of disgust. I never got another chance to speak with her because soon after, Benaki's guards, high on the power of imprisoning a dragon lord, had snapped a steel collar around Savitri's neck, and chained her to a tree outside. They'd teased her mercilessly, and she allowed it, simply curling into a ball instead of facing them with claws and teeth.

I'd been more convinced than ever that her meat was being poisoned, and I managed to convince Krishnan to offer her our leftover pizza as a dead-goat alternative. Not that her health was going to matter.

When Benaki arrived, he ordered Savitri's collar removed. She stood, docile, as the chains were hauled away, and it was obvious that the dragon lord planned to see this plan through and tell the delegation whatever Benaki wished as she held on to the thin thread of hope that the general would uphold his promise to free her mate.

Squinting, I looked up to the sky. Small black dots, around twenty or so, floated like tiny bugs in front of the morning sun. Even from this far away, I could hear dragons roar as they announced their arrival to our ramshackle reception party. They were flying in fast, and the dots grew larger and more impressive by the second as the council representatives drew closer.

A crowd had gathered beyond the thick stone wall that separated Savitri's buildings from the rest of the world, and I heard cheers rise up. I wondered whether they thought the delegation was here to help clean up the chemical spill. People shuffled ever closer to the boundary of the property wall, anxious to get a look at the new arrivals. Their exclamations were followed with a growled order from one of Benaki's dragons to move away from the building. I peered through a small metal grate in the wall, and watched as the crowd only shifted slightly at the warning. With no dragonspeakers to translate, his order was either misunderstood or ignored.

The council representatives, still blissfully unaware of our true circumstances, obliged the excited crowd with awesome feats of aerial prowess. One of the larger dragons, Lady Adelaida's judging by his brightly colored scales, impressed the spectators with a slow, midair roll. A darker, thinner dragon joined in at a faster pace. The second dragon's dark coloring, coupled by the thinner, longer shape of his body as it spun in ever tightening circles, caused him to look oddly similar to the funnel of an Oklahoma tornado.

The spectators crowed their approval.

The dragon guard's second warning—a roar and snap of teeth—was a universal method of communication, and those closest to the angry reptile obligingly moved away from the dragon and the building. But their enthusiasm was in no way dampened.

It was a rare sight to see this many dragons in one place. Those who were attending the conference with

a human counterpart wore bright saddles decked
out in the official colors of their respective territory. The humans seated astride did the same, their
uniforms matching the scale colors of their dragon.
Those dragons who had come alone displayed their
national pride with scarves of colored cloth wound
around their necks, or had painted their territorial
hues directly onto their scales.

The entire delegation landed at the same time in
the usually secluded Savitri territory. And, despite
earlier warnings about chemical spills and quaran-
tines, it seemed as if half of India had come to enjoy
the show. They cheered as if this group would save us
all, when in fact they would likely be the last thing
we'd see before our murders.

I scanned the sea of faces for any hint of a pale-
skinned man with brown hair, and felt tears clog my
throat once again when I failed to locate Daniel's
familiar grinning face. "Move away from the wall.
Your new master has ordered it." The dragon glanced
toward Benaki, who stood beside an obviously sickly
Savitri, the epitome of a concerned subject.

Of course, Benaki's act would have been far more
convincing had he not been staring daggers in my
direction. It wasn't hard to see that I didn't have a
future with this company past today.

That is, if I didn't starve to death first.

Fully aware that Benaki had every reason to make
sure I died of an alleged accident as soon as possible,
I'd been careful not to eat anything. Other than the

pizza, Savitri had done the same. In addition to refusing any food served by Benaki's men, with each hour that passed with no word from Daniel, Savitri had retreated further into her emotionless state. This morning she was barely a shadow of the former Indian dragon lord. The dragon council would have no trouble believing she'd died of natural causes.

Benaki knew it. And quietly reveled in his new power.

Suddenly furious at the dragon responsible for the suffering of so many people—Savitri and her mate, Neetha and her murdered best friend, myself and, as I was starting to realize, likely Daniel—I couldn't even pretend to cower at his orders.

Slowly, and very distinctly, I lifted my right hand and showed Benaki a different, but no-less-universal signal of my frustration and anger at his actions. My bird might not hold a candle to the midair antics of a dragon, but it got my point across. Even from a distance I could sense the general's eyes narrow. Before the dragon beside me could notice his master's fury and decide to earn brownie points by knocking me unconscious with a meaty fist, I turned my back on the entire spectacle and stalked inside.

The window for Daniel's rescue attempt had officially closed.

We were all doomed.

As I LEFT the garden, I was followed, of course, by one of Benaki's dragons. As one of only two dragonspeakers, I was considered a higher risk than the other human employees and was treated accordingly. The general had assigned a dragon to be with me at all times, just in case I tried to communicate with a reptilian member of the delegation. My guard tracked my movements with a bored eye until the delegation members were shown inside.

The other staff was similarly shadowed, although with a lesser degree of suspicion, as Benaki's guards made regular rounds throughout the room under the guise of small talk with the visiting troupe. I could see that the human members of the council felt the tension in the room, but no one acted on it. Savitri was a known recluse; they probably assumed that all visitors made us uncomfortable.

Krishnan hadn't spoken to me since last night. True, as the only two dragonspeakers in the building, we'd been busy trying to calm Savitri's staff when Benaki's dragons got a little too growly for their comfort, but I couldn't help but notice that Krishnan always seemed to leave a room as soon as I'd enter. He too had been furious at my reckless disregard for the safety of Savitri's mate, regardless of my reasons behind it.

The amount of small talk must have made Benaki nervous, because the delegation hadn't been in the building more than ten minutes before the general suggested the council step into Savitri's office and commence the process of choosing China's new dragon lord.

But the other dragons were amenable, and soon the entire party was lumbering toward the door.

"Thank you, Mr. Krishnan," a voice said in English. "I'm glad to hear the chemical spill has been contained to the west end of the building. I trust all the employees are in good health?"

I heard Krishnan answer in the affirmative before he received another question. "Lord Relobu asked that I visit with Lady Savitri privately, on an unrelated matter. With whom should I speak to have that arranged?"

Krishnan was halfway through a bumbling explanation about why that wouldn't be possible before I realized the American voice belonged to none other than Trian Chobardan, Myrna's boyfriend. My roommate had said it wouldn't be long before Lord Relobu sent his right hand man to find me. She'd been right.

By the time I'd wrapped my head around the news, Krishnan had led Trian into Savitri's office. I tried to follow, but my guard stopped me with a rough swipe.

"Benaki gave me orders to keep you separated from the dragon council. You're to remain under quarantine until Benaki determines you're of no threat to the rest of his human staff. Unless, of course, you fall ill." The dragon gave me a toothy grin, fully aware that Benaki had no intention of allowing me to live.

As irritating as it was, Benaki was no idiot. Word of my and Savitri's argument, and the reasons for it, must have made its way to his ears. I'd been locked out of the meeting.

The dragon was still chuckling at his own joke, but I barely even registered his amusement. My mind was still on Trian, and what his presence meant for me.

It really wasn't much of a decision at all. If I stayed here, and followed Benaki's rules, I was dead. But if I turned myself in to Trian, it was possible he could put a stop to Benaki's coup and save the lives of Savitri's staff.

Sure, I'd probably end up dying for Richard's idiocy anyway—most likely at the end of a very long and public trial—but right now, the way I saw it, my chances were better with Trian.

All I had to do was figure out how to get to him.

TWENTY-THREE

BENAKI CERTAINLY DIDN'T make it easy for me. The dragon hadn't been kidding about my "quarantine." I'd been marched straight to the break room and told to sit.

For the rest of the morning, I tried every excuse in the book, from bathroom breaks to fainting spells, and hadn't gotten anywhere near the room where the dragon council representatives—Trian included— were ensconced.

I'd just about decided to take my chances and see whether I could outrun a dragon *and* get through Savitri's office doors when they cracked open and Krishnan slipped through.

He walked across the room and, when he saw me, his eyes widened for a moment as he realized I'd been placed under guard.

"I was trying to help, you know."

When he didn't respond, I tried again. "You know the odds of Eriel being alive are infinitesimal."

He paused, his forehead pressed against the wooden door. "Of course I know that." The words were said in a low murmur, but I could hear his pain, his feelings of helplessness in every syllable.

He faced me. "But Savitri—she's different. Kind. When I was a boy, she visited my school. It was just after she'd chosen Bangalore as her new capital, and there were a lot of humans who were terrified by the thought of a dragon-ruled city. A few of the children got brave, and started throwing sticks and rocks at her. She could have taken off all their heads. But do you know what she did?"

Krishnan smiled at the memory. "She turned to the leader of the group, a boy well-known for bullying, and asked him to tell her why he was afraid of dragons. The boy didn't understand her, of course, but she waited patiently while her translator rephrased the question. I still don't know how she did it, but by the end of their conversation, she had the boy sitting on her neck, whooping for joy as they sailed over the roof of the schoolhouse."

I nodded. I'd come to India terrified of dragons, with good reason. She'd put me at ease almost immediately. "You don't want to hurt her."

"The death of her mate would kill her. I can't stand by and let that happen to Savitri. Even though I know it's hopeless...I just can't do *nothing.*"

I looked behind me for my guard. He was still there, calm but far too alert. I couldn't say more for fear he would overhear.

So I played my American card, and ignored the bounds of Indian custom.

Krishnan jolted when I wrapped my arms around him in a fierce hug, his body stiff with shock and discomfort. "Let me help her. Tell Mr. Chobardan that Carol is waiting for him outside the boardroom." I whispered the words in his ear before I stepped quickly away.

Krishnan stared at me for several moments without speaking. Then, with an ever-so-slight dip of his chin, he acquiesced. As I watched from the break room, Krishnan crossed the room dotted with cubicles and slipped back into the dragon lord's office without using the door mechanism.

I stood, biting my nails, and watched as a long line of live goats were led into the room for lunch.

I DIDN'T HAVE long to wait before Trian came striding from the office, his dark eyes scanning the room until they locked with mine. With almost casual grace, he crossed the room so swiftly my guard barely had a chance to notice him before Trian bowed before me in the typical Indian greeting.

"Pardon me." Trian said, placing a casual hand on my shoulder. "Would you be able to help me with something in the garden?"

My guard, who understood enough English that he'd correctly interpreted Trian's request, tried to step between us, almost knocking me to the ground in the process.

"I'm sorry, sir, but she is unavailable at the moment. Perhaps I can find a serving girl to assist you with your needs."

I fought the urge for hysterical laughter when Trian turned to the dragon, a look of confusion on his face as he addressed me yet again. "By God, I think this dragon just tried to talk to me. What did he say?" Trian's voice and manner matched that of Myrna's old boss, Emory.

The dragon, unsure of how to respond, hesitated.

Trian took instant advantage and grabbed my arm, half dragging me toward the garden entrance.

My guard, shocked, did nothing but hop around me, claws out, like a distressed chicken. He obviously had no idea how to handle a disobedient human guest. Benaki had given specific orders that they were to be treated like royalty.

"Why look," Trian's Oklahoma drawl had returned at the same time he increased his speed until I was having to half run, half hop to keep up with him. The dragon did the same, his wings flapping at his sides as he tried to gain control of the situation. But he was obviously flustered by Trian's act of complete incomprehension and pushy manners.

Trian pretended not to notice the dragon's growing panic. "I think he's dancing. Do all the Indian dragons dance?"

I felt the sunlight on my head as we stepped over the threshold and into Savitri's garden. Trian headed straight for the copse of sandalwood trees near the fountain, keeping up a brisk patter of rude comments the entire time.

In the time it took me to come up with an appropriately ridiculous reply, Trian turned and drew the thin deadly sword strapped to his hip. With one tight motion, he stabbed my guard through the eye, felling the giant animal immediately, and with an efficiency that was scary. The dragon's body fell neatly into the space under the trees, safe from the eyes of any in-sky observers.

"Carol. What the hell happened to your hair?"

I tore my eyes from the dead dragon to stare blankly at Trian. He must have asked me a question, but I hadn't heard a thing.

Comprehension and sympathy clouded his gaze, and he grabbed me into a tight embrace before gently pushing me away with a hand on each of my shoulders so he could see my face. "I'm sorry honey, but I need you to think. Myrna still hasn't managed to get Relobu to budge on the fugitive thing, and Richard is still selling the story that you were the mastermind behind the plan to blow up Tulsa. I'm relatively certain that your life wouldn't be immediately in danger if you came back with me to Tulsa, but I can't promise the same long-term. It's your choice. You want to come with me, you come. But I'll look the other way if you want to slip back inside."

Trian's eyes were solemn, and it warmed my heart to see that he'd be willing to defy Lord Relobu's orders for the sake of Myrna's feelings.

But I'd already given my decision all the thought it warranted.

"I'm ready to go. But only if you promise you'll help Savitri."

Trian's lips thinned. "Krishnan filled me in on most of the situation, and I've figured out the rest with my own research. Never fear, Benaki doesn't know it yet, but he will not be sitting on any thrones, now or in the future. I give you my word that we will rescue Eriel."

I believed him. Because I knew who—and what— he was. Trian was just like Daniel. And when Daniel made a promise, he kept it.

"Take me home."

TWENTY-FOUR

TRIAN NODDED ONCE, then proceeded to unfasten the row of buttons running down the center of his shirt. Handing me the soft, finely woven material, he told me to put it on over my Indian "uniform" before disappearing back into the building.

Moments later he was back, his arms filled with silken saris taken from who knows where.

"It's going to be a little chilly, but these should keep you from freezing to death." Using the saris, he bundled me into a strange semblance of a winter coat before handing me his sword and stepping a few paces away.

"Watch the door. There will be a few moments when I'd prefer not to be attacked."

He turned to face the stone wall, but I saw him grimace slightly before his back rippled with the unmistakable signs of impending dragon wings.

When Trian had first morphed in front of Myrna, I hadn't been around, but her descriptions didn't hold a candle to experiencing the sight firsthand.

Bones seemed to pop out of nowhere, reforming into the shape of a massive dragon. The hair on

Trian's head seemed to disappear completely, replaced with sleek black scales perfectly designed for covert nighttime flight.

He'd kicked his shoes off in the grass, and I watched, fascinated, as toenails morphed into four-inch long talons, and the structure of his foot stretched, elongated, until all signs of Trian the man had disappeared, replaced with a two-ton reptile with fierce but intelligent amber eyes.

"I don't have a saddle, so you'll need to tell me when you have to take a break." His mouth now unable to form English words, Trian gave me the orders in dragonspeak.

I nodded.

Tucking his now-scaled legs until his body lay flat on the ground, Trian extended a wing to assist me onto the space between his shoulder blades.

"Last chance to change your mind."

"Nope. This is what I need to do."

He nodded his approval, giving me a final nudge. Once I was settled, Trian hopped sideways until he had a clear shot from under the trees to the sky above.

Craning his neck, Trian watched until the dragon on security duty dipped into a lazy turn before shooting into the sky with a furious burst of speed.

As I left India behind, it was to the delighted laughter of children who'd witnessed our escape from the other side of the stone wall.

Though it was the middle of the day, Trian seemed

to have no trouble avoiding the guards circling Savitri Enterprises.

In fact, Trian made it look like child's play as we dipped and darted into every available shadow, flying low as we used the trees for additional cover.

Forgetting for the moment what awaited me in Tulsa, and circumstances of the people I'd left behind, I sat back and allowed myself to enjoy the most delicious taste of freedom.

OTHER THAN THE obvious fact that I was riding dragonback, the trip back to Tulsa was relatively uneventful. When my teeth had started to chatter from the cold, Trian landed, stopping only long enough to morph back into his human form so he could buy me a thicker coat and find some food to fuel him for the long flight home.

Within twelve hours, Trian had deposited me on American soil, morphed back into his human form, donned his Relobu uniform, and somberly escorted me into a holding cell at a downtown police station. The officer on duty, a young lieutenant with barely enough facial hair to qualify as a grown-up, took one look at Trian with his professional attire and obvious air of command agreed to Trian's every request.

I'd half hoped that the police station would refuse to hold me—technically, Lord Relobu held no sway over the human legal system. But Tulsa, being the capital city of Relobu's territory, not to mention the dragon lord's home, had long held a reputation for allowing the dragons leeway when dealing with the rare human-committed crimes against dragons.

It didn't bode well that not one of those humans was still living.

"I'll see what I can do about getting you a visit from Myrna."

Trian gave my hand a quick squeeze and left, the sound of the key turning in the lock the last sound I heard for a while.

I paced in my small cell, wishing someone could tell me the fate of my Indian friends. Had Trian arranged a painless reversal of power in the office building, or had more been lost to unnecessary violence?

I had no doubt that Trian, with the full force of Relobu's armies behind him, would have no problem retrieving Savitri's mate, should he still be living. I peeled my eyes open once again, the images of a dead Daniel appearing on the inside of my eyelids too much for my already raw emotions.

It felt like hours before the scrape of metal signaled that I had a visitor. I stood, hoping to see the familiar face of my roommate, come to tell me that Richard had decided to be a decent excuse for a human being and confess to his own crimes.

But the person who walked through the cold metal door of my cell had my heart trying to jump out of my chest with joy. I pushed both arms through the bars of my cage as if I could somehow convince my-self I wasn't dreaming.

"Daniel!"

So overjoyed that he was still alive, it took me a couple of beats to notice that he didn't seem happy to see me.

"What the hell were you thinking!" He stalked across the room and grabbed me, despite his angry words, squeezing until I was sure I'd have imprints of metal bars on my face for the rest of my life.

"Oh my God. I thought you were dead." I leaned into his embrace, awkward as it was, and reveled in the familiar smell of his cologne. The cage rattled with our movement, and I reluctantly let go of Daniel's shirt, pulling back so I could memorize his face.

He did the same, and for several moments, with no words, we drank in the sight of each other.

Finally, he sighed. "Tell me why you lost your mind and turned yourself in to Relobu."

"I had to. Benaki killed all of Savitri's dragons, and he planned to get rid of us all as soon as the del-egation left. I needed to ensure everyone was safe."

Daniel scowled. "I told you not to worry about it. Jovan's contacts came through. We had more than enough dragonpower to free Eriel. I came back to the Bangalore offices, only to have Krishnan tell me you'd flown off in the sunset with Trian not ten minutes earlier."

I blinked as his words sank in. "You rescued Eriel? Well what the hell took you so long?"

He grunted when my fist hit his shoulder, but he grinned.

"Nice to see the slammer hasn't broken your spirit. It took me a while to get Jovan on the line, and another couple of hours before we'd contacted the generals still loyal to Savitri. Benaki had only managed to turn one of the commanders, but it was enough to ensure that none of Savitri's letters were being delivered, and that Benaki's were substituted in their place.

"Savitri's commanders had no trouble understanding my English, but I had no idea how to decode their responses. By the time I'd found someone who could translate for me, the dragons were deep in an argument on the best way to take the house with the least amount of damage."

His lips kicked into a grin. "Apparently Savitri is pretty particular about her furnishings, and her soldiers weren't too keen on facing her if they accidentally broke one of her marble busts. They seemed to be split on whether the life of her mate would keep them out of trouble for messing with her breakables."

He opened his mouth to tell me more but the wide double doors opened, revealing Myrna. A man carrying a rather impressive ring weighted down with what appeared to be almost one hundred keys trailed behind her. He seemed familiar with the set, however, because it took him only a moment to locate the one that opened my cell.

"Carol!" Myrna almost knocked me down in her excitement. "I am so glad you're okay."

Grinning, I gave her a tight hug before moving to step from the barred room.

The man with the keys stepped forward to block the exit. "Ma'am, I need you to stay where you are. Until Lord Relobu gives the word, I'm afraid we need to keep you here."

I turned to look at Myrna. Her face was twisted in displeasure, but she confirmed his statement. "The old lizard still refuses to believe Richard was the man behind the bombing."

Daniel turned to Myrna, shock in his eyes. "How did DRACIM allow that to happen?" His lips had tightened in anger.

I knew the feeling, but my anger wasn't directed at DRACIM. Or even the dragon lord. Relobu seemed to have chosen sides, and he'd picked the poster child for dragon relations. On paper, I *did* look like the one more likely to hate dragons. Richard's father had basically founded DRACIM, so I couldn't really blame the dragon lord for thinking it was crazy for Richard to be the mastermind behind a plot to mass murder the very creatures he worked with on a daily basis.

It was understandable that the dragon lord would finger Emory and me for the crime, especially considering my obvious unease around dragons while preparing for the China trip. It had taken me a full day to be comfortable around the old dragon Trian had tasked to help with my combat lessons. And that dragon had been half-lame and practically toothless.

In contrast, Richard had worked for Relobu since he was a young man. Since I was first introduced to Richard Green, he'd been polite, well-spoken, and infinitely gracious to humans and dragons alike.

In fact, when his attention had turned my way, I'd been understandably flattered. I thought I'd finally gotten over my horrendous luck with men. Here was a man who seemed to have it all together.

His dad had been permanently injured by dragons, but Richard still interacted with them every day.

During our mission in China, I'd spent most of the time in the throes of a panic attack. Richard had remained unnaturally calm.

Funny, I'd really admired Richard's capacity to remain unruffled. What I was only now beginning to realize was Richard's anger wasn't gone, it was burning deep beneath the surface. To everyone else Richard was professional, meticulous, and even-tempered.

I looked to Daniel. His hair was mussed, his shirt wrinkled, and he was currently shouting at my friend for not doing more to get me out of here.

And somehow, this time, I realized I had a keeper.

Too bad I wouldn't be around long enough to prove it.

"Daniel, leave her alone. You've got to admit that

I look far guiltier than Richard. Myrna can't change that, and neither can you."

Daniel scowled but fell silent, jamming his hands into the pockets of his jeans and rocking back on his heels. He turned to Myrna.

"So what can we do to help her?"

I wasn't particularly happy to see that Myrna—the woman trained in dragon problem solving—didn't have an answer.

She shook her head. "Relobu has agreed to allow a human audience to attend the meeting tomorrow, which means at least your trial will more closely resemble a human trial. And it likely also means that an execution is off the table, should you be found guilty."

"Well. That's something, I guess."

Daniel didn't seem too happy about the situation either, but then again, I hadn't seen him anything but frustrated in a long while. He leaned over to give me a quick peck on the cheek. "I'll be back in a couple of hours. I've got a story to turn in."

I nodded, surprised and maybe just a little bit hurt. I mean, I hadn't really expected him to offer to move into jail with me, but I didn't expect him to dismiss my plight in lieu of filing a story either.

Daniel left the room without a backward glance.

"Wow. You've got it bad." Myrna eyed me with interest, and I could tell she was dying to ask me about what I'd been doing in India.

Unfortunately, Daniel's abrupt attitude hadn't put me in the mood to share yet another of my bonehead moves in the dating department. "Yeah, well. Looks like I'm the only one."

Myrna's gaze returned to the now-empty doorway. "Looks like," she murmured.

TWENTY-FIVE

IF I'D LEARNED one thing over the past couple of weeks, it was that boredom was the worst form of torture. Myrna had done her best to keep me occupied, but with Emory's absence and the recent bombing, DRACIM needed her for—well, everything. So when she received the third urgent message requiring her immediate response, I took pity on her and told her I'd be fine on my own.

I chanced another look at my cellmate and sighed. The guy, somewhere in his mid-fifties, had been brought in about an hour ago, reeking of alcohol. Once inside the tiny holding area, he'd promptly staggered to the thin metal bed bolted to the wall and passed out, his snores nearly rivaling those of the dragon in India.

As if he subconsciously knew I was watching, the man shifted on the bed, curling a long arm under his head and rolling onto his side. Unfortunately, during his obviously impressive drinking binge earlier in the evening, he'd managed to lose his pants. And now his movements had caused the thin blanket a policeman had wrapped precariously about his waist to come untucked, giving me a full and unobstructed view of things I'd rather not ever see again.

Naturally the hour I'd been forced to spend in a gin-soaked cell with a naked-bottomed drunk is the same hour Richard chose to resurface. And of course, he was, as usual, meticulously dressed while I looked like a rumpled mess. Even with the clothes Trian had picked up for me on our stop, I knew I looked just as bad as the mug shot I'd taken upon arrival said I did.

Pacing, I waited while Richard spoke to the officer on duty at the door. And when he was finished, I wasn't exactly welcoming. I couldn't believe he'd had the gall to stop by. "What do you want?"

"Hi." Richard's eyes flicked to the sleeping drunk. "I came as soon as I heard you were back. How are you holding up?"

"How am I holding—" I was so angry I could barely speak. "Are you freaking kidding me? How do you *think* I'm doing, Richard? I'm sitting in a jail cell, charged with a crime I didn't commit. A crime, I might add, that carries a very high probability of a life sentence as soon as Relobu gets around to collecting me.

"How dare, you, Richard Green! How dare you walk in here and pretend we're going to be friends? I can barely look at you I'm so angry right now."

My chest was heaving by the time I'd finished my tirade, and the drunk had sat up and was eyeing me with bleary confusion.

Richard glanced toward the bed and winced. "Look, I have something I need to talk to you about, but I'd rather do it in private."

I took a deep breath, ready to repeat my earlier sentiments when Richard said the only words that would even remotely cause me to listen.

"I can get you out of here."

As if on cue, the police officer came back, keys in hand.

"Relobu's cleared me?" That was fantastic news. I performed an impromptu jig, so excited about possible freedom that I was willing, for the moment, to forget Richard was a two-faced liar.

The drunk, inspired by my enthusiasm, decided to join in the fun and dance with me. I wasn't sure whether it was by accident or design, but somehow his left hand found a good chunk of my right buttock, and I gasped in surprise.

"Hey, that's enough there. Back off the lady." The officer nudged the drunk good-naturedly back toward the bunk, then stepped aside to allow my exit.

Richard walked with me down the short hall toward the station's sole interrogation room. "I'm afraid you'll have to meet with Lord Relobu before you can really leave, but we have a few minutes. We'll be able to talk in here."

The officer opened the door and then left us alone, efficiently palming the bill Richard offered in exchange for his service.

Great. Now we were bribing police officers.

I sat down at the table, suddenly much less excited. I knew exactly why Richard had made the effort to come and see me. And his next words cemented the conclusion.

"So. I've scheduled your meeting with Lord Relobu first thing tomorrow morning. And I think it will be best if you avoid mentioning some facts that might be triggers for Relobu's anger. For example—"

"Richard. I'm not going to lie for you."

"Oh no, I'm not asking you to lie, exactly. I just think that it would be best if you didn't mention anything about the night Emory and I met at the hotel."

I didn't say anything. I just stared at him.

Visibly irritated when I didn't immediately agree with his suggestion, Richard reached a hand toward my arm. "Please, Carol. It's just easier this way."

"Easier for you, yes. But Richard, think about it. Say I neglect to mention anything that paints you in a negative light. What are you going to do when Emory heals up?"

He didn't answer, and I suddenly realized what Richard was suggesting.

"You're going to set Emory up to take the fall!" I stood, too shocked to process what I was hearing. "You'd let him rot in prison for a crime he didn't even commit!"

His hand remained clamped to my skin. "For us, Carol. For us. Relobu gave me my job back." His gaze was intense, as if he could mentally force my understanding.

But I understood all too well. "Richard, no matter how amoral, or how downright annoying Myrna's former boss can be, I will not sentence him to death, not even to save my own life. And especially not to save yours."

I yanked my arm from his grasp and motioned through the door for the officer to take me back to my cell.

"Carol, think about this. Within six months, I'm sure I'll be able to manufacture at least a dozen working prototypes of the bioweapon we lost at DRACIM. We sell most of those to the dragon lords and hope they take themselves out in territory wars. We use the money they give us to make even more. And with my job back, I'm in the perfect position to activate one within Relobu's home? By the end of next year we'd finally be free of the dragons' rule."

Even now, it surprised me that beneath his outwardly easygoing demeanor, Richard had a fanatic's view of the world. I still didn't understand how he managed to keep it hidden. I'd known his father had been injured by dragons, but I'd had no idea Richard blamed the entire species for the attack.

His words brought a deep sadness to my heart. This man had been twisted by his hurt, so much so that he couldn't even see reason.

"Do you hear yourself? You're talking about killing people, Richard. Dragons, humans, anyone who stands in your way."

"My father may still be breathing, but he died the day those dragons broke his back. They deserve to be killed."

"All dragons aren't the same." Richard's attitude made me examine my own position on dragons. Before my trip to China with Myrna, I'd thought they were all beasts, with skill enough to communicate with us, but without the spark of consciousness that made them individuals.

And then I'd gotten to know Trian. Who messed up royally the first time around, but who more than made up for his mistakes and loved my friend with a passion that made me jealous. And Savitri, who loved her mate with the same unswerving loyalty.

I thought of Daniel, who I'd believed to be someone special. Someone who cared for me the way Trian cared for Myrna.

But he'd left, more worried about his filing deadline. And I hadn't seen him all day. In my recent experience, dragons had more capacity for caring than most humans.

"They are all the same. They are killers. And I will see to it that every single one of them dies. If you choose to align yourself with monsters, I have no choice but to treat you as one." His statement was a pronouncement of fact.

Obviously, I had no chance of convincing Richard he was wrong. And it made me more sad than angry.

"Goodbye, Richard."

I left the room, the echo of Richard's sudden withdrawal into the smooth and urbane shell he wore so well haunting me the entire trip back to my cell.

"HEY, IS THAT you?" The young police officer was back on duty, staring at an expensive-looking television showing a local news program.

Until he'd switched it on with a small pop, I hadn't even noticed it hanging from the wall—it was clear I was back in Relobu's territory where the dragon lord was not subtle about keeping the human police force as his "friends" by gifting them electronic toys that were prohibitively expensive for the average human.

The officer pointed at the screen, which was indeed displaying a picture of me, pulled from the CreaTV employee directory. I gazed longingly at the long waves of reddish-gold hair that tumbled over my shoulders as I rubbed my shorter, shaggier tresses. Until I caught some of the commentary.

"Carol Jenski, creative director with CreaTV, is accused of orchestrating the attack on DRACIM's Tulsa headquarters a month ago, causing the deaths of eleven dragons. Her trial will be held tomorrow, in the home of Lord Nir Relobu. The trial will be governed by dragon custom, with a short period of arguments followed by a summary judgment from the dragon lord."

Someone had really done their homework. Pictures of me from childhood to just a few months ago flashed across the screen, accompanied by running commentary on my life. The segment was incredibly thorough. I was half surprised they didn't mention my favorite cereal.

"That would be me."

The young man gazed at me with calculating eyes. "That's something crazy that you did to those dragons. I've never guarded someone who's been on television before." He paused, as if mulling over his words. "It's kinda cool."

I gave him a tight smile, unwilling to spend the time and energy it would take to explain that my current situation was, in fact, not "kinda cool."

I wondered whether Daniel would be disappointed that he'd missed the story of the century. By now, the coup in faraway India held nothing to the sensationalism of a dragon murder trial.

I wondered whether he'd filed his precious story.

"Do you happen to have a copy of today's *Tulsa Times Chronicle*?"

The boy hustled over to the lone metal desk and snagged the paper, passing it to me through the bars.

Right there, on the very first page was Daniel's story about the coup. He'd met his deadline. And he'd left me in a jail cell while he did it. After Daniel's impassioned speech about how I deserved better treatment than I'd received from Richard, I'd been nothing but a source to him. A source with convenient bedroom benefits.

As tears smudged the ink on the newsprint, I wondered how it was possible to have my heart broken this many times and still be breathing.

The newscaster on the television had no sooner finished his story when my escorts arrived. Four uniformed officers, with guns strapped to their hips, quickly and efficiently pushed through the swarming media just outside the door and placed me safely inside a waiting vehicle.

TWENTY-SIX

THE OFFICERS DIDN'T bother to cuff me, they simply pulled into Relobu's driveway and helped me out before hopping back into the car and speeding away. Because really, where could I run? The place was swarming with dragons, every single one glaring at me with pure hatred.

I ducked my head to avoid their eyes as an aging human butler showed me inside.

My trial was considerably less fancy than the Chinese dragon lord's had been, though it felt almost as crowded. Unlike the gala in Budapest, the room was equipped with only two rows of chairs, both facing the single podium in the center of the room. Both rows had been filled with humans, most of whom I recognized. A single row of dragon perches had been placed behind the human chairs, their heavy wooden beams providing a sturdy bar for a dragon's birdlike feet to grip. Each and every perch was filled to capacity with unfamiliar dragons, as well as every empty space around the edges of the room.

I'd drawn quite a crowd this morning. When I'd pressed, Myrna had told me most of these dragons were family members of those who had died in the DRACIM disaster. The thought brought tears to my eyes.

Up front, beside the podium, was a single chair that I supposed belonged to me.

I'd been briefed on the format of the proceedings. First, I would be allowed to share my side of the story, and would be asked questions from the audience, including the dragon lord, should he be so inclined.

Then, any party who was willing would be given the opportunity to testify on my behalf, or against me.

Which is why I wasn't surprised to find Richard sitting in one of the empty seats. He was here to call me a liar. Emory sat beside him in a wheelchair, his face almost unrecognizable from the broken nose and jaw. Evidently Richard had managed to bribe his way into the hospital room, and Emory had been all too eager to take Richard up on his offer to "misremember" the details of that night in Budapest. In his lap lay a notepad filled with writing, and I realized he planned on offering his own testimony.

Myrna, seated next to Trian, gave me a strained smile. She was wearing her DRACIM insignia, a small pendant in the shape of a dragon, on the lapel of her jacket. She too had sheets of paper folded in her hand, and I realized she was here to not only offer me moral support, but DRACIM's support as well. I hoped she wouldn't lose her job over this. I gave her a small wave before taking my seat.

There was no sign of Daniel.

I tried to tell myself it was because members of the media had been specifically excluded from the proceedings, but I knew that wasn't the reason he didn't show. Myrna had offered to provide one of the DRACIM passes should he wish to attend and he'd refused, saying he had "other plans."

The great dragon sat on his perch near the back of the room, surveying the area with a sharp eye. Much larger than Lady Savitri, he towered over the human occupants even when seated on a perch. His beard, a rippling waterfall of scaled flesh that reached nearly to the floor, gave Lord Relobu a distinct grandfatherly appearance.

Except this grandfather had neatly severed the neck of a Chinese dragon lord barely a month ago.

And this time, it was my head on the chopping block.

The trial was called to order by a small purple dragon around my height. He stood just behind the podium, and let out a roar. Soon, all of the other dragons had joined in the call just as they had at Hian-puo's trial, with Lord Relobu's deep baritone completing the formal announcement.

Emory frowned at the realization that the trial would be conducted in dragonspeak instead of English.

Myrna took pity on her former boss, though I have

no idea why, and signaled for a translator to move into position beside his wheelchair.

Nervous, I blurted out my testimony in jerky sentences, starting with my reasons for joining the DRACIM and Relobu teams going to China, and ending with my flight back to the United States on Trian's back. Several members of the audience asked me additional questions, though once the dragons realized Lord Relobu planned to enforce a strict anti-heckling policy, the "questions" died down considerably.

Richard was next, and I had to admit that he wove his lies into pieces of the real story so skillfully that I half believed his version of the events.

Myrna and Emory's stories lined up perfectly with mine and Richard's, respectively. I was depressed to note that Richard had prepped Emory well, so that all Myrna's former boss had to do was point at specific sections of his pre-written statements for the answers.

I was surprised when Dreru, the dragon on our security detail in China and the provider of my first flight by dragonback, shuffled to the podium. He kept his remarks brief and unemotional, refusing to state his opinion on anything at all, offering facts only. I'm not sure whether his testimony helped or hurt me—as he was unable to give insight on the most serious of Richard's lies because he'd been busy providing more general security at Hian-puo's trial when the actual bomb movement was arranged. However, the very fact that a dragon got involved in the proceedings helped to settle the tempers of the scaly portion of the audience. I gave him a nod in thanks.

After Dreru's testimony, Lord Relobu stood and asked the waiting crowd if there were any others who wished to share their knowledge of the events. For a moment the audience fell silent.

Then a very welcome, very male voice sounded from the back entrance. As many times as this man had appeared out of thin air, I was beginning to wonder if he had superpowers.

My nerves frayed to the breaking point, I started to laugh.

Slowly the dragons shuffled out of the way, allowing Daniel to make his way to the front of the room. He approached the podium, but instead of taking his place behind it, he came to me, wrapping his strong arms around me and running his hand along my back, soothing the tremors I didn't even realize I'd been experiencing.

"I was going to ask you if you wanted to have dinner with me this evening, but I think maybe I'm inviting you over for a massage and bubble bath instead." He grinned down at me, his carefree attitude going a long way toward raising my hopes for a positive outcome.

Until I heard Richard's voice. "Why is the press here? He's disrupting the trial!"

Very slowly, and without releasing the hand he'd clasped between his own, Daniel turned to face my ex-boyfriend. "My name is Daniel Wallent. I was on assignment for the *Tulsa Times Chronicle* in Budapest during the timeframe in question. And I'm here to prove beyond a shadow of a doubt that Carol Jenski is innocent of the charges brought before her. In addition, I will be able to prove that these two men," Daniel pointed at Richard and Emory, "colluded to destroy the dragon population in and around Tulsa."

Myrna, all smiles, stepped up and translated Daniel's words into dragonspeak. "The cavalry managed to arrive," she whispered into my ear as the surprised murmurs subsided. "Though I certainly wish he hadn't cut it so close."

"You knew he was coming?"

"We've shared a few conference calls over the last few hours." She winked.

Richard, recovered from his initial shock, swung his face toward Lord Relobu. "He's press. The rules state that no press can participate in the proceedings."

"Actually," Daniel said mildly, the only evidence of his anger toward Richard being the way he rhythmically squeezed my hands as he spoke, "I no longer work for the *Tulsa Times Chronicle*. I resigned my post this morning. On this occasion, I serve as the representative of Lady Savitri Sarin, dragon lord of India, Nepal, and Pakistan and guardian of the Chinese territory until such time that a dragon lord can be chosen."

Well, well. It seems some business did actually get finished in Bangalore.

At Daniel's words, Richard's superior smirk slid from his face, replaced by an expression of dawning horror as he realized Daniel would have every right to speak.

Lord Relobu gave his formal permission, and Daniel kissed me once, hard, before turning to take his place at the podium. It was then that I noticed the large backpack hanging from his shoulder. It was large, brown, and worn in several spots. It was also full to bursting.

He sat it on the wooden dais with a hard thunk, and pulled out an awkward metal canister. A series of growls erupted from the crowd, and I frowned. I had no idea what it was.

"This," Daniel said, answering my silent question, "is a replica of the bioweapon detonated within the halls of DRACIM."

He held it up for everyone to see, and several of the dragons hissed or growled. They were definitely not fans, and I couldn't blame them.

Daniel, oblivious or uncaring about the reaction of his audience, continued, "This device, or one similar, was originally requisitioned by the late Hianpuo from Shui-Tech, a Chinese electronics company. After Hian-puo's trial, steps were taken to shut down

Shui-Tech, with the employees to be reassigned to other projects."

"Carol, can you pass these around?" He handed me two stacks of papers, one of large sheets written on in dragonscript and another of smaller pages, the English translation. Daniel continued to speak as human assistants ensured that each person present had a copy.

"This sheet details the current whereabouts of the team previously assigned to build the weapon. If you read the attached interview transcripts, every person on this list has been contacted by Richard Green personally and offered an 'off the books' job in exchange for obscene amounts of money."

Daniel returned to his bag, fishing around until he located an item about the size of his thumb. "This is a data drive found in a trashcan at the Hotel Gellért. Though the drive is EMP-corroded, a contact of mine was able to retrieve a good portion of the information. Please, look closely—this data drive is inscribed with the Relobu family crest, suggesting it belonged to someone with the Relobu delegation at the event."

"The serial number on the device has been traced back to a shipment delivered here on the Relobu estate over a year ago, far before Carol came on board with DRACIM."

Richard stood up, his face red with anger—or maybe even panic. "Now wait just a minute. This drive could have belonged to anybody. Carol could have picked it up from anywhere—a desk, a supply cabinet, hell, even a trashcan here in Tulsa—while she had DRACIM level clearance to Relobu's house."

"True," Daniel admitted easily, "but it seems mighty suspicious that I was able to retrieve several files, many of which identify your Relobu network ID as the author. Some of those network-signed documents held schematics to this machine. It's also quite a coincidence that you've hired the entire Shui-Tech weapons team, and that their new contracts found their way onto the same thumb drive. And yes, before you ask your question, we had the data drive dusted for fingerprints. Yours were all over it. How do you explain that?"

Richard's face twisted. "Easy. I slept with the slut. She probably took it out of my pocket and loaded the schematics on the drive without my knowledge."

"Excuse me? What did you just say?" Daniel's voice was quiet, but I could tell he was furious. I just missed his hand as he stepped from beyond the podium and approached Richard's chair.

"I said, your little slut probably stole the drive while I was sleeping."

Even though I was expecting it, I was shocked at how fast Daniel's fist came up. Richard's nose exploded with blood, and he let loose a high-pitched squeal as he attempted to protect his face from another blow.

But Daniel had already turned back to address the audience. "I'm assuming you all have plenty of questions, and I will be happy to answer them. However, I've brought all the Shui-Tech experts with me, and they're all willing to testify that Richard, not Carol, was the one who approached them with the job offer. They're waiting just outside the room should you wish to speak with them directly."

Lord Relobu rose from his perch. "That will not be necessary. Miss Jenski, you are free to go. And I would like to extend you my heartfelt apologies for the mistake."

Trian let out a whoop and grabbed Myrna's hips, swinging her in a tight circle before kissing her full on the mouth. Daniel mimicked the move with me, and I gladly kissed him back, the relief of my sudden reprieve like a drug coursing through my system.

"You saved my life. I thought you'd left me."

He grinned. "I hate to break it to you, but that's not going to happen for a long, long time."

TWENTY-SEVEN

"So what are your plans now that you're unemployed? Will you try to get back on staff at the *Tulsa Times Chronicle*?" Myrna leaned back against Trian's chest on the couch in our apartment and took a sip of her drink.

I did the same with my glass, snuggling closer to Daniel and trying to convince myself I wasn't dreaming. That this was real life. I had my life back, a man I loved in my arms, and the company of good friends. I was full to bursting with joy.

"I think I'll do some freelance writing for a while. I've got some savings, and I'm not particularly keen on leaving the country just yet." Daniel smiled at me, telling me without words that I was the reason he wanted to stick around.

As promised, as soon as we left Lord Relobu's, Daniel had whisked me away to his home in Tulsa, a cute little A-frame house nestled just next door to a local park. He'd filled the tub with bubbles and water, and spoiled me with a professional-grade head massage—avoiding the still-healing cut, of course—

followed by a more thorough full-body number that had me trying out his mattress for the first time.

At first, we'd lain in bed facing each other, tracing the outline of hips, stomachs, and rib cages, both of us happy just to be together with no dragons or death hovering like a shadow over our heads. Daniel, of course, had gotten a little distracted with my breasts, and soon we'd moved on to some pretty serious tickling, followed by a mind-blowing sexual experience. How he manages that unique blend of laughter and sex appeal, I'll never know.

After that, we'd fallen asleep, the stress and non-stop speed of the last few days catching up to us.

And oh, what a wonderful feeling to wake up next to someone you love. I smiled at the memory.

Myrna caught my eye and gave me a not-so-subtle thumbs-up.

Yes, we were both very lucky women.

Trian and Daniel were in an argument about the latest soccer match, but their raised voices were punctuated by a healthy portion of good-natured ribbing. I was glad they got along so well.

As soon as there was a lull in the conversation, I held up my glass for a toast. "To good friends and lazy Sundays."

"Hear! Hear!"

Myrna gave me another wide smile, her eyes sparkling as she kept her glass aloft. "To good friends, lazy Sundays and to surprise engagements with enormous diamond rings."

Before I fully comprehended her words, Myrna slipped a massive ring onto her finger and held out her hand. "Last night, Trian asked me to marry him. And obviously, I said yes." The diamond twinkled merrily.

"Oh, that is fantastic! When's the date?"

Myrna glanced to Trian. "We're not quite sure yet. We've been thinking." Myrna brushed a stray lock of her hair away from her face. "With all the upheaval between the dragons and humans it would do for both of the races to have something to celebrate—together."

"And you're thinking a wedding might be the perfect setting." I thought about it for a moment. The potential for disaster was high. Placing dragons and humans in a social situation was always a little risky. Add that to the usual craziness of drinking and family feuds and the risk went up tenfold.

"We'd have to hire some guards, and they'd need to be conspicuous." Trian seemed to be on the same wavelength.

I nodded. "But the payoff, if all goes well, would do wonders for the dragon/human agenda Relobu wants to push. Hire a publicist, do some interviews. Are you sure you're ready to be *the* greatest tabloid sensation since dragons were discovered?"

Myrna hesitated only an instant. "If it means getting the species close enough that we can convince them to sit down to negotiations sometime in the near future? Absolutely."

"The wedding will have to be huge."

Myrna grinned. "Don't suppose you know of any good wedding planners?"

I felt my eyes widen. "Yes, as a matter of fact I do. But I have one demand."

She waved a careless hand in my direction. "You don't even have to ask. I'd planned on forcing you to be my maid of honor."

"Oh, I had no doubt. But that wasn't my demand."

Myrna raised an eyebrow. "Do tell."

"You have to promise me that you'll wait at least six months before tying the knot. Because you're crazy if you think I'll allow photos to be taken of me before my hair grows out."

Myrna touched her glass to mine. "It's a deal."

This wedding was going to be fantastic.

* * * * *